Praise for Jayne Rylon's
Men in Blue Series

"This book is full of greatness. [...] The chemistry between these three is just so explosive you can feel it coming off the page."
~ *Guilty Pleasures Book Reviews on* Spread Your Wings

"I had some very high expectations. Not surprisingly, Ms. Rylon and this book far exceeded them."
~ *Sizzling Hot Book Reviews on* Spread Your Wings

"Jayne Rylon manages to combine an intriguing story with captivating characters, creating a sensual roller coaster ride with some of the most sizzling protagonists you're likely to meet. From the moment the story starts, you'll be snared."
~ *Long and Short Reviews on* Night is Darkest

"Jayne Rylon has written a fantastic follow up story to the first Men in Blue book. This book is a lot of fun and has plenty of unexpected twists that lead up to a great ending."
~ *The Romance Studio on* Razor's Edge

"Rylon knows her stuff, providing readers with explicit, clear-as-day details about everything in the subculture from toys to scenery."
~ *RT Book Reviews on* Mistress's Master

Look for these titles by
Jayne Rylon

Now Available:

Nice and Naughty
Where There's Smoke

Men In Blue
Night is Darkest
Razor's Edge
Mistress's Master
Spread Your Wings

Powertools
Kate's Crew
Morgan's Surprise
Kayla's Gifts
Devon's Pair
Nailed to the Wall
Hammer It Home

Compass Brothers
(Written with Mari Carr)
Northern Exposure
Southern Comfort
Eastern Ambitions
Western Ties

Compass Girls
(Written with Mari Carr)
Winter's Thaw
Hope Springs
Summer Fling
Falling Softly

Play Doctor
Dream Machine
Healing Touch
Developing Desire

Hot Rods
King Cobra
Mustang Sally
Super Nova
Rebel on the Run
Swinger Style
Barracuda's Heart

Print Anthologies
Three's Company
Love's Compass
Powertools
Two to Tango
Love Under Construction
Hot Rods

Spread Your Wings

Jayne Rylon

Samhain Publishing, Ltd.
11821 Mason Montgomery Road, 4B
Cincinnati, OH 45249
www.samhainpublishing.com

Spread Your Wings
Copyright © 2013 by Jayne Rylon
Print ISBN: 978-1-61922-162-8
Digital ISBN: 978-1-61921-342-5

Editing by Amy Sherwood
Cover by Angela Waters

This book is a work of fiction. The names, characters, places, and incidents are products of the writer's imagination or have been used fictitiously and are not to be construed as real. Any resemblance to persons, living or dead, actual events, locale or organizations is entirely coincidental.

All Rights Are Reserved. No part of this book may be used or reproduced in any manner whatsoever without written permission, except in the case of brief quotations embodied in critical articles and reviews.

First Samhain Publishing, Ltd. electronic publication: October 2013
First Samhain Publishing, Ltd. print publication: October 2014

Dedication

For my good friend Jambrea Jo Jones who has waited very patiently (ahem) for this story. You truly are one of the kindest and most deserving people I know.

May reality be better than fiction.

Also for one of my favorite Canadians, Shari David. Thank you for always supporting my work, but more for being a friend. I'll never forget our trolley ride around San Antonio and all the ensuing hijinks of that weekend. I knew from the first time we met—when you gave me your marshmallows in exchange for my chocolate around a campfire at Lora Leigh's Reader Appreciation Weekend—that it was the start of something golden.

In memory of fan Marion Tito's lost coworker at the Federal Bureau of Prisons, real life man in blue Eric Williams, who was killed in the line of duty on February 25, 2013.

Prologue

Nine Years Ago

Jambrea Jones didn't flinch when sparks rained around her from a busted out light. A long time ago, she'd given up ducking at the report of rifles in favor of hauling ass. Hiding in the facility under attack wouldn't save her or her patients, but running might.

It seemed to be working so far, considering that she'd already crossed the scrubby yard behind the field hospital three times, transporting those who were at least somewhat mobile to the buried storm shelter. She'd discovered the quiet nook a few weeks ago and kept it her secret for reading on her lunch break.

The dirt enclosure rumbled but held around her stowaways in the face of the nearby detonations that seemed to multiply by the minute. So she'd left them to make another voyage through chaos. The racket of war had never encroached on the walls of the hospital before—that part was new and less than exciting. International boundaries, including respect for the wounded, didn't seem to matter to the bad guys swarming around them.

After all, they were enemies.

She tore down the hallway, stopping to take the pulse of a man slumped against a flipped gurney. No helping him. Recalling the crayon-embellished construction paper card he'd received just yesterday wouldn't make the rest of her day any easier, so she put it out of her mind. Just like the endless gore and cries of pain she'd endured, a vile part of the process of healing soldiers.

Most of this wing had either been cleared out or left to the dead. Maybe she'd join her stowed patients sooner than she'd planned. The sheer number of casualties began to numb her insides. She'd fought to return these people—as whole as could be—to their families.

All that suffering for nothing.

Damn it! She'd never imagined herself a hero. More like a broke kid wanting to go to nursing school, who had no other choice but to rely on the military for training and future tuition. Today didn't make her any more likely to reenlist when her time was up. Still, she was here and she'd do what she could.

Finishing the circuit of what would have been her rounds, she heard a bang that had more in common with a pissed off man than yet another wave of assault from outside. Sure enough, a muffled curse followed.

Him. It had to be the *special* patient. The one only Dr. Riley was allowed to see.

Had no one let him loose?

Jambrea paused, staring down the dark corridor toward the isolated chamber at the end. In truth, it was more like a cell. Wires in the glass reinforced even the itty-bitty peep pane. How dangerous was he really? Could she doom him to certain death, trapped for the invaders to collect? What if he spilled more secrets to them? Which was worse for warriors on the front lines?

Hell, for all she knew, collecting the guy could be the plan. What else could have triggered today's violence after several years of manning the outpost in the mountains of Afghanistan had passed with only minor incidents?

Whispered rumors had reached everyone at St. Joseph's hospital. Their visitor—a super spy double agent—had crossed leaders in every nation on the planet at least once. A compound fracture of his femur caused by a bullet had kept him bedridden, under constant guard, for months.

Supposedly.

"This is what I call a bad fucking day on the job." No sense in being scared. Jambrea scrunched her eyes closed as she weighed her options.

Another crash radiated along the length of the hallway. Sounded like a bed being upended. Even that didn't dent the steel door of his prison. From the other direction, shouts rang in a guttural language she didn't understand.

Swallowing hard didn't dislodge the lump in her throat.

Jambrea unballed her fists and charged. Straight toward the lone remaining occupant of her ward. Court-marshaling threats wouldn't persuade her conscience. She couldn't leave someone in there after witnessing firsthand the atrocities their enemies were capable of inflicting on human flesh. A kill shot would be too quick and painless for someone like their guest.

"Shit, shit, shit." She flew along the hall to the end, hurdling the remains of the pair of guards, who'd apparently paced too close to the shattered windows. When she reached the door to the restricted area, she framed her eyes with her hands and peered into the patient's dim room, which had no exterior windows.

A brilliant blue flash filled her world when the prisoner popped into view, standing directly on the other side of the portal, staring right back at her.

A heart attack seemed imminent when the full force of his gaze lasered into her brain.

"Fuck!" She stumbled away, clutching her chest.

"The keys are on his belt." Mystery patient pointed toward one of the corpses.

Jambrea didn't hesitate. She slid on her knees to avoid crossing in front of the obliterated windows again, in case someone had spotted her during her reckless dash. The blood on the ground facilitated her progress. She'd seen worse.

Unclipping the key ring from the guard's belt, she flipped

through two before finding the scrap of metal that fit into the lock. Her fingers shook as she considered what she was about to unleash.

"I won't hurt you," he promised, though his yell—necessary to penetrate the thick door—didn't do much to calm her nerves. "We don't have a lot of time here. Do it or we'll both be toast."

Eerie echoes chased the ghosts of patients along the hallways now that anyone sane and able had fled. Maybe the ghastly sounds were really the whines and yelps of search dogs. Jambrea shuddered. She'd never been a huge fan of canines. Especially not those monsters, bred to attack.

"Come on, kid." The man before her held perfectly still, as if she might bolt if he so much as sighed.

Quickly reviewing her options left her with no other alternative she could live with. A flick of her wrist disengaged the lock. She barely had time to jump aside to prevent the steel from imprinting on her face.

"Sorry. Afraid you'd change your mind." For a detainee, he seemed nice enough. The guy held out his hand and helped her steady herself. Warm and strong, he immediately took charge. She didn't mind, more of a follower by nature. The go with the flow mentality had helped her survive her stint in the Air Force.

"Let's vanish." He ushered her toward the windows. "Stay low this time. I can't believe your kooky ass ran right in front of those openings."

"Excuse me," Jambrea huffed. "I did it to rescue your *rude* ass. And I did run, not stroll."

He considered her, pausing long enough to make her sure of his sincerity. "Thank you."

"No problem." She glanced away from the intensity of his stare.

"Hang on, not that way." The pressure on her arm, still linked to his, drew her up short. "We'll never make it."

Her guide peeked over the mangled sill. "It's not that far of a drop. I'll go first then help you. Just do it quick so you get the bricks between you and anyone watching over there."

Jambrea nodded. The blast pattern of the shards did seem to have come from the opposite direction. Some of the combat skills she'd practiced in training returned though she'd had little use for them in the hospital until now.

"Move," her unlikely comrade hissed from outside the building. He'd slunk as quietly as a shadow, slipping from his prison before she even noticed.

The jagged remnants of the pane made it difficult to choose her angle of approach. With a grunt and a few mumbled curses, she hoisted herself up and swung over the edge. Dangling by her hands would have likely resulted in her dropping to the ground a few seconds later, upper body strength not her forte.

Except a deceptively well-muscled arm snaked around her waist, supporting her and drawing her onto a tiny ledge in the brickwork that made it possible to cling like some misfit superhero. Not bad.

"That's it." He coached her to another handhold then a third, each one lower than the last by a foot or two. "We're only about five feet up now. Hang on a minute and I'll help you down."

With that, he leapt nimbly the rest of the way to the ground, stirring up a puff of red dust. Silence ensued. "Um..."

"Shh." He quieted her. "Someone's coming. Let's make this quick."

Jambrea peeked between her feet. She prepared to jump, but she didn't have to. The spy reached toward her and she allowed herself to sink into his steady grasp.

"There we go." His reassurance came soft in her ear as he set her delicately on the ground beside him despite her decidedly non-petite frame. Just then, barks shattered the relative calm. They came from the ward, exactly where she would have been if he hadn't rerouted their exit.

Jambrea shivered. When she turned and looked into his calculating eyes, he didn't need her to explain her sudden chill.

"You saved my ass, I saved yours. Least I could do." He shrugged, raining bits of glass from his shirt to his sweatpants. No braces made lumps under the thin fabric.

"I thought you had a bum leg." She watched as he shook his limbs out, shedding glittery giveaways before they crossed the open area. No need to hand a sniper any advantages like the beacons those would become in the sunlight that poked between the stunted evergreens around them. Again she adopted his survival tactics.

"Don't believe everything Uncle Sam tells you, kid." His voice might have been gruff, but his hands were efficient yet tender as he dusted off her backside. "Now zip it while I figure out how we're going to sneak through the perimeter they'll have set."

"I have a place to hide." She pointed. "Over there. Some other patients are waiting too. In a storm shelter."

"Right. Okay." He didn't waste any time in arguing. Instead, he gestured for her to guide them. They kept low to the ground, snaking through the brush, pausing when boots clomped too near or shouts seemed to increase in frequency.

It seemed like days, but was only minutes, before they reached Jambrea's haven.

"In you go." The spy waved his free hand, crisscrossed with scars that caught her attention. The other held the heavy trapdoor as if it weighed nothing. For her to lever the partially rotted wood open, it usually involved a bunch of grunting and a bruise or two. All worth it for a couple stolen moments of precious solitude.

"What about you?" She hesitated when she realized he didn't intend to join them. Descending the ladder, he followed her only enough to say goodbye without giving them away.

"Trust me. You're all safer without me." He smiled at her softly.

She tipped her head and opened her mouth, then closed it again. Arguing about her own protection was one thing, but she couldn't justify putting the rest of the refugees at risk for one man. No matter how much he intrigued her. She scanned him from his slightly crooked nose to the creases around his eyes and mouth. The grooves were too deep for someone not all that much older than her in age, though light years ahead in experience.

"I'll never be out of harm's way again after the things I've seen. And done. Don't worry about me." He ruffled her hair—not much longer than his mop—as if she really were a kid, pissing her off.

"Fine. Have it your way." Her ire flared then snuffed in an instant, short-lived. "But be careful, okay?"

"You got it, Jambi."

"How do you know my...?" She drifted off when he climbed enough to poke his head out of their nest.

"It's my job to find out shit people don't tell me." He winked as he glanced over his shoulder. "And I'm the best. No worries. It'll all be good now. Thanks again."

She almost tried another time to get him to stay since the same instinct she'd used to administer hugs to the surliest patients at exactly the right moments tugged on her insides.

But before she could, he'd vanished.

"Good luck," she whispered.

Chapter One

Present Day

Jambrea rode bitch on the bench seat of Matt Ludwig's beastly black truck. As her date to Lily and Jeremy's commitment ceremony, he'd insisted on picking her up. She supposed the vehicle fit the man himself, who was enormous enough to dwarf her, making her feel petite. Very different than the story Lily's and Jeremy's photos of the big day would tell. Next to the bride and her sister Izzy—especially in these heels they'd insisted she wear to match the rest of the wedding party—she was going to come off like an Amazon. Terrific.

In the background, the radio droned about a missing presidential candidate. It'd been all over the news for weeks now. Annoyed with life and horrible things happening to good people, Jambrea flicked the volume all the way to zero, muting more bad news. Usually she could shake off misfortune, even living with it day by day in the hospital. Lately, that was becoming harder to do.

Maybe because of her present company.

On her right perched Clint Griggs. Her *other* date to today's festivities. He looked deliciously handsome in the charcoal tailored suit his friends had dressed him in. It was odd seeing the pair of cops in street clothes. Despite their dashing good looks in their matching outfits, she missed their crisp navy uniforms—especially the pants that usually hugged their tight asses to perfection. Well, that and the bulge of their *guns*. Plus their handcuffs. Right.

"What's that sigh for?" Matt dropped one hand from the

wheel to squeeze her knee. That didn't resolve any of her issues. In fact, she thought she might overheat when she took in his relaxed posture as he handled the monstrous truck with ease. His walnut hair feathered over his forehead in the breeze from the air conditioning, which did nothing to cool her down. The rugged features of his face captivated her.

How could one man be so damn big, strong *and* handsome? It didn't seem fair.

Clint must not have approved of Matt receiving all her attention since he combated his friend's touch by drawing circles on her upper arm. Bare at the edge of the cap sleeve he toyed with, her skin nearly burst into flames at their direct contact.

Dear God, when were they going to stop torturing her and either make a move—individually or collectively—or pass for good? In limbo, they were playing a constant game of red-light-green-light that confused the hell out of her. Frustrated her too. Or was it a round of monkey-in-the-middle, with her grasping for something they withheld? Either way, she kept losing.

She'd burned through a crap ton of batteries lately. Pretty soon, she'd send them a bill.

"I guess there's just a lot to reflect on today." She didn't begrudge anyone happiness. That didn't mean it wasn't difficult to watch friend after friend find eternal bliss while she waited in the wings. Even a temporary fling would suffice at this point. Anything to get her back on the proverbial horse.

Why did her heart have to be so stubborn? For most of her twenties, she'd had a crush on an unattainable man. Then, when she'd finally decided it could be time to move on, she'd fallen for not one of these sexy Men in Blue, but both of them.

Fuck. Why can't my life ever be simple? She glanced down at the tattoo on her right wrist and reminded herself to be strong. Moping wasn't her style.

"What does that mean?" Clint angled toward her and the

man who'd been his bestie, the guy who still was his partner on the force. The complicated attraction braiding the three of them into a colossal knot had wedged some distance between the men. Awkwardness had snuck in ever since the night they'd both made out with her on her couch, during the case that had brought their mutual friends Lily and Jeremy together permanently.

The brief taste of paradise had only resulted in weird vibes the next time she saw the pair, not any progress. They hadn't mentioned the stolen kisses again. Neither had she.

"Frankly, it means I'm annoyed I had to be stuck with the two of you today." Nothing like rubbing her face in what she couldn't have, for some reason she didn't understand. They supported Lacey, Mason and Tyler—a pair of cops in their precinct and the mens' shared wife—in their unconventional relationship. So that wasn't it.

What was the problem? She wanted to scream but would never risk ruining Lily and Jeremy's celebration with lingering tension from an unfinished fight.

Clint groaned and Matt snatched his hand back as he turned into the lot of Gunther's Playground, where Lily and Jeremy both held positions of high esteem. The sex club was a blend of old and new. Black Lily's respected clientele and a fresh start for all who'd rather leave the horrors of the sadistic chemical aphrodisiac Sex Offender and the elite drug-slash-sex-ring they'd survived behind them forever.

In truth, Gunther's was a place for people serious about the BDSM lifestyle to mingle. That included Mistress Lily and the only man to ever top her, Dom and cop, Master Jeremy. Jambrea understood now that the club was so much more than a means to score an easy fuck. Her eyes had been opened through her friendship with Lily. And while the midnight activities engaged in here might never be exactly her cup of tea, she found it hard not to be jealous of the community of likeminded individuals who had a safe place to express themselves.

Jambrea had nothing but two men who wouldn't be straight with her. They came to a gentle stop as Matt eased into a parking spot. "Let me out, Clint."

She practically shoved him because it was the only way she could escape. Even the short ride to the venue where two of her dearest friends would vow publicly what their hearts had already sworn to each other had riled her. Clint and Matt's powerful thighs on either side of hers had scorched her through her flimsy scarlet dress. It wouldn't have been a problem if they intended to do something...*anything*...about it.

Her hopes of that had long since evaporated.

"What'd I do?" The pinch of Clint's lips made her fingers itch to reach out and reassure him. Reality was, he kept hurting her and she'd had enough. At some point, self-preservation had to come before coddling.

"Nothing." She practically spat the denial at him. "I can't believe Lily stuck me with both of you in the processional. Can't even have a freaking normal date like every other woman in the world."

"You know there was an uneven number of guys and girls." Matt tried to defuse the situation.

"Yeah, *that's* why she did it." Jambrea rolled her eyes. As if Lily wasn't a professional at manipulating people, though not in a malicious way. Surely, her friend had been trying to be helpful.

She ignored Clint's proffered hand and slid from the truck, clutching her purse—embroidered with black lilies and red roses, a bridesmaid's gift from Lily—like a shield against the way his soulful gaze turned her insides to mush.

"You're saying we didn't just get lucky?" Matt joined her on the pavement after circling the hood of his baby.

"I haven't gotten lucky in forever. Certainly not with you two dumbasses." It might not have been ladylike, but she stomped off, leaving them in her wake. It was either that or bash them with her clutch. How could they be so dense? And if they didn't want her, why did they keep sending her mixed signals?

Fortunately, the troupe of cops and wives—including her fellow nurse Lacey—who'd become her dear friends milled out front, available to run interference. Izzy squealed when she saw Jambrea approaching. The pixie practically bounced in place, her blond curls springing, until Jambrea came in for a much-needed hug.

"You look amazing!" Lacey joined in the barrage of embraces.

"Thanks." She scanned what she could see of herself, thinking again that the dress *was* more flattering than she'd imagined it would be. Shapewear to the rescue.

"I almost didn't recognize you out of scrubs," Mason, one of Lacey's husbands, teased Jambrea, though his smile was warm and his gaze appreciative. He gave her a squeeze that set her more at peace.

"Let's check the floof factor." Izzy's fiancé, James Reoser, snagged Jambrea's hand and swirled her in a move he must have learned in his ballroom dancing days. She giggled as the skirt of her dress fluttered outward and her anger leeched away on the resulting breeze, replaced by appreciation for her friends.

Apparently, Tyler—Lacey's other husband—approved. "Pretty darn good. Maybe you'll let me have a turn at the reception, Jambi?"

"You're on." She beamed at the gathering, reminding herself how fortunate she was to have a by-choice family this strong. Which reminded her of their growing numbers. "How're you feeling today, Izzy? How's Razor Jr.?"

Lily's half-sister, bright and bubbly, rubbed her hand over

the baby bump her bouquet couldn't quite hide. She and James were waiting until after their newest addition made an appearance to get hitched themselves. Probably meant another dress, more makeup and someone doing her hair again.

Secretly, Jambrea couldn't wait.

As long as she could swing a real date. Or attend solo.

When Matt and Clint ambled over to the group, probably having argued again for a bit, she didn't feel like ruining the vibe. She fanned herself with the luscious bouquet Izzy handed her, then announced, "I'm going to head inside. Don't want to get sweaty."

"Okay, we'll be in shortly." Izzy waved to her, though her narrowed eyes probably meant she was on to Jambrea's ruse. Sometimes dodging was the right move.

Ushers she recognized as some of Lily's submissives guided her to a holding room off the auditorium, which generally hosted events of a somewhat baser nature. They'd done up the space brilliantly for today, draping crimson and black tulle from the ceiling and lighting what looked like a million tapers held in ornate candelabras of all shapes and sizes. Gilded mirrors reflected light and warmth from every direction.

Moisture gathered in the corners of Jambrea's eyes. The hall, which even vampire nobility would be proud to get married in, was perfect for her friends—dramatic, intense, serious and gorgeous.

Before she could bawl and ruin her face, she stepped into the waiting room.

Inside, two people had already taken their positions. Lucas and Ellie.

"Hey there." She waved at the pair as she joined them. Both had suffered horrific injuries in the Sex Offender scandal. Lucas, physical ones; Ellie, more emotional wounds. If they could carry on, Jambrea scolded herself, then she had no business whining. Again she ran her finger over her tattoo.

"Hi, Jambi." Ellie beamed. It was so nice to see her smile again.

"You look really pretty." Lucas peeled his stare from Ellie for long enough to give Jambrea a cursory glance. She didn't mind. It was sweet to see the two of them together. The more she mulled it over, the more she thought they might be good support for each other. They had a lot in common. Unfortunately, not much of it was good stuff.

"Thank you." The nurse in Jambrea immediately noticed Lucas rubbing his thigh compulsively. She'd facilitated his rehab sessions enough times to know he was overexerting himself by loitering, even with the aid of his cane. He'd pay for this later. Still, she knew better than to dishonor his efforts by calling him out. So she took up a post on the far side of the space and pretended to study a painting of a woman suspended in an intricate web of ropes while she peeked at the unlikely friends from the corner of her eye.

Ellie, however, didn't have the same healthy respect for the temper of an injured man. Or maybe she just didn't give a shit about Lucas's bark. The thin woman had lived through unspeakable abuse. The ire of one pissed off ex-military commando would seem like nothing to her. The fact that Lucas had been maimed while trying to rescue her from The Scientist probably added to her concern. Guilt could drive people to do crazy things.

"If it's sore, why not use your wheelchair? The ceremony won't take long, but it'll feel like forever if you're hurting. I bet your leg is already past numb to burning again, huh?" Ellie didn't shy away from Lucas's foul mood. Not even when he snarled at her. Truth was, she'd endured much worse.

"I'm not gonna let you push me down the aisle like an invalid." He rejected her help. Jambrea had seen that one coming a mile away. She'd dealt with prideful patients enough to know he'd fought to walk again, against all his doctors' expectations. Sentencing himself to the chair so publicly wasn't going to happen unless he had absolutely no other choice.

The man's pain tolerance was legendary. Accounts of his heroics in the dungeon of Morselli's lair were only surpassed by those the nurses and hospital staff recounted from his recovery and therapy sessions.

"Better to fall on your face like a self-absorbed fool and ruin Lily and Jeremy's day? Of course, you're right." Ellie turned her nose up and gave him the cold shoulder. At least for a few seconds.

"Shit. Fine. Hand me the damn thing. I'll rest until the last second, okay?" He crossed his arms over his chest. Still, he waited for Ellie to accept his compromise.

She beamed so quickly Jambrea wondered if that hadn't been the slender woman's goal all along. Crafty little bitch. Jambi liked her.

Ellie rolled the chair into position and held it steady as Lucas sank his jumbo frame into the seat. When she patted his broad shoulder, she let her hand linger to massage the tension there. Lucas didn't stop her. Interesting. "There you go. Want me to do your leg for a bit?"

Jambrea thought he'd erupt again.

Instead, he agreed in a gruff whisper, "Yeah. If you don't mind."

Well, holy shit. Maybe some men were less obstinate than others. Did she know how to pick 'em or what?

Ellie knelt in front of the man who'd sacrificed a hell of a lot for her safety. No, existence. He groaned, his head dropping back, when she showed no mercy. After a few minutes, the rumble of approaching voices echoed outside their door.

"Enough." He called Ellie off and she didn't object, quickly rising to greet their friends.

Thankfully, they'd barely all jammed inside, creating a

buffer between Jambrea, Matt and Clint, before one of the event organizers called them to attention.

Jambrea shuffled around people to help Ellie lever Lucas to his feet once more.

"Thanks." He grunted as his injury bore his weight.

"Anytime." She didn't suppress the urge to hug him, glad when he returned the embrace. Whispering in his ear—easy to do considering her heels and her natural height combined—she coached him, "You're doing great. Remember to lean on the cane. You can keep most of the pressure off."

"I got it." He tightened his grip for a moment then dropped his arms so fast she thought he might have been offended.

"What's this? Trying to steal my girl?" Matt. *Damn.*

"Didn't see your *Property Of* stamp on her forehead. Sorry." Lucas wasn't about to take shit from anyone. Not even the hulk bearing down on them.

Before things could really degenerate, the usher lined them up. With Jambrea smack in the middle of Matt and Clint. Each one of them curled a hand around one of her elbows. And it was as if she'd never abandoned the steamy cab of the truck. Electricity arced between them. Damn men.

Izzy and Razor were the first couple to march down the aisle, beaming at the guests gathered to witness the exchanged vows. Everyone else shuffled forward.

"Look, we only have a few seconds, but…we're sorry, Jambi." Matt wasn't really the smooth-talker of the duo. To see him struggle to right things made her a little more confident.

"Yeah, we know we keep fucking up." Clint took over, making the most of their precious moments. From behind them, Lucas issued a brief laugh and muttered something that sounded like, *No kidding.* "We want to make things right. Later, can we talk about how?"

"Of course." She might have said more except just then

they were called forward. Her two dates escorted her to the front of the room before leaving her with the lingering trail of their fingertips. Minutes later, she still tingled where they'd touched.

From her spot in the line of attendants, Jambrea could see the place of honor Lily had given to her submissives. Ryan and Ben sat closest to the center aisle. Then Ramone. Bruce and Daniel. Cameron and his new Master—whom he'd met at Gunther's—and all the others took up the entire front row. Behind them sat Lily's assistants—Kitty, Dawn, Ive, Suz and Gigi. Each man and woman seemed genuinely thrilled for their Mistress, boss and mentor, who would pledge herself to the only man she'd ever knelt for.

On Jeremy's side, the police chief and a woman JRad had once rescued, Zina, held hands as they sat among a slew of other friends and relatives. Jambrea even thought she spotted Rhonda—a woman they'd all gotten to know and love at barbeques when she and Lacey had shared a backyard—sitting next to Mama Rose, Tyler's mom.

And just then, the music changed. Violins played classical music that might have seemed at odds with the somber interior of the club if Jambrea hadn't become educated on the sanctity of this place for its members.

Jeremy strode to the front of the room. He stood tall in his black leather pants and matching satin shirt. A watch set in a studded cuff adorned one wrist. His wedding present from his soon-to-be wife. The women had all helped her design it. On him, it was perfect.

He looked formidable and knockout sexy. Comfortable in his own skin. Jambrea couldn't believe she hadn't realized what he kept hidden beneath his police uniform back in the early days of their acquaintance.

Maybe everyone needed that one special person, or people, to unlock their inner spirit.

Jambrea glanced across the room at Matt, then Clint. Both

men were staring at her. She fidgeted with her dress, smoothing any wrinkles as best she could given the flowers in her grip. Clint winked at her.

Though she tried to smother it, a smile tipped up the corners of her mouth. Why did he have to be so damn fine? And always know how to make her feel less self-conscious.

A murmur ran through the crowd.

Jambrea glanced toward the back of the room. She could see why. Lily. Gorgeous and austere in her black lace dress—a red leather corset molded her torso with the long skirt and train flowing from beneath—she clung to the arm Gunther extended and accepted his kiss on her artfully rouged cheeks. Lily's locks waved down her back, unstraightened and unbraided. A rarity. Loose and free, they rippled alongside her face then over her shoulder all the way to her waist. If Jambrea had hair like that, she'd never wear it any other way. As hers was thin and fine, she'd always chosen to keep hers short to maintain the illusion of fullness.

Jeremy made a small sound that drew her attention. The computer geek turned Master rubbed his chest over his heart and the bunch of lilies she knew were tattooed there. Razor, JRad's best friend, clapped him on the shoulder for support. The groom didn't appear to notice. Instead, his world seemed full of Lily. The palpable love connecting the two people Jambrea cared about, despite their distance, wrung her guts with joy and envy simultaneously.

She peeked at Matt and Clint. Again, she found them both gazing at her.

Maybe she'd been too harsh on them earlier.

Maybe they could make up at the reception.

Maybe tonight could be different.

Please, let it be different.

After one last prayer, all thoughts turned to her friends and the pledges they swore. It was beautiful. Perfect. Everlasting.

"Can I bring you another drink, ma'am?" The waiter swung past her table in his circuit of frequent rounds. No extravagance had been spared in the party Gunther had thrown for his protégé, who might as well have been his son, and his new quasi daughter-in-law. Fitting since the pair were also the stars of his shockingly successful new facility.

"I'll take two this time." She slammed the last of the prior fruity concoction, then set the glass on the waiter's tray. If it wobbled a little, it was probably because he held the platter precariously balanced on one palm.

"Are you sure, Jambi?" Clint leaned closer to be heard over the music, which all their friends danced to. "The cocktails are stronger than you might realize. They're using the good stuff, so it doesn't taste as much like booze."

"I know my limits." Daring him to object, she stared daggers at him, then Matt just for the hell of it. Talk, her ass. They'd relegated her to the friend zone the moment they'd sat down to dinner together. Sure, it'd been fun. She always had a great time with them, but it was fake. They were ignoring all the other layers deeper than pals.

Pretty soon she was going to lose it. But not here. Not in public.

Awkward, she and her dates comprised the sole occupants of the dais designated for the wedding party. Even Ellie and Lucas seemed to have wandered off somewhere, maybe the gardens.

"Hey, Jambs, come on," Izzy shouted to her from the dance floor, waving to their group. The couples had split up a bit now that something other than endless love songs bleated from the speakers. All too eager to leave her dates, Jambrea shot to her feet.

Clint braced her when she teetered. Damn heels. She smacked his overly familiar hand before it could work any of its hornifying magic. *Enough with the pheromones already.*

Then she sauntered onto the floor in time to the beat and tried to burn off a little of the buzz she might have underestimated. Lost in the music and revelry, surrounded by friends, she forgot about some of her angst. Until Lacey leaned in and whisper-shouted, "Matt and Clint are about to choke on their tongues over there. Show me some hip shimmies!"

Fuck them. Why not?

Jambrea obliged.

It wasn't long before Lacey's face lit up. "Incoming."

"What?" Jambrea peeked over her shoulder. Sure enough, the two men she'd obsessed over for the past year or so stalked closer. She whipped her head back around toward her friends. "They don't dance."

"Maybe they will for you." Izzy grinned as she ground her backside against her fiancé, who wrapped his arms protectively around her and the child she carried.

"I doubt it." Jambrea refused to let them ruin her fun though. If anything, she redoubled the swivel of her ass and dug into the groove of the beat.

And then there were hands on her waist, turning her. From the way her captor's thumbs nearly touched in the base of her spine, they could only belong to Matt. He tucked her close to the furnace of his body and rocked in a basic side-to-side step, mostly in time to the music. She closed her eyes and settled against him, thrilled to feel the growing erection he pressed to the small of her back.

"Hey, mind if I cut in?" Clint asked.

Jambrea blinked when he reached out, cupping her ribs in his palms. Four hands on her at once nearly short-circuited her brain.

"Actually, I do," Matt growled.

"Too bad." The other man wasn't retreating. Instead he pressed closer, flanking her with their gyrating bodies. Her breasts brushed his chest as she undulated, caught between rubbing herself on one or the other. Or both, after Clint took another half-step in.

Instinctively, she wrapped one arm around his neck while the other reached behind her to palm Matt's ass. Her head fell back, resting on his chest. Clint leaned in and took a taste of her exposed neck. When someone whistled, they all jolted. What the hell was happening? Where were they again?

Oh, right. The reception. Jambrea shook her head, clearing the blazing desire from her mind as best she could. Unfortunately that only made the dance floor rock like the deck of a ship. Uh oh.

"I've got you," Matt rumbled in her ear.

"No, *we've* got you," Clint corrected.

For a few minutes, she stopped fighting and pretended that they meant it like it sounded. It was the best one-hundred-and-twenty seconds of the year so far. Then the song ended and the DJ announced the final dance. A ballad.

"We're getting the hell out of here," Matt proclaimed.

The guys corralled her toward the guests of honor. They exchanged congratulations one more time.

"Have a good night." Lily's sly grin didn't allow any room for misinterpretation.

Before Jambrea could respond, her dates whisked her to Matt's waiting black chariot. Clint didn't bother to boost her into the truck. This time he encircled her waist and lifted her onto the seat as though she weighed nothing at all.

"What were you trying to prove out there?" Matt rubbed his jaw. "Every single guy in the room was drooling over you. You've had too much to drink to be advertising like that."

So they hadn't rushed her home to sample the wares she'd been hawking? No, they'd just planned to cock block any other interested man. The wave of disappointment that hit her made her feel sick. Fortunately, she only lived a few blocks away.

They spent the entirety of the ride in silence.

The teeter-totter they'd been balancing precariously on slipped from its fulcrum. She couldn't take another minute of the erratic highs and lows, and especially not these weird, forced, blah middle points. No more.

Despite her protests, they insisted on walking her to her apartment. Granted, she lived in a relatively crappy neighborhood that had deteriorated bit by bit since she'd moved in nearly a decade ago, but she'd never had issues before. Her pair of cops were more dangerous to her than random thugs.

When they held the door, she couldn't help making one last bid for what she felt slipping through her fingers. It was now or never.

"You know, I didn't even see any other guys at the reception tonight. What do I have to do to make *you* like me?" She rubbed against Matt, uncaring about how pathetic she looked or how much she'd hate herself in the morning.

"Son of a bitch. I *do* like you. Too much." He stared at her in horror as they squeezed together into her apartment, Clint close on their heels.

He groaned in the background. She spun on him. "Come on, tell me. What'd I do wrong? How did I screw things up? Am I supposed to pick one of you? Is that what this is? Some stupid male contest? Was it because I kissed you both? Was that some kind of test? Did I fail?"

"Jambi, no." Matt spun her around again. The world tilted and she wondered when the last time was that she'd been so hammered. "You've got this all wrong."

"Then why? Tell me what I did!" She couldn't believe that she raised her voice, but it felt good to finally let off some steam so she kept ranting. "One minute you were sucking my face off and the next time I saw you, you wouldn't even look me in the damn eye."

"It wasn't because of you. It's...us," Clint admitted as he and Matt exchanged a worried glance. Good, let them be afraid. They could share the sour stomach that had been rotting her from the inside since the fallout of that single reckless, yet addicting, moment became apparent.

She waited, but they didn't elaborate. "Really, that's the best you can do? Some *talk*. 'It's not you, it's me' never convinced anyone."

"Maybe this isn't the best time..." Clint hedged.

"It's *never* going to be the right occasion. It's been months already. You're cowards, both of you. I never would have guessed it before. Go home, jerks!" She wrenched off her shoe, then threw it at Clint, catching him in the gut. His *oomph* held a note of surprise. "You're not going to do this to me anymore. I'm tired of waiting, hoping, for something that's never going to happen. If you won't be honest with yourselves, at least be upfront with me. Tell me you don't want me. Say it."

"Jambi, you're dr—" Matt cut off when she swung her furious glare toward him instead.

"No. Forget it. Shut up." She flapped her arms, not caring that she'd lost her temper for the first time...maybe ever. Irrational fury barred them from conjuring some ridiculous explanation that would steal her thunder. "No more excuses."

"I don't think it's smart to leave you like this." Clint looked to his partner for backup.

"I'd rather be alone than babysat by you two. Unless you plan to come to bed with me, get out." She yanked the hem of her dress over her head and launched the gossamer sheath against the wall. It slithered to the floor and lay crumpled.

One of the guys, or maybe both, cursed as they took in her silk lingerie. It only made her feel stupider that she'd pretended even for an instant that she'd get to display it in far more favorable circumstances tonight. When would she learn that just because she hoped something would happen, that didn't mean it would?

She kicked off her remaining shoe, enjoying the *clunk* it made as it joined her dress, then stormed into her bedroom. Alone.

Jambrea crashed onto her bed and thought of the last man she'd wasted nearly a decade of her life over. Stuck in this shithole, unable to grow or evolve, hoping he'd know where to find her if miracles happened and he changed his mind.

No matter how amazing Matt and Clint were or how brilliant the potential attraction between the three of them was, she refused to make that colossal mistake again. Flushing more of the best years of her life down the toilet was not an option.

She had to admit it. The pair of hot cops weren't ever going to cross that threshold for a romp and certainly not for something *more*.

"Get. The. Fuck. Out!" she yelled, then rose her voice to ludicrous level. Who cared if her throat was raw in the morning? "Can't you hear me?"

"Goodnight, Jambrea," Clint called softly from the other room.

"Sleep well, wild thing. Call if you need us." Matt sounded like someone had kicked him in the nuts. Not a bad idea. Why hadn't she thought of it before she'd lain down? If the room wasn't spinning so fast, she might consider climbing out of her nest to give assault a whirl. If they arrested her, maybe they'd break out their cuffs. Probably as close as she'd get to what she really craved.

"Fuck off, assholes." She buried her face in her pillows as the sound of the door closing was followed by the creak of her piece-of-shit metal staircase groaning beneath their muscular heft. "I *do* need you. And you don't care."

Why had Matt decided to call her that? *Wild thing.* Not now. Not tonight. When all the walls inside her were crumbling anyway.

It was the last straw. Though she hated to, she sobbed into her pillow until unwanted dreams of days long gone haunted her sleep. The broken record played again as it had infinite times before. She thought she might have escaped, found a new song to dance to—with new partners—but those delusions had been false.

Again, she was flying solo.

Just like she had A.J.

After John.

Chapter Two

Almost Nine Years Earlier

Jambrea stood on a stage a few months after troops alerted to their plight, surely thanks to her spy savior, had hauled her and nine wounded men from the storm shelter. She wished she could move just enough to shield her eyes from the glare of the sun. Nothing could compare to the intensity of the desert rays she'd left behind, but out in the crowd she thought she glimpsed a familiar yet rare shade of blue before the man in the fifth row donned his oversized sunglasses.

It couldn't be him, could it? Hairs lifting on her nape proclaimed it might be. The eerie sense of being watched for the past twelve hours intensified. Damn military protocol that required she stand at attention throughout the entire award ceremony.

Not that she wasn't honored. After all, from what she'd been told, only three women had received a Silver Star since World War II across all branches of service. The third highest honor in the Air Force—for gallantry in action—seemed like overkill for what she considered simply doing the right thing.

The cluster of men she'd helped rescue cheered from the front row. They might disagree.

And what about the one who seemed to subtly tip his hat before exiting the auditorium?

Jambrea knew it was the spy the military was so grateful to have alive to fight sneakily another day. If she'd had any doubt as to his value and usefulness to their country, the nine bazillion reams of Top Secret documents she'd had to sign and

Spread Your Wings

swear to had clinched the deal.

She tracked the man's progress until he disappeared from sight, with one last glance over his shoulder. Then she smiled, shook the Vice President's hand and accepted the small, velvet-lined box that would showcase the medal they pinned on her dress uniform.

Because after today, she wouldn't wear either again—the clothes or the award.

If nothing else, something positive had come from that nightmare day.

Jambrea was free. With the training she needed to get started and the funding for nursing school, which would allow her to secure her public sector license.

Finally, on to the rest of her life.

She clapped for the other honorees and filed off stage. Passing by the families taking pictures of their proud recipients, she rejected the pang of jealousy that attempted to infiltrate her hard-won serenity. Alone, she'd gotten used to surviving. Her parents hadn't approved of her joining the military, even as a way of escaping the poverty they'd raised her in. When she'd tried to visit on leave, she'd found they had been evicted, their house condemned and no forwarding address given.

Yet another reason to keep building something for herself.

On impulse, she swung her beat-up jalopy into the parking lot of a tattoo parlor she'd passed earlier. The neon sign blinking in the window proclaimed walk-ins were welcome. She wondered if the hundred bucks in her pocket would be enough for what she wanted.

Turned out, the artist refused her cash due to his respect for her service to the country.

And suddenly, things were looking up.

Jambrea climbed the open-backed metal stairway to her

no-frills apartment. She hadn't bothered with an extravagant place, knowing she'd be gone for quite a while. Hell, mostly she'd been proud to have a decent apartment she could afford on her own. No roommate, not even roaches to crash her party. Maybe now it'd be time to look for something...homier. As soon as she got settled at school and into her new routine.

She dropped her stuff on the living room floor, her duffle making a dull thud on the shaggy harvest gold carpet that was functional, if outdated.

"About time you showed up."

Jambrea would have screamed if she hadn't recognized her uninvited visitor's voice. That sensual rasp had haunted her dreams for months. She flipped on a dim light and took in the utter relaxation of his frame as he lounged on the ugly recliner she'd picked up at Mrs. Daisy's yard sale the summer before her deployment.

"Glad to see you made it out in one piece." Suppressing the urge to shuffle beneath his steady gaze, she stared into his eyes. The electric blue irises grew as his pupils shrank in the light. How long had he been sitting in blackness?

How many years had he spent in the shadows?

"Same goes." He rose from the depths of saggy cushions, which had nearly sucked her into their black hole a million times before, as if he were a jaguar unfurling from its perch on a tree limb. Silently, he stalked to her.

Moisture abandoned her throat, leaving it dry when he approached.

"What happened here?" He brushed a finger over the bandage around her wrist. "You didn't try to hurt yourself, did you?"

Jambrea threw her head back and laughed. "I'm not a quitter."

"Didn't take you for one." He squinted. "Though I didn't see those at the ceremony. Your sleeves were long, but I'd have noticed bandages like that."

"It *was* you." A grin tugged at her lips.

"Yeah. Wouldn't have missed it. You deserved that, you know." The power of his gaze struck her once more.

"I suppose." She shrugged.

"So..." His thumbs brushed over her pulse in a circle, careful of applying too much pressure.

"They're tattoos." Endorphins still pumped through her from the inking. "Probably red and puffy... Want to see?"

"Hell yes." He seemed surprised. "Didn't take you for that sort of girl."

"What kind is that?" A raised eyebrow warned him of the thin ice he trod on.

"Hey, calm down. I love a woman with permanent art." He held his hands up in surrender as she unwound the dressings. She could easily replace them with superior wraps when they were finished with show and tell. "It just takes commitment. You're young. And those are really visible."

"I'm not ashamed of expressing myself."

"Tell me you didn't get something dumb or meaningless." He scrunched his eyes closed until she swore she didn't opt for a misspelled Chinese character or, maybe, an abstract doodle.

"See for yourself." The heat of his stare astounded her again, making her feel as if he seared her skin. Even the buzzing tattoo machine hadn't scored her so deep.

"'I never saw a wild thing sorry for itself.'" He grunted his agreement with the quote braceleting her right wrist before scanning the other. The delicacy with which he rotated her arm in his grasp had her knees wobbling. "'I want to live my life so that my nights are not full of regrets.'"

"So?" She waited for his verdict, unsure why it meant so much to gain his approval.

"I'm a D.H. Lawrence fan myself, wild thing." Thrills radiated from the soft kiss he placed just above the text, on her pulse. The damn beat had sped up to something near supersonic. It didn't slow when he recovered her minor wounds carefully. She admired his craggy features, which had not a drop of pretty boy about them but still managed to be breathtaking. His too-long hair was sun-fried and a little shaggy, the dirty blond highlights in it something movie stars had artfully applied. "There's something about you, Jambi. I haven't been able to get you out of my mind since that day. And I'm not the kind of guy who gets distracted easily."

"It's kind of crazy, right?" She hoped he felt half the instant attraction she did.

"Uh huh. I shouldn't even be here." He looked toward the door long enough to make her think he might change his mind and scram.

"Well, since you are, why don't you make it count?" Tentatively, she reached for his jaw, cupping the distinct edge, loving the scratch of his substantial scruff on her palm. He didn't flinch. What else could he have come for if not for this? He must have felt it too.

"Do you know what you're asking for?" A step forward eliminated most of the space between them.

"Pretty sure this falls in the 'no regret' category." She nudged his face lower so that she could do what she'd dreamed of for months.

The kiss trumped every fantasy she'd had. Urgent. Dangerous. Yet ultimately safe.

She trusted him, even if it made her the biggest fool in the universe. The government hadn't conferred the Silver Star on her for rescuing a terrorist. And he hadn't left her in his dust as he could so easily have done in the midst of a war zone. If he'd had to make hard choices along a windier path than most people travelled, so what? That only made him nobler in her estimation.

For tonight, she wanted to help him forget all the people who'd tried to hurt him.

Almost as much as she craved the bliss he could impart. It would wipe away the loneliness of her past and kick-start her brand new life.

She nibbled on his lower lip when he separated them to draw a deep breath. He didn't go far. Especially not with her teeth teasing his mouth.

He walked her backward, toward the only bedroom in the tiny place. It wouldn't have been difficult to spot her pink comforter even in the diffuse glow of the single illuminated lamp. When the backs of her knees collided with the dipped mattress, they tumbled together.

The weight of him didn't hurt. Welcome, it reminded her that another human being joined her tonight, filled the spartan space with something other than her off-key singing or the conversations she sometimes conducted with herself. Maybe it was time to get a pet, at least.

Because she knew her super spy wouldn't be around for long.

Could she handle that?

When his hand massaged her breast while he multitasked, delivering another round of wet, lingering kisses, she figured it was worse to starve completely than to miss out on seconds. Unsure of what to do, she allowed her desires free rein. The flexing sinew of his back called to her fingers, urging them to explore the long lengths of muscle beneath his non-descript gray T-shirt.

No matter how hard he aimed for ordinary, he couldn't disguise how exceptional he truly was. Especially when he saw parts of her no one else had bothered to notice.

"You're so decent, Jambi. Do you know how hot that makes

me?" He murmured in her ear between nips on her neck and traces of his deft fingers over her collarbones. "It's been so long since I met an honest, hardworking, trustworthy person. They're an endangered species in my world."

She accepted his praise along with his physical reward for the attributes she'd concentrated on to stay true to herself. Better than a government issued shiny bauble any day. Muddled thoughts or not, she knew all those times she'd taken the high road were paying off. Being able to say she was proud of herself, and how she'd fought to get where she was, meant a lot to her. It was all she had to cling to sometimes.

"Thanks." A groan cut her short when he pressed his leg between her thighs, spreading her and tucking closer to her core. He activated nerve endings she thought long rusted with disuse. The button on the jeans she'd changed into after the ceremony were no match for his roving hands. And when he slipped his fingers inside her panties, she decided she'd better come clean. Or he'd figure out her secret on his own soon enough.

"I—I, uh, don't do this all the time." She swallowed hard, but supposed he ought to know. Maybe he'd adjust his expectations a bit, teach her to please him. "In fact, I sort of *never* did it before."

"Good to know. It's not smart to fuck strangers." His hips hesitated in their grinding motion, making her need flare even as her logic returned a bit.

"Right. I get that." A deep breath mashed her breasts against the hard plane of his chest. "But I meant that I've never done this before. Like at all. You know, sex."

"What?" His attempt to jerk upright was thwarted by her legs snaking around him and clinging tight. Powerful thighs had never seemed like a blessing before. "Wild thing, no. You should wait for someone special."

The slump of his shoulders made up her mind.

"I did." She hugged him with her arms as tightly as she did with her lower body, for once grateful for her less than delicate build. "Finish what you started."

Still he didn't resume the passionate volley they'd been embroiled in before she opened her big, dumb mouth.

"Please," she begged.

"Are you sure?" The unadulterated confusion in his stormy eyes had her nodding instantly. No way would she allow him to believe *he* wasn't worthy. She'd had enough of feeling *less than* in her life to do the same to another.

"Hell yes."

His muscles tensed, then relaxed beneath her continued kneading. When she lifted one hand to his nape then buried her fingers in his hair, he growled a little. "That's right. For tonight, I'm yours."

He kissed her again before rising only long enough to shed his clothes with brusque, efficient moves that reminded her of a master martial artist. For all she knew, he was one. The sleek, toned physique he displayed as he approached once more made it more likely than not. He'd hidden a hell of a lot of strength in that deceptively lean body.

Jambrea could stare at him for hours. Except they both knew they didn't have the luxury of time. He went somewhat slower as he discarded first her jeans then wrestled her shirt and bra off, careful not to scrape her wrists even with the soft cloth. If his hungry stare and appreciative murmurings were any indication, he savored unwrapping her.

Though she'd never felt entirely comfortable in her body, he erased any lingering worries with every reverent caress and kiss he placed on her newly exposed skin. When he licked his way down her belly toward the top of her rainbow cotton panties, she couldn't help but giggle with pure delight.

"Something funny?" He raised a brow, but didn't pause his descent.

"More like I'm relieved. Never thought I was going to find someone who could make me feel like this," she whispered the truth, glad for the darkness dancing around them.

"Oh, wild thing. You're meant for something big. I'm just the bastard who's gotten lucky enough to have a taste of you before you find forever." He drew slow circles above her ribs then nuzzled her mound through the thin fabric of her underwear. "Never forget that. You deserve the best."

The merits of debate flew from her mind when he walked her panties down her hips. She kicked them into the corner of the room and allowed him to spread her thighs even wider apart. At the first contact of his open mouth on her pussy, she yelped.

He chuckled against her damp flesh. "Hang on. It gets better."

Colors sparkled behind her eyelids when she scrunched them closed to endure the flood of sensation he imparted with his talented tongue. She couldn't keep herself from reaching for him when he proved his promise. Her hands roamed over his cut arms and shoulders then to his hair. Though she tried not to tug, she couldn't help her fingers from entwining in the shaggy strands.

He didn't seem to mind, if his grunts told a true story. In fact, he seemed eager to give her what she demanded, burying his face between her legs and playing her with his mouth as if she were some kind of instrument and he a virtuoso. It didn't take long before the pressure mounting inside her proved too much to resist. She shattered, her hips instinctively rocking in a repetitive arc that enhanced the motion of his lips on her clit.

Though the orgasm was more powerful than any she'd rubbed herself to, she still regretted that her channel clenched around nothing more substantial than air. "Please, fill me. I want to know what it's like. I need you."

"Wild thing, you still have a hymen. I can see it, feel it. Are you sure you don't want to wait? I've never been with a virgin before." He scrubbed his hand over his face, clearing some of the slickness from his chin though that probably hadn't been his intent. "I'd do anything to keep from hurting you. That's not what I planned by coming here tonight. Believe me."

Something in his gorgeous eyes made her wonder if he was talking about more than just the physical intimacy they'd flown into. Could he tell how much she cared? That when he walked, he'd take a piece of her with him? And still she wouldn't deny either of them the experience. How could she when it was so brilliant? Amazing.

"I do." She reached for him, settling him higher on her body, cushioning him as best she could. When they kissed again, somewhat less harried this time, she moaned into his mouth. The thick length of his cock nudged her as they melded together. "This is what I want. You. Tonight. Right now."

"If you're sure..."

"Shut up and fuck me already." She laughed when his jaw went slack. "Hurry."

He dove for his discarded jeans and ripped his wallet from the back pocket. In a flash, he'd opened a condom packet then rolled the thin latex over his cock. She got a good look at the long, hard length of him as he manhandled himself.

Plenty of naked men had passed through her wards. Usually, they weren't aroused. Even those who did get hard while she gave them a sponge bath or while they were sleeping hadn't seemed quite as impressive as him. Would he fit? Would it hurt?

At this point, she didn't really care. She wanted to know what it was like to share that bond with someone. If only temporarily.

Jambrea held her arms out, open.

"Wild thing." He sighed as he stroked himself from base to tip a few times while studying her. For once, she didn't shy away from being the focus of someone's attention. "You're so beautiful."

"I don't need words. Just come here." She blushed, though she turned her head so maybe he couldn't tell.

And then he was there. Blanketing her, holding her close to his chest so she could feel the pounding of his heart, which matched hers. He kissed her, looking into her eyes without blinking as he aligned their bodies. The tip of his cock pressed against the covered opening of her body.

She held her breath as he advanced. At first it simply felt like she stretched impossibly around him. The nurse in her knew the thin barrier would flex and allow him some leeway. But when he rocked against her yet couldn't progress any farther, a spear of pain had her eyes widening.

"Yeah, I'm there. This is it. No turning back…"

Jambrea rocked her hips upward and impaled herself on his shaft. She writhed as a bolt of lightning ran up her spine. Through the madness of mingled lust and pain, he pinned her to the mattress, kept her as still as possible and soothed her with a blend of reassurance and tender kisses.

A ragged gasp inflated her lungs, pressing her and her visitor together completely. He kissed away tears she hadn't realized she'd shed as the world returned to focus. His hands released her forearms and instead roamed over her body from the sides of her breasts to her hips, ensuring the embers of arousal didn't flicker out completely in the face of temporary discomfort.

"How are you doing?" he whispered in her ear as he nuzzled her neck. When had anyone taken such good care of her?

Wrapping her arms around him, she squeezed him tight, hoping her hug could say all the things knotted up in her throat at that moment. And when she felt him trembling between her thighs, she shivered.

The motion reminded her of where they were joined. Her

muscles flexed of their own accord and both of them groaned at the resulting pleasure.

"Wild thing, I can't stay like this much longer," he rasped. "You're killing me. So tight, hot, wet. Damn."

"So don't. Show me why this was worth it." She trailed her hand from his shoulder to his ass, squeezing the tensed muscle there and loving his resulting thrust forward.

"Jesus. Yes." He withdrew a tiny fraction, not enough that the bulbous head of his cock slipped from her though. Then he returned, slow yet steady, feeding her more of his length than she had taken herself.

"Oh." A moan left her parted lips.

"Yeah." He smiled against her neck. "Me too."

He backed up then drove forward, implanting himself even deeper. God, how far could he reach?

Jambrea's mind disengaged. For once she stopped thinking and let herself simply be. Feel. Enjoy life and the moment. Ecstasy infused every breath, every heartbeat, every clench of her pussy around his thick erection.

When he bottomed out in her, they both smiled as their gazes collided. Locked deep, he kissed her again and again. The base of his cock and the solid muscle of his abdomen pressed against her clit as he rocked, knitting them together as tightly as possible.

The beginnings of another orgasm wrung her muscles around him.

"Go ahead, wild thing." He encouraged her to let go. Of everything. And she did.

For the first time in her life, she jumped.

And when the climax had begun to fade, she realized he was moving inside her. He rode her, finding his own rapture in the moist clinging of her pussy. Though she wouldn't have believed it possible, the sight of his desperate desire ramped her

45

up again.

Soon he found his rhythm.

When she realized how ferociously she clung to his shoulders, she uncurled her fingers and hoped she hadn't scratched him too badly.

"I don't mind." He nipped her neck then moved a little faster, harder between her thighs. "Feels fucking great. To know you want me too. It's not for show with you."

What kind of women had he been with? His job didn't exactly make relationships a possibility, she supposed.

Jambrea smothered him. Within her and above her. She curled her arms and legs around his shuttling body, which continued to pump into her with greater force and frequency by the second. His torso became damp with sweat, and she knew it had nothing to do with exertion. More likely restraint.

"Don't insult me by holding back." Her demand came out like a roar.

"You're going to kill me." His head lowered until his forehead rested on hers, his breath washing across her face. "I want you to come with me."

"Twice is more than I've ever managed in a night." She prepared herself to accept his needs, to become the receptacle for his passion. There was pleasure in knowing she could give him that. A temporary respite from the stress of the life he'd chosen, or maybe the one that'd picked him.

"Well, you've never spent one with me before." Arrogance tinged his smirk and he swiveled his hips, applying himself to teasing her even as he slaked his own lust.

He hunched his back, allowing him to suck on her nipples while he continued to plow into her over and over. And soon she knew he'd get his wish.

The comforter ended up fisted in her hands somehow. Her heels dug into the mattress as she held herself up and open to meet each of his lunges. Spine bowed, head thrown back, hips rocking in sync with his, Jambrea yielded.

As she came, so did he.

The man above her cursed, shouted, groaned and shook. He emptied himself into the condom he wore with endless jerks of his body that demonstrated to her just how completely vulnerable he'd allowed himself to become.

For a long time after, they lay boneless and tangled in the quiet. Content to stay still, they surfed the endorphins pumping through their veins. Until she feared she might doze off and wake to an empty bed and hollow arms, only to find this had all been the best dream of her life.

"Are you okay?" His sexy voice had dropped an octave. It sounded scratchier than she remembered.

"Perfect."

"Yes, you were." He squeezed her with one arm.

She kissed his chest, sighing when he rose, going into the bathroom to dispose of the condom. Running water followed shortly after the flush of the toilet. When he returned, and stood hovering over her, she couldn't stop herself from wondering.

"So...what's your name, anyway?" She worried the corner of the sheet draped haphazardly over her as he sat on the edge of the bed and toyed with her cropped hair.

"Does it matter?" A laugh puffed from between his swollen lips. He'd applied himself thoroughly to imparting pleasure, guaranteeing her first time had been worth the wait.

"I guess not, but I'd sort of like to know who took my virginity." A blush stole over her cheeks.

"Right." A pause stretched out until he cleared his throat. "It's John."

"Like John Doe?" She rolled her eyes. "Just say you won't tell me. Can't. Super spy etiquette or whatever."

A rich laugh filled her shabby bedroom as he flopped to his

back, staring at the tan, amoeba-shaped water stains decorating the ceiling. "Tell a woman the truth and see where it gets you."

"Seriously?" Propping up on one elbow allowed her to peer into his gorgeous blue eyes, ones she'd never forget.

"Yep." The edges of his lips curled into something resembling a smile. At least from a man as hard and world weary as him.

"Nice to meet you." She dropped a kiss on his mouth. It quickly became more and would have turned into a whole lot of yumminess if she hadn't paused him by lifting up then climbing from bed. He steadied her as her weak legs grew somewhat coordinated once more. "Sorry, have to use the restroom. And maybe I should grab a quick shower."

He grimaced when he took in the smears of blood on her thigh.

"I'm fine, promise. Be right back."

"Okay. Mind if I take a look around?" He sat up, his long legs folding over the edge of her mattress.

"Not much to see, but sure, knock yourself out." Waving toward the main space of the modest apartment, she wished for once she had something a little more presentable.

She rushed through her shower, not giving a shit about the lukewarm water this time. With every splash she prayed that he'd still be there when she emerged. If not, she'd given him the perfect chance to poof. Up to him.

The prospect of an empty house hurt her insides.

Just a little longer. A little more. Please.

Relief brought tears to her eyes when she exited the bathroom to find him lounging on her bed once more, though this time clothed. He curled his fingers toward his palm. "Come here, wild thing."

She didn't have to be told twice. And neither did she care

that all she wore was a towel. He'd seen every bit of her tonight anyway. Not just her body, either.

Burrowing into the bed and soaking up his perpetual heat, she clung to him. They didn't talk much, but they enjoyed each other's company and the delight of not spending the loneliest part of the day in solitude.

When the rising sun began to turn her bedroom wall the slightest shade of rose, he sighed and kissed her on the forehead. He didn't have to tell her their time was up.

"If you can come back, you're welcome." Saying 'my door is always open' wouldn't matter to a man like him. He'd pick any locks that stood in his way and she'd be none the wiser. But it meant something to her to offer.

"Ah, Jambi, don't do that to us. I can't." He left no wiggle room, though she couldn't squash the hope in her heart. "It was crazy to stay the night, never mind retrace my steps. I won't put you in danger like that. You have no idea the way I live. In twilight. I thought you understood."

"I do." She traced the muscle twitching in his cheek. "But there should be a place where only the things you want to happen, happen."

Of course he got it. He got her. His laugh would be something she treasured. "That's the wrong kind of wild thing. Though I like Maurice Sendak too. What I'm trying to say is that I've worked hard to never regret the decisions I've had to make in my life. Finding that impossible today."

He rested his forehead on hers for the space of several breaths, skimmed his fingers over her obscured tattoo, then crawled from bed.

Jambrea thought it might have been the most difficult thing she'd ever witnessed. The strength and courage it took him to keep going awed her. Now there was a true hero. If she thought he'd accept it, she'd give him her medal. "You can do it, John. Whatever the hell *it* is. I believe in you."

"I'll keep fighting. Until my last breath. I promise that to you and all the other civilized people in this country, even if they never know I exist." He tucked his feet into running shoes. "This meant something to me. Don't ever doubt it, though you'll never hear from me again. On the darkest of nights, I'll have memories of you. There are still innocent people in the world, even if I don't get to meet many of them."

Tears stung her eyes. She wished she could comfort him more, tend to the wounds she could sense lingering inside the valiant warrior.

"That's not how I want to remember you." He swiped at one fat drop that leaked from the corner of her eyes and tracked down her cheek. "Smile, Jambi. And wait for the right man to come along. Make sure he deserves a woman like you, huh?"

"Sure," she mumbled with a sniff. Who else would be able to claim something like that after him?

"Stay safe, kid." He grinned at her half-snarl.

"You too, John." She mourned as he covered the hint of his rock solid abs beneath his T-shirt with a non-descript black hoodie then slipped his gun into the concealed pocket at the rear of his pants. When he'd finished, she'd never guess he carried.

How many other secrets did he hide as effectively?

"So long." He blew her a kiss then melded into the dusk of her living room. The door didn't make a sound when it closed, but the emptiness in her apartment—and her heart—guaranteed he'd left the building.

And her life.

Forever.

Chapter Three

Two Weeks After Lily's Wedding

"Stop laughing. I need your help." Jambrea's usually smiling face, unaccustomed to frowning or self-pity, couldn't quite pull off the scowl she attempted. The impressions of her dimples lingered.

"To get laid?" Lily suffocated her evil *bwah ha ha ha* and refrained from steepling her fingers in front of her. Her less experienced—*way* less experienced—friend wouldn't understand. The inevitable downfall of two cocky cops had more to do with her delight than the obvious discomfort of the woman in front of her.

The fact that Jambi had come to Gunther's Playground the exact same day Lily returned to work after her honeymoon spoke volumes. Jambea had thought about her approach, calculated the best course of action. And she was taking steps to get what she needed. Not so different than most of Lily's clients. Yet worlds away too.

Red cheeks and bright eyes gave Jambi's nervousness away even if her short hair standing on end after dozens of finger-combings hadn't. Lily didn't need such obvious signs to read the cute nurse she'd become such close friends with. Who'd have thought the Mistress and the innocent could nurture so many commonalities? A wolf and a sheep. Both enjoyed their place in nature's hierarchy.

"Well...yes." Jambrea chewed her lower lip long enough that Lily had to restrain herself from ordering the other woman to stop before she hurt herself. Simply because she was dressed in her full Mistress Lily regalia and sitting behind her desk at her private club didn't mean she had any authority over Jambrea.

At least for now.

"Why? What happened with Matt and Clint? I saw them drag you out of our reception." Lily tipped her head, truly curious. "I didn't figure you'd make it all the way home before someone was getting a BJ, at least."

"Maybe *that's* what I did wrong. I probably could have gone down on Clint on the ride to my place." Jambrea shook her head. "No. They won't let me touch them. Honestly, I'm so confused. I don't get it at all."

"Have you asked them what's going on?" Lily often counseled submissives. This would be a hell of a lot easier if she could lock her three bullheaded pals in a room for a few days. If they'd just let her orchestrate a session, all this extraneous drama could be dealt with so they could move on.

Then again, the last lesson she'd tried to teach Matt and Clint didn't seem to have stuck.

"I did." Jambi paused, slumping in her chair. "Well, kind of. I went insane on them. Screaming, throwing things, the works."

"You?" Lily leaned forward. No signs of sarcasm were visible from several inches closer.

"Yep. Not my finest moment. I was kind of sloshed, not that that's any excuse." She smacked her forehead repeatedly with the heel of her palm. "I asked them what I was doing wrong. Why they kept turning me on, then shoving me away."

"What did they say?" A sinking feeling crept into the euphoria Lily had lived with since her wedding day. Maybe... She might know what the problem was after all.

Could her experiment have gone horribly awry?

"Some bullshit line." Jambi's fight started to fade and instead of amped she just looked weary. Bloodshot, puffy eyes guaranteed she'd spent some quality time mourning lately, too. This was bad. *Really* bad. "The standard, 'it's not you, it's me—*us*—'crap. That's when I went berserk. I mean, how could they have made out with me one minute, the night of your Sex Offender incident, then by the next time I saw them, only a few days later, go into this screwed up downward spiral? Just when I was finally growing a damn spine, ready to believe all the things people have been saying about how they look at me and stuff, they go crazy! It pushed me over the edge. And even after all that—God, I acted like a total frothing-at-the-mouth psycho—I woke up the next morning to find Clint smashed onto the couch and Matt camped on the floor with just my rainbow peace sign Snuggie as a blanket. They faked leaving, then came back to make sure I didn't die in the middle of the night. Of course, as soon as I woke up they ran out of there before we could discuss anything serious. Why do they care, but not enough?"

Oh yeah, time to come clean. Because Lily had a feeling Jambrea had suffered weeks of insomnia scouring internally for an external problem. "Are you feeling less postal now? Because I have a confession."

"What? *You?* Did they talk to you? Ask advice or something? I don't want you to violate their confidence." Jambi didn't seem pissed, more inquisitive. She never got that worked up really. It said something that she'd lost her cool with the guys. And no matter how much her heart hurt, she thought of those around her first. So freaking selfless it bordered on unwise.

Lily could stand to learn from her friend, she thought.

"No. They didn't say anything to me. Still, I might have an inkling. Worse, this might kind of be my fault. Oh boy. How can I say this?" Lily considered her options, then decided Jambrea would respect a straightforward approach the most. Even if she didn't like what she heard.

Her guest tapped her fingers on the polished ebony arm of the occasional chair she graced.

"You said they made out with you the night I took Sex Offender, right?" Lily recalled that insane evening. The substance flooding her veins had driven her and Jeremy to extremes. It had been the first time she bent for him. And he'd granted her everything she needed, including access to as many men as it had taken to slake her augmented passion.

Matt and Clint both included. *Shit.*

"Yeah." Jambrea turned fierce. "And I still can't believe you did that. The things I've seen at the hospital, working on addicts and the lab testing for the antidote... You're nuts."

"There wasn't another way to infiltrate Morselli's operation."

"I know, Lily." Jambrea backpedaled. She smiled. "It was the bravest and most idiotic thing you've ever done. You saved countless lives."

"But...did they tell you what happened after?" As an infamous Mistress, Lily didn't often feel the need to squirm, but she did now. Talk about honor, Jambrea topped the list. What would she say about the lengths they'd had to go to in order to end Morselli and The Scientist's madness?

"That they both had sex with you? Yes. Bitch." She looked wistful, not betrayed, when her gaze met Lily's. "Was it good, at least? Let me live vicariously for like two seconds."

"I don't remember a lot of specifics." Lily shivered.

"Sorry, that was inconsiderate of me." Jambrea retracted her wish. "I understand that it was a necessity. That the drug is agonizing if not combated by endorphins released through sex. Truly. I get it. They would never leave you to suffer."

"No, no. It's okay. I'm not going to pretend it wasn't one of the hottest experiences of my life and would have been even without the chemicals poisoning me." Even now, the memories had the power to rev her up. And Jeremy was at work on the graveyard shift down at the station. Damn. She drew on years of experience to focus. "I will say, Matt is one of the biggest guys I've ever seen. And I've seen plenty."

"No kidding, he's built like a refrigerator." Jambrea hummed. "I like that. He makes me feel dainty. I haven't felt like that since I was five."

"Jambs, I mean he's big everywhere. *Enormous*." Since when did Lily blush? She'd developed the bad habit since Jeremy had assumed control. Damn him.

"Oh. Right." Jambrea groaned. "Now I hate you even more."

"I'm just warning you because I think someday you're going to need to be prepared. As soon as we can figure out the rest." She wondered if vanilla relationships would be as easy to puzzle through as the more structured power exchanges she indulged in. In her world, there were rules, understandings, clear delineations of authority. Jambi was living in a free for all. Fucking terrifying. "And unless I'm completely off the mark, I'm betting you don't have a ton of experience."

"Uh." No response was answer enough.

"I'm not saying that's a bad thing. I wish I could tell Jeremy he was shortlisted, one of a precious few, but my dad had me trained by the time most kids go to college. You know that. Your experience is so different from my life. I forget sometimes how wholesome you are."

"Lily, your father was a monster. That's no reflection on you."

"Thanks, and I get that. Really." Her new husband had made sure of it. In such a short time, he'd erased most of her doubts and replaced them with reassurance and love. It would mean so much to help people she cared about find something as precious.

"So, tell me why you're suddenly nervous? Beating around the bush isn't like you." Without flinching, Jambrea challenged Lily despite her complete Mistress mode. That took balls. "What haven't you told me? How could it be worse than fucking the guys? Although, they made out with me *after* that, for the record. Things weren't all wonky yet. Maybe if I hadn't been so timid we could have already sealed the deal by then."

"No use in wondering *what if.* They didn't make it easy on you. They were more interested in butting heads in some crazy bid for your attention than in working together. I think it was that night, that crazy orgy, that might have flipped on a light bulb for Matt and Clint." Lily schooled herself not to squirm. "I think they liked what they saw. Or at least they realized there are many possibilities beyond the conventional."

"So what turned them off again? Me?" Jambrea deflated.

"I don't think they're disinterested. In fact, the opposite is likely true." She chose her words carefully.

"Oh sure. They're soooooooo horny at the thought of the three of us getting it on together they would rather suffer irreparable degradation of their vertebral columns than join me in my shitty, but pretty comfy, bed. Sounds like I barely escaped being fucked to death with Matt's giant cock. Ugh."

"Jambrea. Stop. It's *not* you."

"It's them. I know. They said so." She put her head in her hands and rocked on the chair.

"No. It was me. A couple days after the Sex Offender thing, I was just messing around. I'm sorry. I thought they'd figure it out eventually on their own or maybe that they already had. Plus I like to poke in people's heads a little, you know, bad habit." Lily tried to talk fast. "They pissed me off. And when they asked how to make it up to me, I..."

"Whoa." Jambrea let her fingers slide apart so she could stare at Lily. "You're never speechless. What's going on? What did you do?"

"I dared them to kiss each other. And I think they liked it."

"What!" The chair clattered against the hardwood floor

when it toppled. Jambrea stood, her chest heaving as if she'd sprinted in from the parking lot. "Matt kissed Clint? Like full-on, mouth to mouth?"

"Yep. At first it was kind of more chin to chin. But they figured it out pretty quick. It was hardly anything, but I could see it had the potential to become a lot more." A sigh escaped her at the memory.

"Stop drooling." Jambrea glared at her.

Lily actually swiped her hand across her lips to double check.

"Oh my God, you've been living my dream life." The tall, statuesque woman began to pace after righting the chair she'd so recently occupied. "I can't believe this. I mean, I'm happy for them of course. But why wouldn't they just tell me? I'd have supported them."

"I'm not sure about that part." What a mess. How could Lily fix things?

"So you think they're trying to tell me they're into each other now?" Jambrea's forehead creased as she pinched the bridge of her nose. "I guess I was a convenient excuse for them to experiment. And when they didn't need that pretext anymore...I got Photoshopped right out of the picture?"

"I don't know, Jambi. That doesn't ring true to me." Lily shook her head. "Damn men, I've spent most of my life learning how they think, but sometimes they still surprise me. How do you feel about the two of them being intimate with each other?"

"It's fucking hot as hell." Jambrea paused her circuit when Lily joined her on the lovely area rug. Gunther hadn't even blinked when she'd requested a sizable budget for decorating her workspace. It was all part of setting the stage. She put her arms around Jambi, unable to leave the woman alone another moment. Considering her absentee family, Lily's friend sometimes had issues with trust and abandonment. Didn't they all? Maybe soon she'd believe she'd never have to fight alone again. "Could you imagine...?"

Lily recalled all too well the intimacy of their kiss. Awkward and new, there'd still been something there that had soaked her panties. Well, it would have if she'd been wearing any. Then again, she did like to watch two men together. They touched...differently...than when they were with a woman. It was delicious.

"Well, actually, I don't have to. I saw it, remember?" She winked at Jambrea, giggling when she took in the other woman's gaping jaw. "It was as sexy as you're imagining."

"Great. Now I'm going to have more dreams about impossible things. Unless I grow a dick tomorrow, they're not going to want me." Jambrea sighed. "I give up, Lily. I can't do it anymore. I'm tired of fighting. I'm tired of striking out. Of all the stars misaligning. Luck hates me. I want something fast and fun. A sure thing. Is that too much to ask?"

"No, honey, it's not." Screw this. Lily squeezed the woman on the edge of losing her composure. "I'm just not sure I have the right venue for what you'd like."

"Oh." Jambrea went stiff in her arms. "I didn't think of that. Am I insulting you by asking you to use the Playground as a hook up spot? I don't think of you as some kind of madam. Shit, I have no idea what the protocol is here. I should have asked before I assumed..."

"Shush." Lily chuckled as she swatted Jambrea's shoulder. "You're fine. Sure, this place means more to the majority, but there are some people looking to scratch an itch. What I'm trying to say is that I don't know what you're looking for in a partner, really. We'd need to hammer that out before I could make any suggestions."

At the end of the day, Lily knew what the best match would be. But they could take the long way there. "Are you looking for a strictly-sex, one-night show, a fling or something that could turn into a forever thing, even if there's no pressure right at first?"

"Oh. I guess I'd like a normal relationship at some point. It just doesn't seem like fate has that in the cards for me." She shrugged.

"Why do you say that? I kind of thought you preferred your independence since you haven't dated in all the time I've known you." Not a bad approach, Lily admitted. At least until you meet the right guy, or guys, who sweep all your protests away. Sort of like Matt and Clint had for Jambrea. Definitely like Jeremy had done for her.

"Who says being single was by choice?" her friend countered.

"I got the sense you weren't looking." Lily was impossible to bullshit. "Or maybe even that you were taken. Unavailable. There have been so many times I've seen guys flirt with you and it bounces right off. You don't seem to care."

"I think you're exaggerating. It's not like men throw themselves at me." She waved her hands up and down her body. Lily would kill for some of her friend's height.

"Oh yeah? What about the cute waiter who always gives us free dessert at the Creekside Café? He even puts his business card, including his cell number, in the folio with the receipt each time." Lily shook her head.

"Who, Mark? He probably does that to all his customers."

"No. He doesn't. I've been there with other people too, and he never hands out his info or brings complimentary chocolate raspberry cake." Lily crossed her arms.

"Then I understand why you like to go there when we eat out. Whatever, I tip well." Jambrea shrugged, still oblivious to her attractiveness. "Okay, though, you might have hit it with unavailable. Emotionally anyway. I guess I have a knack for finding exactly the wrong men. Ones who aren't really up for grabs. There was someone once. I thought maybe he was my forever guy… It was dumb. There was never any chance. I just couldn't shake off the way I felt for him. No one else compared, until Matt and Clint."

"Who was he?" Lily sat, riveted to the devotion practically making her friend glow.

"John."

"John who?" Not that she expected she knew the guy. More that Lily could sense there was more to the story. Curiosity mixed with professional interest. If she planned to set Jambi up, she had to know what her triggers were.

"I don't know." Jambi sniffed. "I never knew. He was a spy. In the military. I met him overseas. The day our hospital came under fire."

"Isn't that what you got your medal for?" How romantic. And tragically bold. Leave it to Jambrea to lust after the most impossible of lovers.

"Yep. They said it was for saving the nine soldiers, but it wasn't. We all knew it was because of John. He breezed through the ceremony, then showed up at my place later. We…we made love. In the morning, he disappeared. And I never saw him or heard from him again."

"Wait." Lily had to have misunderstood. "When did you get that award again?"

"Nine years ago." Her friend sank onto the chair once more. This time she buried her face in her hands. Splayed fingers allowed her to peek out at Lily's gaping mouth.

"You're telling me you hung on to a one-night stand for nearly a decade?" Lily regretted her unusually shrill tone when Jambi flinched. "Honey, you didn't have a crush. You were *in love*. I'm so sorry he didn't deserve it."

"He told me it couldn't ever happen again. It's not his fault I didn't listen. To be honest, though, there's still a place in my heart for him." Jambrea cleared her throat. "They say you never forget your first."

Lily couldn't help herself. She plopped to her haunches in front of her friend, clasping Jambrea's knees in her hands. "Are you saying?"

"That I'm a one-hit wonder? Unfortunately so." She laughed. "Or maybe a solo act. I'm an expert with my rabbit vibrator."

"No shit." Lily was starting to see why the trio was having so much trouble hurdling their obstacles. There were land mines in every direction.

"And after all this time, I finally find not one but two guys who can make me forget those old dreams, but I waited too long and now they don't want me either. I feel like if I don't do something to get over it quick, I'll waste another decade of my life wondering what could have been. It's hopeless. Why do I sabotage myself like that?"

"It's not you, Jambi, it's them. This time the line really is true."

"So can you help me or not?" Quiet desperation radiated from her friend. If Lily didn't facilitate a session for her, she'd likely put herself at risk. Maybe troll for a partner at an unmonitored site on the Internet or something. No way would the Mistress in her allow that to happen.

Guests at the Playground were screened. Their health records were current and they had to demonstrate skill in certain arenas before being allowed to practice riskier acts on other members. The club was as safe a place to experiment as could be reasonably expected.

"Yes. I can." Lily smiled. "Why don't we go grab some lunch and dessert from Mark? While we're there, you can fill out a survey about what kinds of things you'd like to experience. We'll get started on the required health forms and background check too. For you, I'll push things through quickly. How's Saturday?"

If they didn't act fast, Jambrea might change her mind and ruin the plan Lily had begun to form in her mind.

"A lifetime away." The taller woman giggled, finally showing some of her usual pep. "Perfect. Thank you."

"That's what friends are for." They rose together. Lily enjoyed the hell out of their complimentary confection before returning to her duties, and her matchmaking plots.

Chapter Four

"I feel like we've been called to the principal's office," Matt grumbled as he and Clint took chairs side by side in Lily's stronghold at the Playground.

"She didn't sound real pleased with us, did she?" Clint winced.

"What gave it away? The 'get your dumb asses down here, pronto' part of her rant or the ice in her tone—cold enough to freeze my balls off over the phone?" The bigger cop stared at his partner as he crossed his arms. The way Clint eyed his bulging muscles made him shift in his seat. Part of him was pissed right back at Lily. She'd gone and screwed with their minds just when they'd sort of committed to doing something about this crazy thing with Jambrea.

The sweet woman had been all he could think about for months. She proved over and over again how compassionate, diligent and easygoing she was while he and Clint had danced around a solution to their problem—being massively attracted to the same girl. On the verge of having it all—even in a way he'd never imagined, with his best friend at his side—the game had changed...*again*...when Lily had introduced another kink in the plan.

Why had he agreed to that dumb kiss with Clint?

And why the hell had he liked it enough to hesitate on joining his best friend in bed with their dream girl? Or even asking her on a date. Probably they should start there. Part of the problem was that he had no idea how to do this when three people were involved.

End result, they'd let their insecurities fuck things up. Twice. Maybe irreparably this time. They were rapidly running out of strikes. Worst of all, they'd hurt the one person they were falling over themselves to claim, however they could.

"You do know this is all your fault, right?" Clint channeled the spark of arousal in his eyes to fuel his anger, as they both had so often lately. Never before had he and his partner argued this much. It sucked. Both of them were as irritable as the old lady on Seventh, who'd racked up a fistful of warnings for hollering profanities at neighboring kids for everything from saggy jeans to laughing too loud as they walked by. She probably hadn't gotten laid in half a century either.

Okay, so it'd actually been more like six months since he'd realized no woman but the adorable nurse inspired him to get it up anymore. But it felt like ten consecutive life sentences.

"Really? *I'm* the problem here?" He glared at Clint. Reputed to have one of the longest fuses of any of the Men in Blue, Matt was rapidly approaching his melting point. Sexually frustrated, terrified of losing his best friend, angry at himself for the wreckage he knew they'd made of Jambrea's feelings—soon...

Kaboom!

As it was, they might have to call in the bomb squad to defuse this situation. Kids hadn't called him The Hulk in high school—before he'd learned to control himself—only because of his size. "How do you figure, asshat?"

"This has got to be about Jambi." His friend took a shaky breath. "If it weren't for you and all your morals...that preconceived junk, we could have had her already."

"When? While she was drunk off her ass after the wedding?" Matt wasn't sure he knew the guy sitting beside him anymore. What happened to his funny, badass, honorable partner?

One amazing woman had waltzed into their lives and he lost all his sense.

Maybe they both had for that matter.

"Or any of the other chances we had before that." Clint grumbled. "While you were still in denial over the fact that you and I had a massive hard-on for the same damn woman."

"See! That's what you can't fucking jam through that hard skull of yours." He leaned in, snarling in his former-friend's face. "It was never just about sex for me with her. I wanted more. Not something to risk on a weekend of fun or some novelty arrangement."

"Who says I hoped for anything different?" For once it seemed like Clint might be listening. He tilted his head and got real still, like he did when they were on the prowl for a criminal in hiding.

Unfortunately, that's when a paneled door in some rich chocolate-hued wood opened to admit Lily and her husband, their fellow cop-turned-Dom, JRad.

"Thanks for coming so quickly, boys." In total Mistress form, Lily impressed even as she could have terrified men who didn't know her as well as they did. Hell, she still scared him in some ways. Blood-red leather clung to her figure as if she'd been shrink-wrapped into it. Studs and buckles alone didn't account for her junkyard dog tenacity.

Knowing their friend had tamed a woman like her had increased the already ridiculous respect he'd had for the guy. Clint too seemed awed.

"That's what she said, *never*." Jeremy cracked himself up as he leaned a shoulder against the rear wall of his wife's office and kicked one ankle over the other.

Matt had never seen his friend so comfortable in his own skin. Happy looked good on the bastard, even if Matt had to remind himself that the dude dressed in black leather and chains was his same old computer geek buddy.

"Jeremy." Lily rolled her eyes, completely shattering the last of her stone-cold bitch façade. "This is serious."

"I know, tiger." He held his hands up in front of him, palms out. "Go ahead, rip 'em a new one."

"Hey, wait a minute." Clint glared at their teammate. "What the fuck?"

"I sleep with her every night. Not you." Jeremy shrugged, not looking a bit sorry. "And personally, I think she's right to smack some sense into you idiots. I can't believe you're still screwing this all to hell."

"You're talking about Jambrea." Cutting to the heart of the problem, Matt met Lily's gaze head on.

"Of course." She sighed.

"We're capable of handling our sex lives on our own. Thanks." Clint started to rise and likely storm out of the club.

Lily's breaking news stopped him cold. "Oh yeah? Then why did she show up here a few days ago and practically beg me to set her up with a fuck buddy?"

Neither of them spoke. To do that, Matt would have had to breathe. Except everything inside him froze. Stuck as solid as the Tin Man, because without the lovely nurse he was afraid he didn't have a heart. Especially if he had to journey down life's winding paths missing his partner too. Surely, they'd never survive this intact.

Lily took advantage of their stunned silence. "Well, to be completely frank, she requested two men to pleasure her. And I can't imagine any reason why she shouldn't have her wish."

Clint found his tongue first. "A ménage? But...she's been running scared from us for months."

"One thing the three of you have in common, then. To be fair, you did a lousy job of seducing her while you were too busy trying to one-up each other." Lily perched on her desk, facing them as she crossed a slender thigh over the other. She swung one of her extreme-heeled boots in time to a beat only she heard. "The way I see it, you have two choices. You can man up, both of you, and give the lady what she wants. Or I'll pass the opportunity of a lifetime to any of the seven capable and oh-so-willing pairs who applied for the position. Jeremy and I could select a duo that will guarantee her a night to remember."

"The hell you will!" Matt roared as he bolted to his feet. He hadn't meant to knock the chair over in his haste, but the thud it made as it tipped onto the plush rug satisfied him.

Lily only smiled as she checked-out the prostrate furniture and murmured, "You're so much alike. No wonder this is tough."

When he planted his hands on the immaculate surface of her desk and leaned in, trapping her inches from his face, undaunted by the fierce Mistress, Jeremy took a step closer too.

"Settle down." JRad might not have possessed Matt's physical strength, but something else inside him allowed him to dominate men and women alike. Hell, even Lily bowed to the man. If Matt hadn't seen that himself, he never would have believed it.

The force of his quiet warning brought Matt back to reality.

"Lily didn't have to give you a head's up. It wasn't easy for her to break Jambi's confidence and figure out the right thing to do in this situation. This has been eating at her for days. Especially since you've blown so many chances already." Jeremy paced beside his new wife, his fingers trailing across her back from shoulder to shoulder. "I don't appreciate you knuckleheads upsetting my wife. So I think you should be thanking her. And listening. Really *listen* to what she has to say."

Matt took a deep breath, then another. He righted his chair and plopped into it, staring at the intricate carving on the foot of the desk. He'd never felt more like a failure than at that moment. "Sorry, Lily. I don't know what to do anymore."

"Me either." Clint surprised him by reaching over and squeezing his shoulder. The contact helped ease the crush in his chest.

"I think you two need to start by figuring out how you feel about each other." Lily raised a brow when he glanced up. "Unless you think I'm a moron and that I imagined the spark between you when you kissed."

"There wasn't—" Clint instinctively began, snatching back his support so he could wave his hands in front of his chest.

"There *was*." Matt decided she had it right. He wasn't willing to risk his best friend any more than he'd throw away a chance at the woman they'd both fallen for. Going further down this path would doom them. They couldn't live in denial forever.

At least it hadn't worked so far. Time to be bold, to make some moves.

Because continuing like this would kill him.

"There was?" The other guy angled toward him as if to search for signs of humor in Matt's face. No joke this time. "So why didn't you do anything about it? You know, after the case closed and we went back to our beat."

"Why didn't *you*?" Matt swallowed hard. "You never mentioned it, so I thought…maybe I had it wrong."

"Holy shit, you two are stubborn." JRad shook his head. "You're partners on the force. I've seen you save each other's asses. There you can communicate like you live in one brain. Why is this any different?"

"Cut us some slack." Clint leapt to Matt's defense too. Relief flooded Matt as he realized they might still be on the same side. "This is a lot to take in. We'd already shifted our whole perspective on relationships and what our future might look like in order to fit what fate had handed us in Jambi. Then this on top? It's like nothing I ever pictured about how my life would go."

"Maybe it's better than you could have imagined before you knew what was possible?" Matt couldn't stop himself from wondering aloud.

"Yeah." The hiss of breath from his partner was followed by the guy clearing his throat. "Maybe it is. Or it could be."

"I'm not saying we're going to solve everything overnight, but I'd like to try. You. Me." Matt paused, long enough for the other guy to finish his thought.

"And Jambrea." There was no room for argument in Clint's conviction.

"Exactly." He extended his hand and Clint grasped it firmly. Their stares burned into each other as they sealed their silent pact. After a few seconds, the intensity had him looking away, to Lily. "And it seems like our girl is the pressing issue. So why don't you tell us more about what you had in mind for her?"

The sheen of tears in the Mistress's eyes surprised Matt. Too much more of that and he might join her. Unacceptable now that they were getting some damn traction. Time to move forward, out of this colossal rut.

"Just one more thing. While I'm glad I pointed out what idiots you've been—" Lily hopped down from her perch and joined them. "—honestly, I feel bad for you. Partly responsible. I know we weren't in an official scene that day. Still, I should have followed up with you guys. Made sure you processed the interaction. It's what I would have done for my submissives. I accept I had some part in this. And that's why I'm willing to help you fix the mess you've made."

"Y-you will?" The waver in Clint's question socked Matt in the gut like a perp's errant fist or maybe a roundhouse kick. It hurt worse, actually. Struck deeper.

"Yes, honey." She hugged Clint, making Matt kind of jealous. It sucked watching the other man in a state of distress. Hell, that's all they'd really existed in for months now. He wanted to be the one to comfort his best friend, to support him as they had done for years. They'd never had a problem they couldn't figure out between them. Until now.

"Would you like Jeremy to leave?" She looked to Matt, her serious stare promising they were about to get really personal.

"Nah. JRad is one of our brothers. There's nothing we would hide from him. Or any of the Men in Blue." Matt sighed. "Do you think this will change how they see us?"

"Seriously? You've wasted even a single second worrying about that?" JRad chuckled, not in an entirely amused or polite kind of way either. "Considering the example Mason and Tyler have set for us all, why would you think anyone would judge you? None of us exactly conform to the traditional view of a relationship. Well, maybe Razor and Izzy. Even the boy wonder knocked his girl up before they were hitched, though. Would you think less of them for that?"

"Hell no. You know I don't." Matt couldn't believe JRad would assume he'd be such a prick.

"Then what's the problem?"

"I don't want the guys to think I was like...in the closet or something." Matt winced. "I didn't lie to anyone. Not myself. Not Clint. And not any of the Men in Blue. I didn't feel this way until I met Jambi. And honestly, not really until your wife stirred up trouble. Like she said..."

Before JRad could get riled, Matt clarified, "Despite what you might assume, I'm glad she did. But I felt like if I suddenly jumped Clint's bones or something that he'd think I'd always harbored some secret crush or some shit. It wasn't like that."

"Hey, don't you think you could have talked to *me* about this?" Clint interrupted. "I wouldn't have thought that. Hell, it never crossed my mind that I'd consider being with another dude until that night either."

He cleared his throat.

"Look, Matt's right about one thing. You guys have more issues than we can fix in an hour or two. Or hell, even a day." Lily stopped them before they drowned themselves in overwhelming emotions. That's what'd ground them to a halt so many times over the past couple months. "So why not take it one step at a time?"

"Which one first?" Clint rubbed his chest over his heart. Matt wished he had the right to hug the other guy.

"Well, if you two don't step up to the plate, Jambi's going to be getting it on with some of my clients in about three hours. So, that probably takes priority." She had the manners to look a little sheepish.

"Tonight?" Matt's heart raced.

So soon? He wasn't ready, was he?

"I didn't want to give you enough time to freak out." Lily came over and petted his hair. Whether he wanted to admit it or not, the reassurance in her fine touch was welcome. "You two are overthinking all of this. Go with your instincts. I know you have them. It's what makes the Men in Blue great at their jobs. Trust yourselves."

Clint blew out a long breath. "Just do it, you mean."

"Literally." JRad chuckled from where he leaned against the wall.

"Remember, this is all about her. That should make it easier. Your only purpose is to bring her pleasure. As much of it as you can give. Certainly a selfless goal like that should keep all your individual nonsense at bay, right?" Lily rested one hand on Clint and one on Matt, binding the pair together.

"I guess. One thing..." Matt couldn't shake a sliver of doubt.

"What now?" Lily's narrowed eyes dared him to ruin her plan.

"What if we do this, tonight, then can't work stuff out? Between us. Or her. Long term. I don't want to set her expectations too high and not be able to deliver. I couldn't stand it if we disappointed her more than I feel like we already have. Jumping right into sex might not be smart. What will she say if she learns later that Clint and I are into each other? Will she feel like we lied to her?"

"Well, about that…" Lily glanced away for the first time.

"What did you do?" Clint practically squeaked.

"For tonight, she'll be blindfolded. It was one of the things she marked on her wish list for this experience. She won't know it's you ravaging her if you don't talk or reveal yourselves. It'll be risk-free for you all. She'll get what she wants. And you can try out a ménage and see if you both can really do it without freaking out. Also, I might have sort of spilled the beans about your kiss already anyway."

"Lily!" Clint gripped the arms of his chair.

"If it makes you feel better, she thought it was sexy as hell." Lily bussed Matt's crown. "And so do I, boys."

"JRad, are you going to spank her for all this interfering?" Clint asked, making Matt burst out into a fit of laughter that had been sorely missed lately. His partner could always have him rolling during their long and sometimes boring-as-hell stakeouts. "Please tell me you are. Hard."

"I'll consider your request." JRad nodded. The subtle shift of his package guaranteed he liked the idea.

"Hey!" Lily smacked Clint upside the head. "Be nice! I'm helping you out here."

"Of a pile of shit you dumped on us," he grumbled. Then, after a pause, he admitted. "At least it'll all be worth it if tonight goes like I think it will."

"Someday you'll be thanking me," she promised.

"Sure, sure," Matt grumbled.

"No, seriously guys." She hugged first Clint than Matt. "I love all three of you like the family I never really had. Jambrea's a sister to me. I want nothing more than to see you happy. I'm sorry I might have jeopardized that. I only meant the best and I hope that tonight I can start you down the path to something as amazing as what Jeremy and I have found. You were there for us, and I want to offer the same support to you. My brand of helping might not have been the best, but I had good intentions."

JRad pushed off the wall and closed in on his wife again when he detected the husk of unshed tears in her confession.

"I know you didn't mean any harm." Clint wrapped his arm around Lily's tiny waist and yanked her into his lap.

Matt smiled, imagining Jambrea there instead. They wouldn't have to worry about snapping her in half like they did with this sprite, no matter how strong her spirit might be. "We love you too, Lily."

"Thanks." She grinned. "So why don't we go over Jambi's wish list and gather some toys so you can make up for lost time?"

"There's still one problem." Clint's shoulders slumped. He looked over at Matt with such hopelessness he thought his friend might wither on the spot. "The Chief put extra security on the presidential debate tonight because of the missing candidate, Rudolph Small. Guess who got the honors?"

Matt groaned. Fuck! They'd been so close.

"Razor, Mason and Tyler already volunteered to take babysitting duty for you." JRad grinned. "You're clear on that end. And they wanted me to tell you to pull your heads out of your asses and make tonight count."

"Sounds like a plan." Matt held his palm up and Clint high-fived him. Finally, something they could agree on.

It felt like the first time in forever.

He couldn't stop smiling.

Chapter Five

Jambrea clenched Lily's hand as she padded down the hallway into the depths of Gunther's Playground. Radiant heat beneath the floor felt nice on her bare feet. Management had truly thought of everything to ensure the comfort of their guests.

This became even more apparent as she passed rooms, some with open doors that allowed her to spy the decadence inside—from a woman shackled to a wooden X, surrounded by an admiring crowd who appeared to be taking turns playing with her, to a bathhouse complete with a lush array of live plants, waterfalls and what appeared to be a trio of mermaids giving a lucky sailor a blowjob. "Something for everyone" would have been an appropriate marketing line.

Compared to the elaborate spider web of ropes suspending a man in the last room they passed, Jambrea figured her requests to be basic. Simple. Rudimentary.

Foolish?

When she stutter-stepped, Lily drew her forward. "You're doing great, Jambi. It's just around the corner here."

From behind one of the closed doors on her left, an earsplitting smack was followed by a yelp and an even louder moan. She jumped, then shivered.

"I feel like the slow kid in an advanced class," she admitted.

"Don't let all this scare you." Lily wrapped an arm around Jambrea's waist. "Everyone starts somewhere. The weekend brings out a lot of experienced players. It doesn't have to be that complicated. Passion is a pretty straightforward thing on a fundamental level."

"Will the guys I'm with be bored?" She nibbled her lip. "Will they want more than I can give? I don't want this to be a chore for them."

"Are you kidding? I can assure you I reviewed your requests and limitations extensively with all prospective matches. There was no shortage of eager volunteers." Lily turned to her. The honesty in her friend's gaze settled some of the butterflies in Jambrea's stomach, beneath the soft robe she wore. Even that pointed her out like a newbie when all the other club members either strutted their stuff naked or were decked out in fetish gear like the head Mistress.

Jambrea could have just stumbled out of her shower. Right down this alluring rabbit hole. She tugged the lapels tighter, crossing them over her chest. Unlike most of the women here, she didn't have perky breasts or a trim waist to flaunt sans support. Maybe this had been a stupid idea.

"Oh no." Lily smacked Jambrea's ass when she balked. Even through the terrycloth it stung a little.

"Hey!"

"Get it in gear, sister." The Mistress toned down her command with a slight smile. "Remember how you made me pinky-swear I wouldn't let you back out?"

"What was I thinking?" Jambrea rubbed her eyes with one hand while the other clutched the overlapping panels of the fluffy garment she wore like armor. The last thing she needed was for the robe to gape open and expose more of herself than she had already revealed to her friend.

"That you deserve to know boundless pleasure?" Lily hooked an arm around her elbow, leading her onward. Slower this time, they no less inevitably aimed toward their destination and the possibilities that awaited her there. "That this is the first step toward something you've been dreaming about for a really long-ass time?"

"Fine. There's that." She swallowed hard. If she didn't go through with their plan, it'd probably be another decade before she got the nerve to try again. No way would she doom herself to extending her isolation. Even if tonight's sexcapades were anonymous—given her selection of blindfolding from Lily's menu of delightful possibilities—the connection of physical touch would suffice for now. And she could superimpose whatever faces she preferred on her mystery partners. For most women that'd probably be a couple of Hollywood stars. Not for her.

Clint. Matt.

She blinked a few times as she realized the cops came to mind first, before John. A long way ahead. After all, she'd really gotten to know and adore the two guys over the past six months or so. Seeing them in action, on the job and in their group of friends, had endeared them to her. Still, John had been her first. A delicious infatuation with a specter.

Part of her was sad at the revelation. Doubly so when she realized none of the three men were truly within reach.

Habit drove her to swipe her fingers around her wild thing tattoo. No feeling sorry for herself tonight. It would accomplish nothing. If she chickened out on the other hand, literally, she'd doom herself to regrets. Going ahead with this insanity could help her break her dry spell and, hopefully, her unlucky streak too. She hadn't ruled out the possibility of a rematch if tonight didn't totally suck.

It wouldn't. She had to stay positive and trust her friend.

"That's it," Lily goaded her as they picked up the pace once more.

Before the pendulum could swing the other direction in her never-ending, "Do it, don't do it" battle, they'd arrived at a cozy chamber. When Lily ushered her into the unoccupied space and shut the door behind them, they could have been anywhere—a lavish hotel, someone's fancy house or maybe the set of a movie.

Perfectly staged, the space invited her imagination to run wild. Relaxing, she sat on the edge of the bed, curling her feet beneath her. Jambrea watched her friend roam around the room lighting candles and even a fire in the gas-powered hearth.

"You'll appreciate that when you're naked." Lily winked. "At least until your playmates warm you up."

A horrible possibility had her throat going dry. "What if they don't? I mean, what if I find I can't do it or it doesn't turn me on like I thought?"

"Don't get ahead of yourself." Lily poured a glass of water from the crystal decanter on the sidebar. She handed it to Jambrea, displaying her superb observational skills. No wonder her submissives adored her. "You're safe here. No matter the reason, if you don't want to go forward, you remember what to do, right?"

"Oh. Yeah." She actually might have forgotten. The combination of terror and thrill distracted her mightily. That was before she factored in the impact of truly touring Gunther's for the first time when things were in full swing. "My codeword. *Blue.*"

Lily chuckled. "Well, we usually call it a safeword, but, yes."

"So why is it blue instead of red?" Jambrea tilted her head, as if that trivia mattered in comparison to all the other things she had no clue about yet had dived headfirst into.

"The word itself is irrelevant. In this case, your partners selected it. Will you remember it? If not, I'll have you tell me something meaningful to you and I'll inform them of the change. It's critical." Lily seemed as if she might continue until Jambrea waved her off.

"No, I can go with blue. Blue, blue, blue." She repeated it a few more times. "I won't forget."

"There's another option." The concentration Lily paid to lighting candles seemed unwarranted.

"Go ahead." Why would she hold back now?

"This room is equipped with cameras. I can watch. Or Jeremy can. Or Gunther, or one of my assistants. Anyone you're comfortable with, if you want the extra layer of protection afforded by real-time monitoring."

"Oh God, no." She tried to think beyond instinctive denial. "You trust these guys, right? You wouldn't throw me to just anybody, would you?"

"Give me a little credit." The spitfire returned full force. "Of course. You're in good hands. *Great* ones."

"Then, no. I don't need you to babysit." She squirmed. "I feel self-conscious enough as it is."

"No need for that, Jambs." Lily scanned her from head to toe. "You look really pretty. Flushed and natural. It's probably best you opted for two men. In case you make one of them come too quick, you'll still get your fill. Alternating partners is always a great tactic to keep the party rolling."

"Uh, thanks. I think." She couldn't help but choke out a laugh. "Can we get the show on the road already?"

"Of course." Her friend leaned in for a hug before surveying the room to make sure everything met her standards. In one corner, a dresser draped with a maroon sheet had lumps beneath.

Were those the toys Jambrea had expressed interest in? Oh, God, what had she gotten herself into?

"The guys are waiting for my signal. They're in the room we passed just before this one." She winked when Jambrea glared at her. Knowing she'd waltzed right by her educators tormented her.

Maybe she shouldn't have asked for...

Too late. Lily took her hand from behind her back. In it, she clasped a black silk blindfold. "Last thing before I send them in."

"You're *sure* this is a good idea?" A tilt of Jambrea's head didn't shake any more sense into her brain.

"Yeah. Sensory deprivation allows you to focus on what's important. Especially given your insecurities, this will help calm you down. Make you worry only about what you feel instead of trying to compensate for reactions or judge what you think you look like as they're playing with you."

"I'm that obvious, huh?" Jambrea sighed.

"Only to me. It's my job to know these things. And I think I understand you pretty well by now." Lily reached out and squeezed her hand. "So believe me when I say that you're ready for this. Tonight is going to be amazing. You've earned it. Enjoy your reward."

"If you insist." She grinned as she closed her eyes. "Go ahead, slap that thing on."

Lily's laugh was musical, something Jambrea hadn't ever quite noticed before. Maybe the Mistress had it right—without Jambrea's vision, every other sense was enhanced. Immediately, she heard the lap of the flames in the faux fireplace, the rustle of the sheets and even her own ragged breathing.

She concentrated on regulating the uneven respiration while slowing the pounding of her heart.

"Better already," Lily murmured as she secured the patch of luxurious fabric with three separate ties. One in the middle, one at the top—around Jambrea's forehead—and one at the base near her cheekbones. The deceptively simplistic mask seemed to be padded and weighted around the edges. It conformed to the contours of her face, leaving no gaps whatsoever for peeking.

A wash of air over her cheeks made her wonder if Lily had tested that theory, maybe by attempting to make Jambrea flinch. If so, she never would have known a blow was coming. Pitch black surrounded her in artificial midnight, deep enough to get lost in.

"Time to let go of your security blanket. Let's get that robe off." Lily pried Jambrea's fingers from the fuzzy edge of the fabric. Still, it was hard to release the shield. "Are you positive you don't want to be restrained? It might help you, like the blindfold, to relax. Knowing you can only lie there and soak in the rapture they bring you is another kind of freedom...from having to respond or act. I promise you'd enjoy yourself."

"That'd have me calling *blue* for sure." Jambrea shook her head though she didn't even know if Lily was watching. "Maybe some other time. Not tonight."

"Okay, then I have some instructions for you. From your playmates." Lily helped Jambrea stand only long enough to peel the terrycloth from her entirely. Then she aided her friend in sinking onto the mattress once more. This time the Mistress nudged Jambrea's shoulder.

She reclined, getting as comfortable as possible on the divine mattress. Her own bed had never felt so inviting. This was like lounging on a cloud. "Go ahead. I'm listening."

"I bet you are." Lily chuckled. The woman liked this entirely too much. "They're not going to speak to you. They don't want you distracted from how they make you feel. Tonight is all about you, not them. So ask for anything you want. Tell them if they do something you like or hate. Give them feedback. They'll shape their advance into exactly what you need. They're here to take direction, not give it. Since you've opted not to be restrained, they want you to know that when they place you somewhere, they expect you to stay until they show you what they'd like you to do next. Really, it's about positioning you where you need to be for them to pleasure you best. It sounds weirder than it will be. Just go with them. Don't fight. If it's not something you're into, speak up. Tell them to slow down. Or if it's way off track, use your word. Say it again."

"Blue." Jambrea pressed her thighs together, embarrassed by how ready she was and what the idea of two men strategizing about their approach to taking her together did to her. Premeditated desire. They'd thought about this, just like she had. Probably not quite as obsessively, but they had dwelled on it at least a bit. Knowing they had a game plan reassured her.

"That's right." Lily patted Jambrea's shoulder then stroked her hair, maybe arranging the lock that always tried to stand on end. "Though I'm confident you're not going to need it, it's better to be safe than sorry."

"I'm ready, Lily." She allowed her fingers to uncurl. Her knotted muscles loosened until she melted slightly.

"I know you are. I'm glad you're finally noticing that too." Her friend bracketed Jambrea's wrist, over her *no regrets* tattoo. "Above all, have fun."

The instruction came softer as Lily must have retreated to the threshold.

"I don't want to be alone." Jambrea could have kicked herself for admitting that. But something about the blindfold did make it easier to forget about her inhibitions and judgment by the world around her. Hopefully Lily assumed she meant only for the moment.

"I'll always be here for you." Too shrewd for her own good, the Mistress caught on to both implications. "And no one's leaving you tonight. I won't be far. There's an intercom next to the bed. And here come your guys. They're peeking out of their door like kids on Christmas morning. Get over here, you two sexy beasts."

Heavier footfalls approached, inciting a wave of gooseflesh to break out over Jambrea's skin. Lily surprised her by sticking around for a minute. She introduced the first man to her by saying, "Give me your hand."

Shortly after, a wide palm pressed to Jambrea's belly. She drew in a breath and held it at the imprint of broad, splayed fingers that curled softly into her rounded stomach. He didn't seem to mind her curves when his thumb brushed back and forth over the area he touched.

"Very nice." Lily approved. She couldn't help her nature, though. "Say hello, Jambrea."

"Nice to meet you," she choked out.

"And your second soon-to-be lover." This time an even larger hand caressed her, gentle for all its meaty size and the slight rough patches on the heel of his palm. Maybe he was a weight lifter, like Matt, who had calluses in the same location. She'd patched blisters for him once or twice when he'd pushed his workouts too far.

It'd be so easy to imagine this pair as those guys. The ones she couldn't stop lusting after even while another man caressed her. In truth, that was why she'd agreed to Lily's blindfold. Trust her friend to guess and give Jambrea's imagination fodder. Her mind could easily transform these two into the pair they were sadly a substitute for.

"Believe me, Jambi. This one is eager for you. I've never seen someone quite so…ready to play. Tell him you feel the same."

"It should be obvious." Jambrea rubbed her legs together, trying to ease some of the ache between them. When no one responded right away, she caved. "But yes, I'm looking forward to tonight. To you. Please get the hell out of here, Lily."

A huff was all the answer she got from the man now petting the underside of her breast with reverent passes of his giant hand. Warmth radiated from his skin to hers, and yet her nipples began to pucker.

Oh, yes, this was what she'd come for.

Begged for.

Suffered the embarrassment of confession for.

"Your wish is my command." Lily snorted, the sound coming further away than before. "I'm closing the door now. Remember your word."

"Blue." Jambrea quickly clarified, "I'm not saying it. Just... Yes, I remember."

Lily flat out laughed this time. A delighted peal that Jambrea didn't hear often. Or at least hadn't. More and more, the happy expression leaked out. She smiled knowing she was responsible for it tonight. "Okay, I'm gone. Have fun, kids. I'll be here when you're finished, Jambi. You're not alone. Ever."

Jambrea winced as the door clicked shut. Maybe her temporary guys wouldn't realize how deeply that fear rocked her. As if they'd taken it to heart, they were there.

Four hands roamed over her from her feet to her ankles and her fingertips to her wrists. They massaged, relaxing the renewed tension from her bit by bit. Though she'd never expected to find herself in this situation, Jambrea relished the freedom to simply absorb the sensations without having to make small talk or suffer the sometimes awkward social necessities she had avoided like the plague.

Somehow, this sensory introduction felt so much more honest than the intricate dance she'd done with Matt and Clint for months. She didn't have to worry about what one would think when she enjoyed the touch of the other. They coordinated instead of clashing in a war for her attention. Fuck it. The guy at her feet with the longer, more deft fingers, she thought of him as Clint.

And the guy who had such beefy, heavy hands, which didn't treat her like a china doll, she decided he would be pretend-Matt. She had no doubt Lily had selected them for those specific roles. What if they were hung like her real-life pair?

Lily had said Matt was large. Really thick. Could she

handle someone like that?

Surely, they would have been filled in on her sparse sexual history.

As if they could sense her derailing slightly, they advanced. Again, Jambrea was thrilled by their silent communication. Two men that in tune had to have some kind of bond. Like Matt and Clint, if they'd ever tap into it instead of playing tug of war with each other. They'd left her flapping around between them like the flag in the middle, keeping score.

The bed dipped as Clint climbed on beside her, the better to reach her calves and then up to her knees with his sensual exploration. Matt followed shortly after, causing a full-on tilt to the mattress. He snuck his hands beneath her shoulders and propped her up far enough to slip beneath her. Bulky, his thickly muscled torso made sure she didn't worry about squashing him into an all-beef pancake.

She moaned at the contact of all that heated flesh with hers. Nine years hadn't been long enough for her to forget the intoxication caused by bare skin pressed to bare skin, especially with a light mat of chest hair trapped in between. An instant chemical reaction flipped her brain to off and turned her hormones to raging.

Taking advantage of her newfound pliancy, Clint slid his thumbs up the insides of her knees. With slight pressure, he parted her legs, nudging until she arranged herself with one thigh draped over each of the living, breathing—hard—props beneath her.

The ripple of Matt's six-pack on her lower back thrilled her. She wriggled a bit in his hold until she realized she'd aligned the cleft of her ass perfectly with his shaft. And that was one mystery solved. Matt's stand-in was enormous. Everywhere. Lily hadn't exaggerated.

She froze, a little frightened at the prospect of holding all of him within her or, worse, of disappointing him by not accommodating his girth. But they had a while to go before she had to worry about that, right?

Would they rush to the finish or savor her complacency?

Hope sprung eternal that they'd take the scenic route. After all, they had a whole covered table of delicacies to enjoy together throughout the night, didn't they? Maybe they planned to take her to the top over and over.

As if on cue, Clint left her to Matt. The man supporting her didn't waste his opportunity to monopolize her body and attention. He nuzzled her neck, letting her feel the scrape of a modest five o'clock shadow. It looked so sexy on him, making his jaw seem even more imposing. Well, at least it did on the real Matt. She imagined it would be the same for this mystery man.

Arching her neck, she granted him better access. He took full advantage. Hungry nips and licks had her mewling. The plaintive sounds might have embarrassed her if they weren't a big part of her limited communication. Without eye contact or the ability to read body language, it was easier to let them hear how they affected her with primal feedback than to explain with something more articulate, words she never could have found or uttered without dying of mortification.

Jambrea didn't think before she lifted her hand to cup her breast in an attempt to smother the pulsating heaviness there. These guys had hardly touched her and already she had surpassed her own personal best records for being turned on. Just as she was about to grant herself some relief, Matt clamped down on her fingers, engulfing them easily in his grasp. He tucked her hands at her sides with enough force to make her positive he intended for them to stay there.

She wasn't about to complain since he replaced her timid kneading with deliberate pinches that definitely didn't hurt. No, he satisfied her longing for pressure and alleviated her restlessness, at least temporarily. Plumping her nipples, he tugged first one then the other with precisely the right amount of force to have her straining for more.

When the mattress shook this time, something rattled. A metallic click sounded in the quiet space a moment before something cool and smooth traced her areola. She gasped as she considered whether her interest in nipple clamps had been wise. Damn Lily and her questionnaire full of tantalizing options. Probably she shouldn't have looked at it so much as a wish list but instead as more of an I-know-I-could-handle-that kind of guideline setter.

Too late now. Unless...

For one moment she considered using *blue*.

Until Clint went for a sneak attack and secured the tip of her other breast in between what felt like a matching contraption. Light pressure built as he slowly introduced her to the device. While it could surely bite more, she was glad when he didn't push her limits. Instead, apparently satisfied, he waited for Matt to make her symmetrical.

"Shit!" She would have slapped her hand over her parted lips to prevent more curses from spilling from her mouth if Matt hadn't told her, with his actions, to keep them at her sides.

Instantly, Clint removed some of the tension from the device.

"No, no. Put it back. Hurry." She groaned when he complied. It felt so delicious, she never would have expected the way her new jewelry amplified the sensation in her breasts. Or maybe that exponential impact was courtesy of the men bookending her.

One of them chuckled the tiniest bit, enough to remind her of the real Clint. He loved to act as Razor's sidekick when the recent ex-rookie played a prank on another member of the Men in Blue. A sense of humor attracted her more than most any other feature on a man.

She writhed in Matt's hold.

Spread Your Wings

Clint stilled her by leaning in and covering her lips with his. A soft, tender kiss had her quieting to make sure she absorbed every nuance of the exchange. Lily had left no detail out in guiding the three of them to fulfilling her every yearning.

Jambrea would have to think of an epic birthday present for her friend.

Mouth to mouth contact had been high on her list of preferred activities. There was something about kissing that struck her as more intimate than a host of the other proffered temptations.

Ah, damn, the guy plying her with his mouth was good at it too. Not that she'd made out with a ton of guys, but still... The night she'd shared her couch with Matt and Clint, while they'd waited for the Sex Offender antidote to save Lily, they'd proved to her that they excelled at a heck of a lot more than their roles on the force.

Hell, imitation Clint even tasted right, like the banana candies he squirreled away in their patrol car. Jambrea wouldn't put it past Lily to have had each man use Clint and Matt's brand of soap and deodorant, or their aftershave, to enhance her fantasy.

Her nostrils flared as she breathed the scent she'd begun to associate with arousal. All the time she'd spent around the duo of cops had imprinted their characteristics on her senses. Picking them, or carefully crafted imposters like these, out of a crowd in a blind taste test would be easy.

Clint broke her from her reverie when he separated them. She cried out and sought his mouth again. Before she could connect with his plump, inviting lips, Matt took the other guy's place. While he was busy distracting her, or maybe simply enjoying their clash of energetic nibbles, the bed shifted once more.

This time the brush of something light and soft had her toes curling in the lush bedding. The feather. It had to be a feather, careening up her leg. Stroking her on the insides of her calf, knee and thigh. Up, up—to the moist apex of her thighs. It fluttered over her clit, which was sensitive enough at their handling to respond to even that barely there contact.

Her moan was devoured by the man at her mouth. He nudged her jaw with his thumb, encouraging her to open for him. So she did. Gladly. And when he let his tongue dance with hers, she sucked on the tip before rejoining the duel.

Right when she thought she'd leeched as much pleasure as possible from their interaction, he slipped the backs of his knuckles down her throat, across her collarbone and to the instrument hugging her nipple. He flicked it in a repetitive motion that had her vibrating with the result of his manipulation.

Damn these men. They knew all the tricks in the book. She wished she could return the favor. But all she knew how to do was lie there and take it. Next time she would let them bind her as they'd requested of Lily. Then again, knowing they'd wanted to, maybe they wouldn't object to her passive nature, enhanced by lack of experience.

The feather passed between her breasts and must have nudged Matt as well. His breath caught and his sizable cock leapt at her back before he sealed their mouths yet again. She didn't notice the absence of the plume until something much warmer, and wetter, replaced it in creating the swirling path being traced all over her body.

It took her a moment to realize what instrument of pleasure wreaked havoc on her system. But when she figured out that it was Clint's tongue lapping at her, drawing ever nearer to her core, she couldn't stay quiet or still. "Yes, please."

Matt facilitated her immobility, pinning her to his mammoth chest and ensuring she stayed widespread for his partner in crime.

The man crawling between her legs nipped her inner thigh,

making her squeal. Then he nuzzled the dampness that had spread there, overflowing from her pussy. Enthusiastic swipes of his tongue cleaned the juice from her skin. In search of more, he rose higher and higher.

His mouth opened and closed on her flesh, drawing lightly as he approached the place she needed his attention most. "More. Please."

She arched in Matt's hold, adoring him for grasping her hips and raising them as if she was as light as the feather they'd teased her with. He presented her to the man delivering rapture. Their coordinated attack poised her on the edge of flying.

Before she could shudder, moved by both the anticipation and realization of her fantasies, he paused his advance. She whimpered and reached for the man between her legs, but he'd left. Just for a moment. Matt returned her hands to her sides, this time pulling them behind her back, catching them between their bodies.

She didn't complain when she realized she could touch him too.

Her hand closed around his cock, at least as much of it as she could handle.

A hiss of breath dusted her short hair against her nape. His teeth lightly scored her shoulder, though he didn't stop her from manipulating him as much as she could given the awkward grip she had.

Her fingers rippled along his length, testing his solid erection. The need to be filled grew, making her desperate for attention. She writhed in his hold until his partner rejoined them, slithering between her legs as though he planned to crawl inside her.

This time he didn't fool around. He closed his mouth over her clit, making her first shriek, then hum at the moist pressure he imparted on the swollen nub. Something cool nudged the opening of her pussy, adding to the sensations bombarding her.

Matt banded an arm around her waist, tucking her tight to him as force built on the tight rings of muscle at her core. Then it vanished as something round and modest popped into her pussy. Before she could discern the intent of the toy, another similar marble pressed against her. This one seemed slightly larger.

In it went too. She sighed, desperate for more. Clint accompanied the now steady stream of beads entering her with the flick of his tongue on her clit, long laps along her slit and gentle sucks on her lips. Soon she lost track of how many segments he'd shoved inside her.

All she knew was that she couldn't take much more before she would shatter.

Hanging on to the delicious cusp of pleasure had her willing to scream in delight. But the gentle petting of the man behind her drew her from the overwhelming rapture enough to tolerate touches that lit her nerve endings up like fireworks on the Fourth of July.

Once he'd given her all there must be, Clint changed tactics. Now instead of filling her, he withdrew his present.

She groaned when he tugged between her legs and the last introduced, largest bead lodged against the inside of her flexed muscles, which guarded the entrance to her body.

A wheeze escaped her, and her fingers tightened on Matt's cock, when she couldn't clamp down hard enough to prevent the ball from escaping her at Clint's persistent pulling. He suckled her clit as her pussy surrendered the toy. The rapid expansion and contraction of the muscular ring sent a shockwave zinging through her.

When Clint did it again and again in a slow, predictable rhythm, her body began to anticipate the decadent sensation. Before she could warn either of the men supporting her, raising her higher, she shattered.

"Oh, God." She cried out as a powerful orgasm ripped through her. The rocking of her hips probably painted her desire across Clint's face. Still he never stopped eating her.

The release cleansed her soul of all the doubt she'd had about her decision to pursue a night of no-strings ecstasy. How could she have lived without this for so long?

In the arms of two amazing men, she unraveled. And still they pushed her.

Clint withdrew the beads in time with the pulses of rapture spasming through her pussy. He kept refreshing her orgasm with new waves of stimulation that his roving mouth only enhanced.

On and on, she came.

Matt kissed her, devouring her cries. He saved her from slumping to the bed, exhausted, as Clint moved into another phase of his indecent assault. This time, the man holding her caressed every part of her over-sensitized skin, bringing her back to their realm in a slow descent that never quite reached the ground. No, by the time she could think logically again, she had already started a new climb.

A squeak snuck past her guard when the snick of a cap was followed shortly by Clint probing her asshole. She'd declined anal sex but hadn't been able to resist the option of introductory backdoor play. And that was when she realized what the man between her thighs intended.

Already coiled, she didn't make it easy for him to insert the first bead despite Matt grabbing her ankles and hauling them toward their hips so she was wide open. From there, Clint made it work. With gentle spirals, he coaxed her into accepting the toy, slick with her own arousal and probably some of the lube he'd acquired. A groan accompanied the intrusion of a hard plastic ball when it slipped through her instinctual resistance.

A tiny bit of pain could do nothing to erase the pleasure he gifted her with in spades.

Again the mammoth guy holding her had his work cut out. He kept her relatively still when all she wanted was to rub herself along the length of his body and that of his counterpart like a cat in heat. Anything to soothe the fire raging beneath her skin.

This time she'd only accepted about half of the string of beads before the combination of a novel sensation, the heat of two men, their constant caresses and Clint's deadly mouth on her pussy had her flying apart. When Clint jerked on the beads—enough to make her feel them though not enough to withdraw them—he extended her climax, or maybe generated another one. Soon she lost track of how many times they made her crest with their hands, mouths, toys and the honest lust with which they claimed her. No holds barred. Exactly opposite of how the real Matt and Clint had run from her, left her hanging.

No, this time she got her wish.

They brought every dream she had to life.

And when she thought she might be tapped out, Clint crawled up her body. He skimmed along as he slunk on top of her, and his friend by default.

The crinkle of a foil packet had Jambrea's eyes scrunching closed beneath the blindfold. Oh, thank God. She would be full of him and his heat. Soon. Matt ran his hand down to her pussy and spread her saturated folds for his friend.

Then, finally, the unmistakable weight of a real human cock—no vibrator for her tonight—nudged her, notching in the vestibule of her pussy. Clint paused, as if giving her one last chance to object, like that would happen, then rocked his hips forward and embedded himself a few inches in her pussy.

His soft grunt made her feel better about the abject pleasure bombarding her. At least she knew he wasn't unaffected by their shared experience. The subtle sound had

Spread Your Wings

her spreading wider, arching her back and relaxing to welcome him into her body.

The giant cradling her hugged her, more with fondness than the urgent squeezes he'd been imparting until then. He must have been able to tell she was trying to admit his friend, though she feared they might also have snuck into her affections after their careful, yet ardent, handling.

Damn her soft heart.

Matt cupped her breasts, then tugged lightly at the chain connecting the clamps on her nipples. She hissed and shifted. The new position allowed Clint to fuse more tightly with her. They became one as he slid home, then out a bit before driving deeper within her. Each motion jiggled the beads in her ass and added another dimension to his invasion.

When he'd drilled as far as he could reach, they both sighed.

She swiped a thumb over the tip of Matt's cock, surprised to find a large pool of precome cupped in the slit at the top. For a moment, she wished she could taste him. But abandoning the claiming that had just begun held no appeal. Instead she reveled in the advance and retreat of Clint's sizable hard-on. He stretched her, boring deeper on every stroke of his cock within her.

She moaned, loving the way the blindfold really had made her super aware of every tiny sensation. The rub of his cock within her nudged the beads still lodged in her ass. The combination of sensual delights nearly drove her insane. Uncaring about how it made her look, she surrendered completely to the mastery of the pair of men claiming her.

She cried out with abandon, embracing the sexual freedom they'd granted her.

Powerful and liberated, she squeezed Clint tight. The head of his cock slammed into the locked muscles at the opening of her pussy before coaxing her to accommodate his length. It didn't take long before she trembled in their grasp, clinging to the razor's edge of passion for as long as she could before one deep, grinding pass mixed with the possession of his lips on hers. The blend of sensory inputs drove her straight into another soul-rending orgasm.

The jerky thrusts of his hips made her sure he joined her. The thought of his come filling the condom he'd donned put her through another round of wringing spasms.

Before she could even stop shuddering, Clint had withdrawn. She whimpered as her body mourned the loss of him. Matt didn't seem to mind the trickle of moisture steadily glazing his balls while she rode out the storm of her passion. He caressed her, adding both arousal and gentle reassurance to the other stimuli bombarding her. The beads in her ass felt divine, shifting inside her as she clenched.

As she continued to tremble, Clint removed the clamps from her breasts.

He soothed the intense sensation, caused by blood returning in a rush, with light kisses and laps of his tongue before taking hold of her hips. For a moment, she wondered if he were some superdude, planning to fuck her again, rocking her into Matt's solid chest as he ravaged her, until she realized the guys were working together to rotate her. So she gave them as much help as her jellied limbs would allow.

And soon she found herself draped over Matt's enormous body, hugging him to her, nuzzling her face in his sweat-slicked pectorals while Clint continued to assist behind her. This time, the other man must have taken over her job, stroking Matt's ever-growing cock.

At least that was what she thought until she heard the crinkle of another wrapper. Not just any touches there. He must be sheathing his friend. Even the thought of the two men being so intimate, finally admitting a tiny bit of their attraction, had aftershocks running through her body.

She got to her knees on the bed and planted her hands on Matt's knotted shoulders. This time *she* kissed *him*. Well, at first she nibbled on his chin, then his cheek before she landed on his mouth. When she did find her target, she unleashed a flurry of pent up lust on the mystery man beneath her.

Lips collided and their teeth clicked once before they established their place, their rhythm, and their ideal approach. A frenzy of sexual energy electrified her, giving her permission to ravage him even as he settled his cock at the entrance to her body. She shifted, lowering her hips instinctively to accept him into her still-pulsing channel.

Saturated, she eased his entry, though his girth imprinted her with simultaneous burn and satisfaction. From behind, Clint embraced her, guiding her while helping to facilitate the joining of his lover and the man he shared her with.

Dear God, could they be any more sexy?

A flash of Lily's story cut through even the haze of arousal they'd billowed around her. She imagined Matt and Clint kissing as she had at least a million times since her chat with the Mistress. The idea of the partners' mouths on each other, soliciting rapture even while fulfilling their best friend's longing, had her thermonuclear in a second.

She slid another few inches down Matt's impressive length, uncaring about the way he stretched her to capacity. If only she could have both of her cops here with her, like this. She swore she'd make it good for the guys who allowed her to dream while thrilling her body.

Over and over.

Feral now, she kneaded the pecs of the enormous man beneath her, a little sorry—though not much—that her fingernails must have been leaving dozens of crescent marks on what felt like flawless skin interrupted only by a light dusting of hair.

Clint's hands encircled her waist, helping her grind

downward. When her spine arched and she stiffened, he held her still, not allowing her to progress until her body had adjusted further to the mammoth intrusion. Then he let her have a bit more. And a bit more. Until, finally, she had all of his cohort. She and Matt didn't fuck hard or fast like she had with Clint.

Instead, they ground together in a sinful figure eight that did unbelievable things to her pussy, and her soul. Relief poured through her when she realized that she could still revel in bliss and physical relief even when her penchant for attraction at first sight had been avoided.

Lust, pure and simple.

She was capable of it. She could make do with it. She could soar because of it.

No more lonely nights—or years of them—for her.

That promise alone had her contracting on the man entrenched in her pussy. He grunted when she began to rock with the help of Clint behind her. It didn't take long before she could feel extra definition impressing the ridges of Matt's cock on her engorged tissue. Even better, her clit rubbed his body, proving again that they fit perfectly together.

Jambrea dropped her hands backward to his powerful thighs, loving the way twenty fingers now careened over her from her stomach to her breasts to her shoulders. She fucked him with a primal energy she hadn't known she possessed. Clint assisted her wild ride and kept her from going too far, dislodging Matt. Because by then all three of them were quite clear that letting him vacate her pussy wasn't on her agenda anytime soon.

All the while, his fat cock teased the beads in her ass. They rolled and shifted as he prodded them and her abdomen undulated with the ripples of her contracting muscles.

Before long, Matt tensed beneath her, nearly quivering with the energy they generated simultaneously. Could he feel the straining of her body and the toy inside her, separated from him by only a thin layer of tissue? She bet he could. He trembled. The tendons in his neck stood out sharply beneath her roving fingers as he must have thrown back his head in an attempt for restraint. And she was right there with him. She shouted, "I'm going to come."

And then she did.

Her pussy wrung the giant cock filling her, squeezing it with concentric constrictions that ran along the tunnel of her pussy. Right when she thought she couldn't feel any more, Clint began to withdraw the beads from her ass. She screamed as she clenched around each and every one. Her eyes rolled back behind her blindfold. She milked Matt, causing him to fall with her into the most powerful climax of her life.

He joined her, slamming upward even as she bore down. His cock flared inside her then pulsed as he flooded the condom he wore.

The enormous guy groaned and shuddered between her legs. As they spasmed together, he cried, "Jambi."

Her orgasm redoubled. It burned like an out of control wildfire that nothing could douse. The man behind them—Clint Griggs—held her tighter, his arms squeezing her at the sound of Matt Ludwig calling out her name in ecstasy.

She might have manufactured some of the other clues, but not that one.

His voice, his smell, his one-of-a-kind body. There was no mistake.

No more lying to herself.

She knew these men.

And now they knew her too.

Chapter Six

"Matt!" Jambrea answered his cry of completion even as part of her died inside. She should have known a connection like this was impossible between people she'd never truly met. Her body continued to come while her mind spun at his inadvertent disclosure of their identities. And soon, questions took over. Why had they tricked her?

How dumb had Jambrea been to assume the Mistress's office was as confidential as a confessional? Lily had betrayed her trust.

"Uh oh." Slightly clearer-minded now that his afterglow must have faded, Clint's entire body went stiff behind her. Well, most of him anyway. That fucker.

Even as the majority of her continued to be disloyal, thoroughly enjoying the ruse they'd concocted, Jambrea began to thrash. She disengaged herself from Clint's embrace, causing Matt's cock to slip from her still-clenching pussy, and ripped the blindfold off in enough time to sear the last moments of his orgasm in her mind. His expression, unforgettable.

Why had he withheld that from her?

"You bastards!" she shouted as she rolled off the bed and snatched her robe from the side chair. "What the hell did you mean by this? Did you think it was funny to fuck me? Would you have laughed behind my back every time we were together with the rest of the Men in Blue?"

Clint opened his mouth, but no excuses came out. Matt braced himself on one arm, still emptying himself into the condom he wore, which bulged with his seed.

They reached for her. She stumbled backwards.

"You know what? I don't want to hear it anyway. *Blue!*" Jambrea didn't care if it was cowardly. She ran, while she still could. Before they concocted some justification that would have her falling back into bed with two men who couldn't be straight with her.

Jambrea tore along the hall, swinging a right at the enchanted pools where the mermaid population seemed to have boomed. Squirming between the crowd watching the erotic-aqua-ballet, she didn't give a shit if her robe hadn't quite closed properly. The edges flapped in the breeze as she bolted for the front doors. Common sense began to kick in gradually.

How would she even get home? Lily had picked her up this evening and escorted her personally to the Playground, knowing damn well she'd have chickened out otherwise. How could the woman who was supposed to be one of her closest damn friends have done this to her?

Sure, she specialized in mind games, but this time they'd all gone too far.

Jambrea slowed, bending so she could rest her palms on her knees and attempt to suck in a few breaths. Her traitorous body still hummed in the aftermath of the pleasure her dream guys had given her before they reminded her that their relationship actually had more in common with a nightmare.

"Hang on a second. I see her." A familiar male voice filled her with dread. Of course she'd be easy to track in the camera-covered club. She couldn't outrun the speed of light. Jeremy called out to her, "Jambi, is that you? Are you—"

Shit! Another one of those damn sexy Men in Blue. Exactly who she didn't want to see right then. She refused to show him how weak they'd made her. The tears she barely held at bay threatened to spill over. Even after all Matt, Clint and she had shared, it hadn't been enough.

Sex alone would never tick all her boxes. She knew that for

sure now.

"Leave me alone." Childish or not, she yelled as she dashed toward a staircase. Up had to lead out, eventually. "I'm getting the hell out of here."

"Let me drop you off. I swear I won't say a single word." His plea faded as she put some distance between them.

And not an instant too soon.

"Which way did she go, JRad?" Matt bellowed as he closed in. He must have gotten dressed in record time. "Answer me! I'm not fucking around."

Fortunately, Jeremy didn't take orders well. She didn't wait to see if his Dom side or geek side won out. Instead she shoved through the fire door at the top of the landing marked *Emergency Exit.*

Stones sprinkled across the blacktopped alley jabbed her feet. The minor pain of the pebbles gouging her arches had nothing on the all-too-familiar gash in her heart. This was why she didn't mess around. Never again. It hurt too much to think she might finally have what she needed only to have it ripped away endlessly—each time with greater awe then more painful rejection. The party wasn't worth the hangover.

Too close behind her, only a few seconds delayed, the steel door slammed into the brick building as first one then the other of her never-would-be lovers were ejected from Gunther's Playground. For a brief moment it had been her amusement park too. *Jambiland*, she thought with a wry twist of her lips. Short-lived, the sarcastic smile turned into a grimace when her heel clomped onto a particularly sharp piece of rubble. She yelped and hopped on one foot.

Her rapid deceleration probably saved her life.

Because a split second later, the sparks from something hitting the wall beside her were followed by a blaze across her upper arm. This kind of heat had nothing in common with the decadent variety she'd experienced at the talented hands of her asshole fuck buddies.

"What the—?" She slapped her right hand over her left biceps, noting the stickiness she was all too familiar with from her time at the hospital. And as a medic.

Blood.

Before she could even complete her thought, she found herself sprawling on the ground. A heavy weight landed on top of her, knocking the wind from her lungs. "Stay down. Who the hell is firing shots?"

Clint's arms wrapped around her head, muffling his shouts even as he protected her with his own vulnerable body. Two other people ran past, jumping over their prone forms. Gooey liquid oozed between her fingers, making her wish she could grab the belt hanging, limp, through the loops at the waist of her robe.

Next thing she knew, she was being dragged behind a dumpster. Add abrasions to the list of damage tonight had done to her. Ignoring the revolting smell and the sludge beneath her knees, she curled as tight as possible into the man shielding her. He whispered into her hair, "I've got you, Jambi. Stay quiet. Still."

So she did. Her ancient training kicked in, yes. But also, she trusted him. In this he was an expert. Proficient and cool, he gripped his gun and aimed at the only remaining angle of approach.

A minute passed, maybe two, and her immediate fight or flight response began to wane. Adrenaline gave way to logic. She counted her heartbeats, judging her pulse to be remarkably normal. Forcing herself to calm even more, she slowed the rivulet of blood pouring from her. Sooner rather than later, she'd need to elevate the limb. Until then, she tilted toward her right side, getting her left above her heart.

Clint drew a huge, shuddering breath that caused his firearm to waver.

Horrible thoughts snuck into her mind. She tried to put a gap between them so she could scan him for injuries, but he held her too tightly for that.

"Are you hit too?" She asked what she couldn't verify herself. Despite the unfortunate end to the evening, she still cared for him. Even if he hadn't shown her what it was like to fly again—so much higher this time—she'd never leave any human being to suffer. The nurse in her wouldn't permit it.

"No. I'm good." His heart raced against her cheek as he surveyed the area, his gaze sweeping from side to side as loud boot-steps pounded the pavement, approaching. Neither one of them had to be told who they belonged to. Clint would know his partner anywhere, she bet. "Wait, what? Hit *too*? As in also? Matt! What's up?"

"They poofed. Two dudes in black dropped off the roof of the building next door and piled into a dark SUV. Either green or blue. Couldn't get details in the shadows. JRad is checking surveillance. Doesn't look like an accident. Let's move. Inside. Somewhere safe." The hulking man cast a shadow as he stepped between the spotlight in the alley and their den. He crouched down, making as small a target as possible despite the lessening chance of violence.

"No, I meant *you*. You okay?" The concern lacing Clint's question made Jambrea snuggle against him despite her best intentions. "JRad too?"

"Fine. Both of us." Matt scrubbed his hand over his chin as he tucked his gun in his waistband at the small of his back. "Other than shitting our pants. What the fuck was that all about?"

"I don't know, but thank God. Jambi thought you'd been tagged." Clint sagged. His arms trembled briefly around her as if he shivered. On cue, her own quaking began. Her teeth chattered as she crashed from all the excitement that had coursed through her.

It wasn't enough to obliterate her pain anymore.

She hated the whimper that escaped when she adjusted her grip on her upper arm.

"Not him," she managed through gritted teeth. "*Me*."

"Holy shit!" Clint tucked his gun in his waistband and bolted to his feet, dragging her into his arms. "Where? Why didn't you say something? Are you nuts? You know, sometimes there's such a thing as too tough for your own good."

"Jesus." Matt scoped out the droplets raining from her. "Stop jerking her around. It's her arm. You're making it worse."

Story of their lives, really. She almost—though not quite—laughed.

"How bad is it?" The pale cast to Clint's face had her wondering if he would drop her. He never flinched.

"Why are you asking me?" Matt shrugged and looked to her. "She's the nurse."

That he trusted her, even in these circumstances, meant a lot to Jambrea. Forcing herself to be objective, she peeked down at the laceration, visible through a tear in the robe. Relief flooded her even as the numbness granted by shock began to wear off. "It's not horrible. Going to need stitches though. And it'd be good if you could help me elevate it and increase the pressure."

Matt scooped her into his tree-trunk arms. Clint whipped off his T-shirt and wrapped it around her upper arm. He helped her lift it and banded his hands around the impact area. She tried not to ogle his bare chest and the sleeve of tattoos she admired. For the distraction factor, she allowed herself a glimpse or two. Damn him.

"Son of a bitch," Matt grumbled as he and Clint took off in unison, jogging side by side. "Can we transport you or should we wait for an ambulance? Hanging around here doesn't sit well with my gut."

"As long as we're not going far." She yelped as they swerved toward their truck. Sprinting, they covered the open area in a quasi-crouch before she quite realized what they intended.

"How about to Mason, Tyler and Lacey's house? It's closer and more protected than the hospital." Matt looked to her as he jammed the key in the ignition and whipped his truck from the parking spot. He'd already merged onto the street and floored it through a yellow light by the time she confirmed that would be fine.

Clint pressed his fingers over hers once more, stemming the blood flow while he hauled his phone out with his free hand. "JRad, change of plans. Jambi's got a flesh wound. Upper arm. Left. We're taking her to Mason. Call Lacey. Have her ready, please?"

A pause.

"It's not your fault. It's ours. We shouldn't have taken the coward's way. Let's get Jambi cleaned up, then we can figure out the rest. She'll be safe there for now. In a few hours, we'll relocate. When we have a plan. Thanks, JRad. Keep your Lily close. You'll meet us there as soon as possible, right?"

Another pause.

"Of course we want you both there. You're still one of the Men in Blue, aren't you?" Clint ignored Matt's cursing to make sure Jeremy understood. "You couldn't have known anyone was out there. The rest is on us. Unless you think we're putting you in danger, get your ass to Mason and Tyler's place. With Lily. See you soon."

Jambrea tipped her head way back so she could meet Clint's worried gaze. "Do you think he's going to be okay?"

"Yeah. Lily will whip him into shape. Actually it might have to be him that does the spanking. I could hear her crying in the background." He snuck in a caress over her wrist and the tattoo there. She hadn't realized he'd noticed it before. "Quit worrying about everyone else for a change, wild thing. You're most important."

"Don't call me that. And...it's nothing." Well, it felt like *something*, but the technician in her knew she'd survive just fine. "Skin and bones are a hell of a lot more durable than hearts and souls."

"You can tell JRad that yourself in a bit." Matt cleared his throat. "I'm sorry we fucked up tonight. The look on your face before you split. Shit. You didn't seem half as hurt when you got shot. I know how badass you are. And we managed to crack your armor. We really screwed this all up, didn't we?"

"Yep." She wasn't about to argue.

"What can we do?" Clint tried to jump in.

"Haven't the two of you done enough?" Suddenly exhausted, she slumped against the seat. "Just shut up and don't remind me of what an idiot I was. Ever again. We'll be there in a few minutes, and then you can go. Leave me to Lacey. She's damn fine at her job."

"That's not..." Matt began.

"You asked. That's my answer." She snipped at them to help her ignore the throbbing starting in her shoulder. "Zip it. Now."

For once, they actually listened.

Sick as it made her, she missed the sound of their arguments.

Fortunately, before she could really start to pout, they pulled into the wooded drive of her fellow nurse's home. She'd known Lacey for years. They'd gone through a hell of a lot together, including the murder of Lacey's brother Rob. A broken heart was nothing compared to that.

"Put me down." Jambrea squirmed out of reach when Clint attempted to haul her from the mammoth vehicle. Lacey, Tyler and Mason jogged down the steps of their newish house to meet them.

She was thankful for Tyler's subtle steadying hand on her uninjured elbow when the ground turned a little wavy. Accepting help from their neutral friend was much easier than relying on the sneaky bastards who'd carted her here. She went willingly into his arms. "Come on, Jambi. Let's get you upstairs so you can lie down and let Lacey work her magic."

"Get her some juice and a cookie or two if she can stomach them." Lacey directed Matt toward the kitchen as she wrapped an arm around Jambrea's waist. If any of them noticed her strange attire, they didn't bother to comment.

Probably everyone had been in on tonight's fiasco except her. The idea made her snarl at Clint, who attempted to follow them. "Stay away."

"But..." He attempted to persuade her into allowing his tender faux-caring at her bedside.

"No. Don't rile her up any more than you obviously already have." Lacey cut that shit out immediately. "This isn't the time. Her arm doesn't look too awful. Still, it's bad enough. She needs to stay quiet and keep her heart rate and blood pressure down."

"I'm sorry." He stopped instantly when he heard he put her at risk. If only he'd had the grace to do that before he'd screwed with her affection, and her body. He stared into her eyes when she peeked over her shoulder and she wondered about the extent of his apology.

"JRad is on his way. Razor too. He said Ellie, Lucas, Ben and Ryan were over there watching movies. Probably going to be a full house soon. Why don't you guys start a list of all our favorite perps including those who've been sprung lately?" Tyler didn't stop his progress toward the guest room.

Almost there now. She could make it.

From down the hall, Clint promised, "I'll find out who did this, Jambi. You won't be hurt because of us again."

His vow trailed off as Tyler shut the door. The moment she was safe behind the barrier she collapsed, sobbing. Or would have if Tyler hadn't carried her the last ten feet to the bed.

"There you go, don't worry about him now. Matt either. You can figure out what to do about them when you're in fighting form." The sensitive guy always had a knack for reading people's feelings. He'd know it wasn't her arm causing all this agony.

"I don't want to ruin your comforter." Jambrea tried to resist, but he helped her sit on the cheery yellow linens anyway.

"Mind if we lose this robe?" Lacey nudged the fabric from her shoulder.

"What's the point now? I think everyone's seen my goods." She tried to laugh. Instead, tears dribbled out of the corners of her eyes.

"That's some fine merchandise, if you don't mind me saying." Tyler scanned her with a friendly yet assessing stare. And hell if it didn't seem like he was serious.

Lacey smacked him on the ass. "If I were the jealous type I might not appreciate that, husband of mine."

"Well, you've got two guys. Maybe I should get to check out two girls." He shrugged as he swung his stare toward the woman he adored. No contest. The green heated up when he saw her imitation ire.

"How about you hand me some towels and a garbage bag instead? I'll lay her down on them and the comforter will be plenty protected. The bleeding is mostly stopped now. You're doing good, Jambi." She strode to the restroom, washed her hands thoroughly and grabbed the supply kit she kept there. It wasn't the first time she'd had to patch one of their friends. "I've got some topical anesthetic in here. I'll clean you up and we'll see how much is burn. Pretty sure a handful of stitches will take care of it."

"I trust you." Jambrea smiled up at her friend, and it was true. Not that she'd wish it on any of the Men in Blue, but if she had to return to a war zone, she knew who she'd want at her back. Hell, the hospital was pretty much as crazy as that deployment had been some days.

"So why don't you tell me about the rest to take your mind off this. It's gonna sting like a bitch." Lacey got to work as soon as Tyler spread out the items he'd gathered. The tall, charming guy took Jambrea's hand and she didn't try to shake it off.

"It's embarrassing." She scrunched her eyes shut, and not because of the needles of pain that even Lacey's deft touch couldn't avoid creating. "Horrifying, really."

"Worse than getting shot?" Tyler laughed. "Come on. It's not like you to be dramatic."

"I had sex with Matt and Clint." She sighed. Why had it been so damn good?

"About time," Lacey muttered.

Before Jambrea could correct her friend, she heard a squeak of a floorboard to their left.

"Um... I wasn't eavesdropping, that was just a bad time to come in unannounced." Izzy stood at the bedroom door, rubbing her distended belly. "Sorry, should have knocked. I can go downstairs."

"Don't bother." Jambrea waved her off, then winced at the resulting sting. "It's not like anyone can keep a secret around here. Especially not your sister, that bitch."

"What?" Izzy came closer. She tucked onto the mattress beside Jambrea, opposite of Lacey since blood kind of freaked her out. Or maybe she simply hadn't built up a tolerance to gore like the nurses had to in order to survive. The pixie rested her head on Jambrea's shoulder and squeezed her tight. "What does Lily have to do with this?"

"I asked her to hook me up with a couple of guys at the club..."

The door squeaked again and Lily joined them. What was this, Grand Central Station?

"And I fucked up big time. I swear, Jambs, I interviewed a bunch of couples. But none fit you like Matt and Clint. I know how much you wanted them and they were down too. I thought if you could get past all your hang-ups you could work things out. I see now how that might have been a really, *really* bad idea. Forgive me?"

Lily joined them, crawling onto the foot of the bed, still encased in her leather garb.

Though Jambrea would like to give the Mistress a flogging of her own, she wasn't really pissed. Deep down, the woman had done what she thought best. "Look, I know you all think that Matt, Clint and I are a perfect match. But obviously they don't. Or they wouldn't have waited for some arranged hookup to screw me. They wouldn't have needed that out. So can we forget any of this ever happened and move on? I've wasted too long on something that's never going to work."

"But was it good?" Tyler asked, seriously. "Because you have chemistry. I can see it. The rest can be fixed. If you want it bad enough."

"Fuck. Yes." She winced more from the admission than Lacey's light needlework.

"Jambi, why does it sound like you're not happy? We've all been rooting for you three to get together." Lacey hugged her gently, offering what comfort she could as she clipped the thread and moved on to bandaging the wound. Next she attended to the myriad scrapes dotting Jambrea's front. "I'm not sure why this took so long, honestly."

"Because they're dumbasses." Jambrea didn't hold back.

"Gotta point there." Razor nodded as he came in and stood near his fiancée and their unborn baby. "And they're probably about two seconds behind me. JRad and the rest of the gang too."

"Perfect." Jambrea wished she could close her eyes and drift off. Even if the ruckus hadn't been enough to keep her conscious, the tenderness setting in would have. Plus, she really wanted to hear about who they thought had done this.

None of their group would be secure until they figured that out.

"I can't believe they waited forever to act on the sparks between you all. Why waste time? All of us know you only get so much before it's too late." Izzy might have been the littlest, but she was tenacious. They'd all done a lot of living in the past year or two.

"Hell, I didn't even know it was them. Your sister blindfolded me. It could have been any two guys fucking me for all I knew or cared." She tried to blow off the impact of their union, but inside something shattered, cutting her to pieces.

"The hell it could've." Matt didn't usually get riled like that. Thunderclouds brewed in his gaze. As soon as he noticed that Lacey had fixed her up pretty good, he continued, "I admit we should have done things differently. But blindfolded or not, some part of you knew it was us. Didn't you?"

She didn't answer right away.

"Don't lie, wild thing." Clint stood shoulder to shoulder with his partner, making it difficult for Lucas, Ellie, Ben and Ryan to fill up the last of the free space in the room.

"Jesus. Could this be any more mortifying?" She would have buried her face in the pillows, but Izzy, Lacey and Lily had her surrounded in an infinite group hug. "Does everyone need the details on my pathetic sex life?"

"No." JRad saved her. He put one hand on his wife's shoulder though he didn't take his stare from Jambrea. "We need to know anything that will help us figure out who shot at you and why, though. Can you think of anyone who would be pissed that you'd go to the club?"

Jambrea shook her head. "No one in my life would give a shit. Other than Parker, I only have you guys."

More heat flooded her cheeks.

"Same for a bunch of us." Lily patted her shin. "It's the family you choose that counts. But you're right, none of us mind if you want to flash your freaky side. Indulging at the club is your business."

"Speaking of..." Matt took his shirt off this time. With both him and Clint naked from the waist up, Jambrea felt her pulse spike. Not helping.

Especially because his cover up attempt—as he clearly intended to drape the material over her—only highlighted the marks they'd left on her and revealed her handiwork. They all got a good look at the scratches she inflicted.

Razor whistled. "Nice job. I think I see why they're calling you wild thing."

"It's because of her tattoo, asshole." Matt whapped the youngest of their cop brothers upside the head with the lightweight cotton before stalking closer to her and holding it out. He helped her thread first her head then her good arm and finally the bad one through the holes. She swam in the damn thing, but it was better than flashing them all any longer than she had to.

"Sure, sure." Razor winked at her.

"Knock it off." Clint growled at the kid. "Why don't you take a nap, Jambrea? I'll stay if you'll let me, but I get it if you'd rather one of the girls keep you company instead. We need to compile the list of people we've pissed off and then, when you've rested, we'll go get your things. You're staying with us until this is resolved."

"Do you think just because you both fucked me, you get to boss me around?" Jambrea propped her hands on her hips despite the sting in her muscles.

"Holy shit. It's a trap. Don't say yes." Razor took a whap from Lucas's cane for that one though Ellie giggled a little in the corner. The light titter was enough to make it worth it. Jambrea hadn't heard her that relaxed since the Men in Blue had rescued her from Morselli.

"You'd rather stay alone in your apartment when there are crazy people on the loose?" Matt crossed his arms. Nothing could get past that broad expanse of chest. The one she'd lounged on so recently. *Shit.*

Psychos taking pot shots or certain death by sexual frustration.

She couldn't say which would lead to a more hideous demise.

"I think it might be best to lock the three of you alone somewhere until you sort all this out anyway." Mason looked to Tyler and then to Lacey. "I can't say we were much better than you guys, but hell, don't throw away years. We could have had so much more, if only I would have admitted..."

"Your dad made sure you couldn't." Tyler hugged his partner. Tears sheened Lacey's eyes. "No sense in second guessing. We're all who we are now because of what happened. No one will ever break us apart."

Jambrea wished she could say the same. She peeked up at Matt then Clint to find them both staring at her. Clint rubbed his fingers over her skipping pulse, conveniently across her matching *no regrets* mantra. Damn them.

"Fine. But I'm not going anywhere without Parker. He'll be hungry." She wouldn't budge on that point. "Give me a little while and then I'll go with you. We'll pick up my things and his travel bowl."

"You're worried about the stupid fish again, seriously?" Matt let his head bang on the wall beside him. "Someone tried to kill you tonight. Came too fucking close. Going to your apartment is crazy. Can't we send one of the guys over instead?"

"He's not *just* a goldfish. And he's not dumb." Jambrea knew it was ridiculous, but she crossed her arms, gasping as her wound scraped against the dressing Lacey had fashioned.

"You've got to learn to take what you can get, boys." Lily patted Clint's tight ass. "There is such a thing as compromise. If you're each stuck in your corners, demanding all or nothing, you'll only ever have three discreet points. Come together, just a bit, and you can draw a triangle, where you each get what you need."

No one bothered to argue with the relationship expert.

Besides, fighting took too much energy.

"I could use a nap too." Izzy volunteered. "Why don't you all go brainstorm and come get us when you're ready to head over to Jambi's place? The rest of our guys can watch your back while you collect your stuff."

"Sure," was all she could manage before her lids grew heavy and she snuggled into the fluffy covers.

"If you need anything, we'll be right downstairs." Matt leaned over and kissed her forehead. He whispered in her ear, "I'm so fucking glad you're okay. We'll fix the rest. I promise. I won't disappoint any of us again."

"Whatever he said." Clint approached her, then brushed his lips against her knuckles. "Me too. Because I like it when you smile like that. I missed it. I thought what we did tonight would make you happy. I'm sorry we screwed that up too."

She might have responded if he hadn't pressed his fingertips against her mouth, then retreated slowly. "We've got your back. Never doubt that."

Chapter Seven

The soft orange glow of dawn limned the horizon. Birds sang in harmonic chirps as if everything in the world were as perfect as a new day in the suburbs. Jambrea hadn't meant to sleep all night, but the painkillers Lacey had administered worked their magic. Next thing she knew, she'd staggered down the stairs of Lacey's pretty house to find the guys still going strong on fact-finding in the living room while their women supported them—cooking breakfast, taking notes or keeping them company as they dozed nearby.

Matt had paced the hardwood floor, his shoulders tense as he tipped his head side to side until his neck cracked. The moment Clint spotted her, he'd raced to her and wrapped her in a hug. Brain fuzzy, she hadn't fought him. And soon after, her friends had fed her, helped her shower and dress, then prepared to send the three of them off.

She figured it was for the best, to keep everyone else isolated from their trouble. It didn't seem like any major ah-ha moments had cropped up during the darkest hours of the night. Putting some distance between the three of them and the rest of the Men in Blue would be wise for the whole group.

So here they stood, in the driveway of Lacey, Mason and Tyler's home, hugging out their farewells.

"If things get too intense, you can always come stay with Jeremy and me." Lily put her arms tentatively around Jambrea. Her friend swallowed hard. "If you're still comfortable at our place..."

Jambrea didn't hesitate in squeezing back. Her reputation

as cool-headed and forgiving had been rightfully earned. It was hard to stay angry when she knew the other woman had acted with positive intent. "It's all good, Lily. We're okay."

"Thank you. I'm not used to having a best friend, you know. I promise I'll get better at it." The tiny lady with huge personality smiled and snuggled into the crook between her husband's chest and his arm, which curled protectively around her shoulder, in a rare display of vulnerability.

That Lily could allow glimpses like that to her new family awed Jambrea. It wasn't so long ago that the tough-as-nails Mistress had shocked everyone in the hospital Jambrea worked at when she recounted years of abuse at the hands of her father without so much as a crack in her façade. Hell, she'd planted herself deep undercover and worked tirelessly to free sex-slaves without her enemies ever catching on. That poker face didn't exist around their group of allies anymore. Hopefully it never would again.

So much had changed so quickly. Once Lily and Jeremy had found each other, allowing their love to blossom, a million other possibilities opened up. They were strong for each other, both of them growing into something new together.

She glanced between Matt and Clint, who kept an awkward distance between them, not quite meeting the other's gaze, never mind hers. Was there any hope things could be different someday?

"Time to move. No one should be out in the open longer than necessary." Mason ushered the rest of the Men in Blue onto his porch and through the front door even as Clint boosted Jambrea into the cab of Matt's truck. Medication kept her zen enough that blinking her eyes open was a struggle. As the informal head of their group, Mason sent them off as he hovered over the threshold. "We'll keep mining the databanks."

"I can check with military info bases too." Lucas spoke from halfway up the stairs, slower than the rest in retreating, seeing as he refused all help. Jambrea worried that his limp seemed more pronounced than when she'd observed him struggling through the wedding. She'd have to follow up with his doctors on her next shift. "I still have contacts that will help in a bind. Plenty of favors to call in. You never know if these dirtbags are local or federal criminals. Hell, international, even. They could trip flags in any number of systems."

"JRad is usually pretty good at poking around across the board." Clint shrugged as he levered himself in gracefully beside her then continued their discussion through the open window. "But we won't turn down any help at this point. We really have nothing. There weren't any particular standouts on the list. Not that it couldn't be someone from the Sex Offender ring who's bitter about being locked up and working from the inside. I just...I don't know. It doesn't feel right. Why Jambi? Or us? To get back at JRad, it seems like they'd target Lily or vice versa."

"And no one could mistake me for her." Jambrea snorted. Size-wise, she easily counted for three of the petite Mistress.

"No, you're much more beautiful," Matt murmured from beside her. "Feminine. Soft. Wild."

Before she could tell him to knock it off with the false compliments—since they wouldn't save him from her wrath at being lied to and fucked, once she got around to unleashing it—Mason thumped on the front door with his fist.

"It doesn't make sense to me either." He waved them off. "Go. Get her essentials. Quickly. Then move out. Maybe you should try bunking in a hotel instead of one of your places. Let's keep communication minimal and untraceable so they don't figure out where you're stationed. You know how to reach us if you need backup, but I think it might be better to lay low than to attract attention at this point. If we spread out, we'll have a better idea of who they're after. Check in three times a day from someone else's phone or a public computer away from your headquarters. The Chief gave us as long as it takes..."

Spread Your Wings

"Got it." Matt nodded his agreement with the plan. It seemed overly cautious to Jambrea, but this was their wheelhouse. The Men in Blue were damn fine at it too. And if it seemed like Mason was hinting at something more, well, she couldn't deal with that right now.

"I'm trusting my gut on this one. I'll ride behind you. Recon the parking lot of her place while you're inside." Lucas reversed his trajectory and hobbled to his car without complaint, though his leg had to hurt a million times more than what amounted to a fancy scratch on her arm. She wasn't the only one who noticed.

Jambrea spied Ellie peeking from behind the curtain, frowning as the injured man left her without so much as a goodbye. When she caught Jambrea's stare, she blew a kiss, then disappeared into the house, which overflowed with friends.

Mason held his hand up in farewell before joining the others.

Then they were backing down the gravel driveway, the ruts in the road lulling her with the sway they caused when paired with the springs of the bench seat. A particularly large bump sent her careening into Clint's side. She didn't have the energy to extricate herself from his careful grasp. Instead, she laid her head on his broad shoulder and tried not to remember what it had been like to have him inside her yet be robbed of the memory of his expressions while they shared something so precious. Or what should have been.

Thieves. They'd stolen intimacy from her by keeping her blind.

Sure, she'd checked that box on Lily's survey, but it seemed like they'd gamed the system, making her the loser.

Jambrea dozed on the ride to her apartment. That might have been because of the chemicals lingering in her cells or maybe because she wasn't ready to hash things out just yet. In any case, she shouldn't have worried, because the guys were on red alert, focused on transporting her unharmed as if she were precious cargo instead of some girl they'd pity-banged.

Because what other reason would they have had for hiding their identity? They could have shown themselves *then* blindfolded her. The point was sensory deprivation, not hoodwinking.

Drained, she floated in and out of consciousness. Each time her eyelids fluttered open, she caught the cops scanning the horizon or the truck's mirrors for any sign of danger. As she expected, there were none.

"Wild thing, wake up." Clint shook her gently, careful not to aggravate her arm. "We're here."

She wished more than anything she could scramble up the metal stairs and into her den. Crappy and old as it might be, it was home...at least for a little bit longer. Instead, she drafted a mental checklist of all the things she'd need to gather.

"How long should I plan on this taking? You know, the investigation." She tilted her head, but didn't argue when Clint slid from the truck and held out his arms. Being carried sounded nice at the moment. Might as well make good use of the convenient excuse letting her give in to unwise urges.

"Why not stay a while? Permanently, maybe, if we can keep from killing each other?" Clint smiled at her, a little wistful. His adorable factor shot off the charts when he winked. "A guy can hope, right?"

"Clint and I have always kicked around the idea of getting a place together. Save on rent. It's not like we spend much time apart anyway. Even on days off, we end up hitting the gym or grabbing something to eat and stuff." Matt shrugged. "It could be a nice arrangement."

Jambrea allowed herself a moment of weakness. She inhaled the scent of Clint's skin, sadly covered by a borrowed T-shirt. Still, he smelled nice—a little sweat mixed with his soap.

When she considered how he'd exerted himself, she shivered. Then she laughed. "You guys hid from me when we fucked and now you're talking about sharing an apartment. Come on. That's a little much, don't you think?"

"Yeah, don't rush." Clint glared at Matt. "We've got a lot of talking to do. Explaining. Listening."

"I hate that shit," the bigger man grumbled as he raked his fingers through his hair.

"Well, you're going to have to learn to communicate better if you want this to work out," Clint snapped. Tension crept into the muscles cradling her. When his hand tightened a little close to her bandages, Jambrea couldn't help but whimper. At least she tried to convince herself it was the physical discomfort—not the reminder of the emotional sensitivity plaguing her—that ached so badly.

"Am I hurting you?" He shifted his fingers away from her wound. Of course that meant he only inflamed the rest of her more.

"Not at all." She rested her cheek on his shoulder, burying her face in his neck as they rushed to her door. Maybe being carried caused the world to bounce more. She didn't remember the stairway swaying so much when she ascended. Then again, all three of them made a much heavier load than her alone. It was only because of Clint's dedication to the gym that she didn't doubt him capable of lifting her in the first place.

Matt had all the bulk of a refrigerator.

And damn it had felt fine beneath her. A sigh buffeted Clint's neck.

"Almost there, wild thing. We'll be quick then we can call it a day." He promised her heaven. If only they were all sleeping together, she might get some rest.

Matt flicked a hand signal at the non-descript sedan parked in the lot below them, at enough of an angle to allow its driver, Lucas, to keep an eye on her door. Two seconds later, he'd unlocked it and let them in.

"Where'd you get my keys from?" she wondered aloud, realizing she'd abandoned her set with her purse in Lily's office.

"Uh." He cleared his throat. "Remember the night Mason and Tyler broke your door down? Because the three of us were...*busy.*"

"You mean the night we sucked face, before you two got all messed up and acted strange around me? Well, even more weird than you were when you were fighting over me?" She shoved Clint, glad when he set her down gently.

"Yeah." Matt grimaced. "Well, when it got fixed, the contractor gave us a copy. I guess he thought it was our place too since we picked up the bill for the installation. I meant to give it to you and forgot. Then I kind of liked having it on my key ring. Sorry, that sounds creepy when I say it out loud."

Jambrea scrubbed her hands over her face. What the hell had been going on all this time? She'd thought they didn't want her enough to risk messing up their friendship when both had actually been interested. Had she gotten it wrong for so long?

And how would they make things work now that she suspected they were running as scared as she had been? From her...*and* each other.

"It does sound a little sketchy, uh huh." She dropped her evil eye act. It warmed her to know they'd looked out for her. Hell, the door they'd paid to replace, insisting it'd been their fault the original had gotten broken, had been at least ten times as secure as the old one. "But I guess I don't mind. I trust you guys. Or at least I did before last night."

"Shit." Clint cursed. Then he looked beyond her and did a double take. "Going somewhere?"

She followed his gaze to the stacks of white cardboard boxes she'd begun packing her belongings in. "Actually, yeah. Handy now, but I'd decided to move. I've outgrown this place and there's...nothing...holding me here anymore."

"There was before?" Matt caught on to her hesitation.

"Maybe." She walked past before he could ask what, or who, she'd been waiting for. She knew it was stupid, but some part of her had worried that if she left John wouldn't know where to find her when he came back. From wherever he'd gone.

Stupid.

For two reasons, really. First, because any super spy would be able to track her in half a second or less, even if she moved to the opposite side of the world. Also because he obviously had meant it when he said he never planned to see her again.

"Where were you going?" Clint looked at her with one brow raised.

"I'm not sure. I haven't found the right place yet." She shrugged.

"This never did seem to suit you." Matt pivoted to face her. "It's not bright or cheery or open or cozy. It's too sterile."

"It was my first home I had on my own. All I could afford. Felt like a castle back then." She smiled, remembering how proud she'd been of her achievements.

How could she have let herself get stuck in a rut? If she wasn't careful, these guys could suck her into another one. Maybe a habit so tempting, she could never claw her way free. Before that happened, she had to make sure they could give her what she needed.

No more settling.

No more sacrifice.

She prevented the partners from digging deeper than she was ready to venture at the moment by pointing them to a stack of boxes. "Most everything I need is in these. Clothes, extra supplies for Parker. Shove aside the ones with memorabilia and we can take the rest. I'll go pack some toiletries and transfer Parker to his travel bowl. Ten minutes tops, I swear."

Matt wandered to her heap of cartons. While she piled them, she'd heaved and grunted more than she cared to admit. As if it were nothing, he bent and gripped the handles on the bottom of the stack. Her jaw fell open a little when he bent his knees and picked up five containers at once. "There's plenty of room in the truck. Why not bring them all? I'll run these down while you and Clint get the rest of your stuff. Let's not waste time sorting through them now."

"Showoff," Clint grumbled beneath his breath.

Jambrea couldn't help herself—she laughed. It felt so good to see them bicker like she was used to. Never did that back and forth amount to more than friendly competition between them. They always recovered their balance, reclaiming their camaraderie.

Another thing that worried her. She never wanted to come between them when they were so obviously a pair. Why hadn't she seen it before?

Thank God for Lily and her insight.

But if the Mistress had been right about that, could she also have been correct to toss Jambrea in the mix? Even in the sneaky way she had?

Biting her lip as she tossed toothpaste, shampoo and other necessities into a bag, she was surprised when Clint came up behind her. "It's going to be okay, Jambi. We'll find out who wanted to hurt us and make sure they can't ever again. I'm only sorry you got caught in the crossfire. Another mistake I'll never be able to forget we made with you."

She turned, surprised when his arms caged her against the sink. Blinking into his bright green eyes, the honesty there stole her breath, giving him a chance to continue.

"If you'd gotten hurt. Worse...I'd never have forgiven myself." He leaned his forehead on hers.

She couldn't help but splay her fingers on his chest, soaking in the warmth and strength of his pecs, kneading them

Spread Your Wings

a little. "It's all right. We're okay."

"Not yet. But we will be." He shuffled closer until his feet were bracketing hers and his body pressed against her full-length. Wrapping his arms around her waist, he held her loosely. They both knew she wasn't going anywhere. Couldn't escape the attraction between them. Especially when he whispered, "I promise I'm going to make this right. I'll bring him around. I know what I want and I won't let it slip through my fingers. Last night showed me what I could be missing. And how quickly everything can be stolen."

Her heart melted when he nuzzled her nose with his. Then he kissed her.

If she hadn't been shaky before, she would have dropped to the peeling linoleum floor when he stole every last bit of her spine, leaving her a mass of rubbery nerves and blubbering sentiment.

She could have kissed him—soft, vital and devoted—for hours.

Except Matt broke up their party.

"Ahem." He cleared his throat roughly. Rather than fuming, he looked away. The glimpse of hurt in his eyes affected her more profoundly than if he'd been jealous or angry at their dillydallying. "We should head out. Lucas thought he saw someone hanging around downstairs. Not the old lady with the thirteen cats, either."

Mrs. Wilkenson had lived on the ground floor since this complex had been new and spotless, in an up-and-coming neighborhood instead of one on the cusp of revitalization. Jambrea shook her head, trying to clear the daze Clint had inspired. She pledged she wouldn't end up that way. She'd do what it took to make these guys live up to the potential she felt every time she found herself between them.

Oh God, it had been heaven *between* them.

"Sorry." Clint stepped away from her, looking as dazzled as

123

she felt. He adjusted the crotch of his jeans as subtly as possible, then tried to barge past Matt, out of the tiny bathroom. Not possible when his partner easily blocked the entire doorway.

"I don't blame you." The massive man smiled at his partner, then clapped him on the shoulder, taking away the guilt in his furrowed brows. "We're going to have to figure out the rules of this thing soon, though, so we quit trampling each other when we don't mean to. Let's find someplace quiet first, huh?"

Clint didn't answer, but he held his fist out and Matt bumped it.

Jambrea imagined them doing a lot more than that. What if Matt had kissed Clint like the other man had just done to her? She moaned, then clapped her hand over her still tingling lips.

"I'm hoping we hear a lot more of that later." Matt grinned at her. The expression had become increasingly rare lately. To see his bright white smile again filled her with optimism. Together, they could figure this out.

Couldn't they?

"Come on." Clint snagged her toiletry bag and held his hand out to her. "The sooner we get on the road, the sooner we can work on that."

Matt strode to the few remaining boxes. She couldn't believe he'd cleared out the majority of her apartment so quickly. Her head spun as she inventoried the blank, dusty shelves that had held her military memorabilia, a few pictures of her family and awards from the hospital. Only generic kitchen stuff and her threadbare furniture would stay behind.

"Parker..."

"I took him out to the truck already." Matt smiled. "I think he remembers me. He hopped right into the net thingy and splashed me like he was saying hello. I even took his castle so he has somewhere to sleep."

Jambrea couldn't help herself. She crossed the living room in two big steps then reached onto her tiptoes to lay a smacking kiss on his cheek. She couldn't believe how tiny he made her feel. And how loved.

What other man would humor her pet fish? Especially when Parker clearly was annoyed by being uprooted. He never slapped his tail at people he liked. Matt didn't need to know that though.

"Okay, kids." Clint cleared his throat this time. "We're ready?"

Jambrea looked around, knowing this place would never truly be home again. Part of her had checked out from this life. Permanently. She ringed her wrist, pressing on the *no regrets* part of her tattoo. Then she nodded.

Matt heaved her remaining boxes into his arms then looked to Clint. "Get the door, would you?"

His partner complied and held it while Matt passed through. Matt clomped down half a flight of stairs before Jambi and Clint made it to the landing outside the door. While Clint fiddled with the lock, a blaring noise had Jambrea nearly jumping.

Lucas.

He honked the car horn again. And a third time.

Still, it wasn't enough warning. The metal beneath them groaned. This time she realized the creak she'd heard a second ago had been caused by more than Matt's hulking form traipsing down the wrought iron.

Matt looked over his shoulder at them even as the staircase began to separate from the building. "Run!"

He screamed at them, but nothing would have allowed them to sprint the entire length before it gave way. Farther down, he made it most of the way before the metal buckled.

"Jump!" Lucas's bellow reached them clearly from his spot

in the parking lot.

Clint grabbed her hand. He peered over the railing then back to her as they lurched downward about three feet then held temporarily. The last remaining bolts wouldn't dangle them in mid-air for long.

A horrible crash sounded as the lower sections collapsed, dumping Matt and her belongings to the pavement. Oh shit, would he be okay?

She didn't have time to check because next thing she knew, Clint tugged her roughly. He set her on top of the railing then shoved.

Jambrea only realized what he intended at the last second. She pushed off the deteriorating structure and cannonballed into the dumpster below, thankful pickup day wasn't until tomorrow. Brimming with trash, the receptacle met her halfway to the parking lot. She only fell about eight feet before rotten vegetables and maybe even some bubble wrap halted her tumble.

A split second later, Clint crashed beside her with an *oomph* quickly followed by a hissed, "*Ew.*"

Sparks flew in the air beside them when the rest of the stairway hit the blacktop. Clint covered her from any debris raining into their safe, stinky haven. Something bounced off his shoulder yet he didn't even flinch. The instant the barrage stopped, he launched himself for the edge and hauled himself up with impressive upper body strength.

"Matt!"

No answer came to the frantic shout.

"Matt! Are you okay?"

This time a groan echoed in the stillness. Then a curse or twenty.

"I think that's a good sign, right?" Jambrea swam toward the edge of the refuse bin.

"Yeah, I'm all right. Had the wind knocked out of me. Everything seems to be moving mostly the way it's supposed to, though," Matt confirmed.

Clint turned to her with a relieved smile. He plucked a noodle from her hair then vaulted to straddle the lip of their landing site.

"What is it with you, me and dumpsters?" She cringed as something squished beneath her sneakers.

"I don't know, but let's not make it a habit, okay?" Clint fished her from the garbage. With the aid of his hand, locked around her wrist, she scampered up and over the side. He lowered her to the ground as gently as he could manage.

It had taken him a few seconds, but Lucas reached them in time to assess the structural wreckage. "Too fucking late. I didn't see it until you all were on there. Fuck. There was a cut straight through the center post. That piece of shit was rickety to start with, but...someone sliced that beam."

"Why didn't they want me to leave?" Jambrea wondered out loud.

"I have no goddamn idea," Matt snarled. "But we're not waiting around to find out."

He tried to haul her toward the truck as she peeked at the wreckage of her possessions. All the sentimental things had been in that last box. Unable to let go, she trotted back and plucked her family pictures from the debris of her shattered glass nursing awards. Estranged or not, she couldn't bear to lose the last link to them.

Lucas tried to help. He couldn't kneel beside her quick enough.

Clint finished the job while Matt hauled out his gun and covered them.

"Wait, I think you missed one. There." Lucas pointed to something shiny, which caught the first rays of sunlight to crest the top of the building.

Jambrea gasped. She lunged for the Silver Star but couldn't quite reach. Especially not with her limited range of motion in her now-pounding arm.

Lucas helped. He plucked the medal of honor from the wreckage and stared at it.

"This isn't the time for fucking show-and-tell." Matt snatched the velvet-lined case and jammed it into a box.

"You were military, Jambi?" Lucas studied her. A newfound respect colored his tone.

"Yeah, Air Force. A medic. I needed scholarships for school." She didn't glance up as she used her good arm to shove her spilled property into the cardboard crates.

"They don't give those to any old G.I. Joe." The injured man looked to Matt and Clint. "You should ask her about that. I bet it's a hell of a story."

Honestly, she wished they wouldn't. But they seemed to take Lucas's advice to heart and tossed her a few questioning glances before corralling her toward their waiting truck.

Matt tossed the not-so-pristine boxes into the back, then did practically the same to her while helping her into the cab.

Without instruction, Lucas nodded. "I'll go tell the guys. We'll bring someone over to study the scene and see what we can dig up. Get out of here. Take her somewhere safe."

"What if she's better off without us?" Clint asked quietly. "We're the ones dragging her into this mess, aren't we?"

"I'd say it's too late." Lucas's mouth was set in a grim line. "They were here. They set the trap. They know they can get to you through her or why else would they have pulled this stunt? Not to mention trying to turn her into Swiss cheese last night."

"Right." Matt swiped a trickle of blood from his cheek with the sleeve of his T-shirt. "We're in it together. The three of us."

Somehow that declaration made all the difference in the

world to Jambrea. No matter what shit hit the fan, they'd handle it as one unit.

She was okay with that.

"Stay safe." Lucas waved them off as he made his way, slowly, to his car. They waited for him to get situated before peeling out, on their way to someplace better.

Chapter Eight

Instead of a rundown roadside motel, like she expected, the glamorous Crystal Suites left Jambrea speechless. She'd driven past the gorgeous high-rise many times, but never dared to consider staying there. Matt and Clint had scored a room using some secret handshake or, more likely, the flash of their badges. Gleaming marble floors were only outdone by an enormous chandelier that dangled over the fountains that graced the lobby like Parker's wet-dream villa.

Out of the corner of her eye she spotted the local celebrity who'd hosted the reality dancing show Izzy and Razor had won two seasons ago. Though she wanted to gawk, she kept her stare cast downward and her face averted.

"Shouldn't we be keeping a low profile?" Jambrea whispered to Matt, as if the polished wood paneling of the elevator they stepped into would amplify the sound of her voice.

"Security is way better in an upscale place. They'll protect our privacy and won't be swayed by petty bribes. They're used to serving guests discreetly, even when odd requests are made." He shrugged. "Plus, their bellman will help us lug all your stuff upstairs."

She swatted his ass, though it probably stung her palm more than his buns of steel. "I told you we didn't have to bring everything."

Clint laughed hard enough to slosh a few droplets of water from Parker's bowl. He looked so adorable carrying her pet through the elegant surroundings, it made her stomach do cartwheels.

"Wild thing, it's not like you have some ungodly number of shoes or a ridiculous collection of cocktail dresses. Have you ever seen what Lacey packs to go on an overnighter? You travel light, even when we're talking about most of the contents of your apartment." Matt tucked a strand of hair behind her ear. "You know I'm teasing, right?"

"Oh." Her cheeks flushed. "Sure."

"We really need to get better at this, don't we?" Clint looked to them both. "Saying what we mean and hearing what goes unsaid."

"I guess." Jambrea mostly wanted to ignore it all, curl up in a corner somewhere and hibernate until the world made sense again.

"I think I'm starting to figure out that look." A smile tipped up the corners of Matt's mouth. "That tone too. It means you don't feel like arguing, not that you agree."

"True." She nodded.

"Well, we don't want to fight either, Jambi." Clint propped Parker's bowl on one lean hip so he could use his index finger to lift her chin and force her to meet his gaze. "That's not at all what I have in mind right now."

"The woman got shot because of us then was nearly turned into a shish kabob on that deathtrap staircase. We all reek of trash and now we have to hide out together in a hotel room for who knows how long—" Matt seemed like he was going to ramble for a while.

"You forgot the part about screwing me while hiding your identities." Jambrea couldn't believe they'd think any of the rest mattered as much as that. All of it together, months of missed connections, didn't hurt as badly as their deception. Because even though she'd dwelled on it for hours, she couldn't come up with a reason they'd go to such extremes other than tossing her a pity fuck they never intended to repeat.

So what was with the mixed signals? And Clint's kiss?

"—I hardly doubt the last day has turned her on. Hurt her, for sure. Scared her, maybe. Made her horny, doubtful." Matt glared at his partner, continuing his rant as they filed out of the car into a lush hallway. Jewel-toned runners led the way toward the room marked on the parchment envelope containing the electronic key Matt clutched. "So keep that gun in its holster until we can hash things out."

Jambrea couldn't help it. She stole a peek at Clint's crotch. *Holy crap.* Matt wasn't joking. Though the fact that he'd noticed his partner's erection spoke volumes to her.

"Keep looking at me like that and I'll risk Gigantor over there kicking my ass for what happens next." Clint's pupils dilated as he registered her appreciative glance.

"You're fast, but there's probably not much room to run in here." Matt inserted the key and waited for the indicator to flash green before confirming his theory.

Richly appointed, the space had a seating area complete with a sectional couch that faced a fancy flat-screen TV, which hung on the wall surrounded with an ornate picture frame. The furnishings were all composed of graceful lines and tasteful fabrics. Nothing gaudy. The elegant simplicity spoke of high-end luxury. On a raised dais at the far end of the long, though not-so-wide, room sat an enormous canopied bed.

"I claim that sucker. Jambi and I will be super comfortable in it." Matt stretched. "I'm too damn big to be cramped on the couch."

"You may be wide, but I'm taller." Clint waved his hands in front of his chest. "I'm definitely getting the bed with wild thing. Don't worry, the sectional looks pretty decent."

"How about the two of you share the bed and leave me the hell out of it." Jambrea propped her arms on her hips and spread her feet apart, standing strong. "I've had about enough of you two making decisions for me. Especially about who I do or don't sleep with."

Spread Your Wings

Clint sputtered, whether at the thought of doubling up with his partner or at her ire, she wasn't sure. Either suited her just fine. Before he could regain his balance, or the upper hand, she moved on.

"Look, I'm starving. I need to eat to take another dose of antibiotics, which I don't want to miss since we went dumpster diving. Could we order room service, maybe? Then I'd love to get clean." She couldn't handle feeling raw all the time. A warm meal and a steamier bath would go a long way to soothing her ragged nerves.

"Shit. Sorry, Jambi." Matt encroached on her personal space. So she held out her arm, elbow locked, palm perpendicular to the floor in the universal signal for *stop*. For once, he obeyed.

A quick flip through the menu and she had her order ready. Everything looked delicious, but she settled on a basic egg-white omelet and some orange juice. As she relayed the choice to Matt, who took down her request as well as Clint's, a knock echoed throughout the room.

She flinched. It hadn't quite set in yet that someone had tried to hurt them. No...*kill* them. Twice. More than herself, she worried about the guys and whatever wackadoodle they'd seriously pissed off. If something happened to them...

Clint stepped between her and the door, his gun drawn but held flush at his thigh, invisible to anyone in the entrance to the room. Matt took in the stance and nodded. The way they worked seamlessly together on the force had her squirming. If only they could capitalize on that groove in their personal lives, they'd be set.

It would be just like last night.

Except better, because she'd know who it was rocking her world.

Matt pressed his face to the door, using the peephole before permitting the bellman to wheel her belongings into the center of the room. In less than ten seconds they'd unloaded the cart, encouraging the man to be on his way with what looked like a big tip. "Thanks."

"My pleasure, sir." He dipped his hat toward the open menu on the desk. "Would you like me to take an order to the kitchen for you? I can fast track it if you like. The best cook downstairs, Greta, is my wife."

"That'd be great. But, seriously, call me Matt." He probably didn't mean to rattle the guy's bones when he clapped him on the shoulder.

"Yes, sir. Matt." The bellman nodded. "I'll be back with your food as soon as possible."

"Thank you." Jambrea added, her stomach growling loud enough to make the guys chuckle.

As soon as the door shut, she rummaged through a box. The arm of a worn, comfy T-shirt hung out of it. She'd gotten the thing as a souvenir when she'd run—somewhat slower than her old boot camp pace—in a charity race for wounded veterans last summer. After retrieving the soft cotton and a pair of yoga pants, she spun on her heel, heading for the open door that could only lead to the bathroom.

She hadn't made it more than two steps into the sanctuary before she gasped at the overwhelming beauty and serenity surrounding her.

Clint and Matt piled in behind her, guns again held at the ready.

"What is it?" Matt swept from side to side while Clint covered him.

"Sorry, no national emergency. It's...beautiful, that's all." She sniffled and blinked back tears. How could things be so messed up and yet so terrific in her life all at once?

It ticked her off that she couldn't savor the moment, or her company.

Spread Your Wings

"Wow." Once the guys determined no threat had followed them into their haven, Clint took a better look at the amenities. An enormous shower with a clear glass front and tinted glass looking out onto the city took up one wall. It had rainfall showerheads on each side and a bevy of chrome sprayers dotting the entire surface. "Looks like you could have one hell of a party in there. I think I'll try it out."

He didn't waste a second before setting his gun on the sink, after double-checking the safety, then whipping his shirt off. His tan skin, embellished with a three-quarter sleeve tattoo on his right arm, had her entranced. The black and red dragon wrapped around him flexed and danced as he moved.

Totally understandable. She was pretty sure she'd writhed like that when she'd surrounded him too. The memory of his cock, sliding into her for the first time, was indelibly marked on her soul. What if it was also the last time?

Did she want it to be?

Or had she had enough of fabulous one-night-stands to last her a lifetime?

If she was honest, she knew the answer without a doubt. She needed another taste of these sexy cops. Preferably sooner rather than later. Unfortunately, her brain wouldn't disengage long enough to permit her to do something so foolish until she ironed out some of the serious wrinkles chafing between them.

"I guess I'm left waiting for the food?" Matt scrunched his nose. "I'm starving and I hate cold eggs. But there's no way I'm touching anything I put in my mouth before I wash this stench-by-association off. Can we hurry it up?"

"I have a timesaver. Let's do this all at once. Simulclean. It's not like we haven't seen each other naked. Oh, wait...I haven't actually gotten a good look at you guys." Jambrea smirked. "I need the tub to keep my bandage dry. But nothing says you two can't take either end of the shower. I'd like that view better than the skyscape over there anyway."

She stared at Matt, daring him to blink first. He did. Then he glanced at Clint from beneath those lush lashes that belied his gruff exterior.

"It's not like we haven't done this a million times at the gym." Clint shrugged. "It doesn't have to be weird. You stay on your side and I'll stay on mine. I'm not going to molest you or anything, asshole."

Matt took a second more to consider before he growled as he stripped his tight-fitting black T-shirt from his immense chest. Imagining those muscles sweaty from a strong workout did nothing at all to cool Jambrea down.

She practically skipped over to the claw-foot tub, then rotated the flashy handles until it began to fill. From a basket hanging on the side, she plucked a glass bottle and cracked it open, taking a sniff. Rosemary and lavender essences delighted her nose.

Anything would smell better than garbage, to be honest.

A dollop into the stream of water seeded a fragrant cloud of mist that hung over the area. She bit her lip and looked up in time to see Clint and Matt divesting themselves of their jeans. Unbuttoned, unzipped and uninhibited, they slid their thumbs in their waistbands and shucked the low-rise denim damn near simultaneously. A couple quick flicks and their socks landed in a little pile on the polished floor.

With their backs to each other, they both turned their heads to the side to focus on her.

"Your turn, wild thing." Matt winked at her.

"Didn't think that one through, did you?" Clint grinned. "I'm up for an encore performance. I didn't finish adoring you before you took off last night. Good thing these shower doors are glass."

Matt grumbled as he followed his partner into the enormous stall. "Don't remind me. And don't go bragging about how *up* you are. It's kind of a regular occurrence."

"No kidding. At least since we met Jambi." Clint didn't bother acknowledging his partner with a glare or even his middle finger, which Jambrea thought kind of a likely response. Instead he kept his gaze locked on her. "I've been hard so much I'm afraid I'm going to get stuck this way. Not that I'm complaining. Better than the other way around. Though it does make my uniform pretty uncomfortable. And I'm getting tired of carrying my hat around like a shield over my crotch. The guys don't need any more material for ragging on me."

"No, you give us plenty of that on your own." Matt flicked on his shower.

Jambrea swallowed hard as she studied his high, tight ass and tree-trunk thighs when he reached over and adjusted some of the fixtures.

"Go ahead, wild thing." Clint smiled at her. "Seriously. You don't want to miss out on warm breakfast. Although I'd bring it to you in here if you want to soak. You've got to be sore."

She choked as she gingerly removed her clothes—both to avoid tugging on her arm and to keep from getting any of the rank slime on her hands. At least any more than she had to. When Clint's concern soaked in, she blushed. "Was it that obvious I haven't been with anyone in a long time?"

Matt cursed and dropped his soap.

"What?" Clint tilted his head. The honest curiosity in his captivating eyes deterred her from devouring the visual banquet before her. Nothing could be more alluring to her than getting them on the same page. Finally.

Jambrea wiggled her lace panties down her hips, noticing how Clint's throat flexed and his Adam's apple bobbed. She dipped a toe in the almost-too-hot water and sighed. Using her good arm, she steadied herself and sank beneath the layer of bubbles forming.

"Jambi, I think Clint was talking about your swan dive into last week's lo mein. Or possibly the damage to your arm." Matt spoke slowly, as if he chose his words carefully. "How long has it been?"

She scrubbed her hands vigorously with the artisanal soap provided then buried her face in them, breathing deep of the fresh scent. "Oh. Shit. Never mind."

"No." Clint surprised her with his determination. Inflexible wasn't how she would normally describe him. But he didn't blink as he hastily scrubbed shampoo into his short hair. Suds tracked down his neck and over his pecs, making her lick her lips, wishing she could have him for breakfast. "Hiding shit hasn't worked for us so far. And this is important. We could have hurt you."

Insulated from them, Jambrea felt like she could stare her fill. The scenery made for a pleasant distraction from the humiliation sure to follow. Tenacious, they'd never leave this alone.

"Jesus, Jambi." Matt scoured his abs as if he was trying to wash away some imaginary sin. "I'm not exactly an average guy. Why wouldn't Lily have warned us?"

"Because she knew I could handle you both?" She settled into the curved porcelain, allowing it to cradle her, imparting some much-needed comfort while keeping her arm resting on the brim. "Because your overprotectiveness seems to be hurting us all instead of helping?"

"Maybe." Clint sighed as he nodded. He rinsed and stepped from the shower without bothering to dry off. Instead, he knelt beside her, taking the soap from her restless fingers. "But you haven't answered us. When was the last time you were intimate with someone?"

Matt's low growl didn't scare her. Not when she was about to reveal just how special their liaison had been to her. How could he be jealous of a single one-night-stand that happened a decade ago?

"Almost ten years," she murmured as she traced the

intricate detailing on the lip of the tub with idle flicks of one nail.

Clint closed his hand around hers gently, drawing it to his lips so he could nibble on her knuckles. "Jambi—"

"Not so wild now, am I?" She allowed herself to look at him. Into his gaze. It seemed senseless to withhold information at this point. "And honestly, that was a one-time thing. If your hymen could regenerate itself, I'd be a born-again virgin by now."

It was bad when he didn't laugh. Wasn't it?

Matt startled her when he knelt beside Clint then rested his hand on her bent knee. He stroked the sensitive skin there with his damp thumb, which glided back and forth lightly. "Who could be crazy enough not to fight for you? For more?"

"It's complicated." She shrugged with her good shoulder. "We were in the military together. He had a...special assignment. I never heard from him again."

It surprised her when tears stung her eyes. Would they think she was stupid to cling to the ghost of a temporary lover for so long? Maybe they'd run when they realized how stalkerish she could become.

They didn't.

"And you were loyal to him, all that time?" Matt winced. "Sometimes you have to know when to give up on people, Jambi. Or maybe you've learned that by now. Is that why you kicked us out after the wedding?"

"Not that you fucking listened," she grumbled, but part of her perked up as she recalled their groggy "good mornings" and their tousled hair.

"We're not quitting when it comes to us. This." Clint took over for her, washing her with a tenderness she hadn't realized him capable of before. He used his hands, not a cloth, lathering them before gliding them over all of her that he could reach.

About the time his fingers caressed her breasts—which betrayed her with hardened nipples—Matt urged her to scoot forward until he could lay her back. He supported her neck in order to wet her hair. He sat her up as Clint rubbed her more than cleanliness alone could dictate.

And then Matt massaged her scalp as he worked shampoo into her short locks. "You're so beautiful."

His reverent touches told her more than his words.

As if Clint could sense her getting overwhelmed with the possibility of something she'd had to write off in order to protect her squishy, emotional center, he cut in, cracking the jokes that made him so easy to be around. "I know I am, thanks."

Matt groaned and knocked his shoulder into Clint, nearly toppling his friend. For a minute it was as if they forgot they were naked and nearly pressed full-length against each other. In that instant, all that mattered was her.

Jambrea couldn't say she disliked their attention.

Except right then a rap sounded from the other room, followed by the bellman calling, "Room service."

From the pitch of his near-shout, she wondered how many times he'd already announced himself.

"I've got it." Matt rocketed to his feet, snagging one of the plush robes off the back of the door along with their dirty clothes, which the hotel would launder. "Hurry, though. You really do need to eat."

"That's probably Matt-talk for, 'Don't ravish her in the bathtub, fucknugget.'" Clint wiggled his eyebrows at her.

"Damn straight. Unless you want a code one-eight-seven on your hands." Matt cinched the belt at his waist the best he could.

"That means murder," Clint said in a stage whisper.

It was impossible to take Matt seriously when the fluffy fabric didn't remotely cover all his important bits. Well, at least

Spread Your Wings

he had nothing to be ashamed of. His bits were intimidating.

Clint and Jambrea cracked up together at the sight of him stomping into the other room, a towel clutched in the gap between the fuzzy lapels. When their gazes intersected, she quieted, but the smile etched on her face refused to flee.

For the first time in forever, she thought there might be hope.

They were teaching her to believe in dreams again.

That was either the most dangerous thing she could do or the bravest.

Maybe both.

Chapter Nine

Clint tried not to drool on the woman cradled in his arms. To have her pliant, snuggling into him—while aware it *was* him—ranked high on the list of things he'd craved for a while. Regaining his camaraderie, and maybe evolving it, with Matt was right up there too.

Could he have both?

Sure as shit, he planned to try.

When he leaned over the bed, setting Jambrea in the center of the mountain of pillows, she squirmed a bit. He easily held her in place with a hand on her uninjured shoulder. Just thinking of the wound on the other had him seething and wishing he could kiss it better at the same time. Who had done this to her?

Matt ambled over with a tray piled high with flat-topped metal plate covers, which hid platters of amazing-smelling grub. He set the bounty beside Jambrea.

Then he glanced over, practically punching Clint in the gut with his hesitation. When had they become so wary of each other? Always bickering, they fought like an old married couple or a pair of the drunk chicks they arrested from time to time on a bad Saturday night shift.

It sucked.

"Let's fucking eat, okay?" He waved at the food and Jambi, both sitting there in front of him like the best presents he'd ever gotten. Sure to satisfy all his hungers.

"Yeah." Matt nodded, though he didn't climb on the mattress just yet.

Their indecision spilled over to the wild thing between them. Again. Damn it. She was too sensitive to their discord. It might have been creepy if it didn't seem so sweet that she was perfectly in step with them. Except she kept misinterpreting the real cause of their friction, applying all their faltering to her involvement when that wasn't the case at all.

"Maybe the two of you really should take the bed. I'll bunk on the couch. I don't mind." She raised a brow at them. "Hand me my omelet and I'll leave you two to enjoy alone."

Matt's mouth opened and closed several times in rapid succession until he resembled Parker when the fish begged for its dinner of tri-colored flakes. If the situation hadn't been so damn serious, Clint might have busted a gut laughing.

"Uh, it isn't like that between us, wild thing." Clint's sour face could have come from sucking on one of the lemons garnishing the iced tea in a fancy crystal decanter. He poured her a glass, then handed it over, stealing quick contact with her fingers, supple from the too-short bath.

"Lily told me you guys made out." Jambrea seemed as if she didn't plan to pull her punches ever again. Certainly she wouldn't let them get away with half-truths. He was cool with that. Direct and no-nonsense, the new her attracted him even more than her shy veil had. All along he'd sensed the fire hiding behind that thin veneer of civility. Finally seeing it unleashed had him hard. Again. And that wasn't helping his case right now.

Christ.

"We didn't French or anything." Clint shook his head. Though part of him wished they had, either that night or sometime in the seemingly endless months between then and now. At least then he'd know if the weird feeling their stupid dare had given him had been some kind of turn on, or simply indigestion.

"You didn't?" She tilted her head to the side a bit. "Why

would Lily lie to me? I trusted her."

With that, he couldn't stay away. He rounded the bed and settled onto the mattress as carefully as he could. When both he and Jambrea propped their shoulders against the headboard, Matt began dishing out plates and silverware. Then he climbed onboard too, rocking them with his bulk, though he sandwiched Jambi as gracefully as possible.

"It was just a kiss. One little peck." Matt stepped in to help. "We pissed Lily off. And to make it up to her, she dared us to do it. It was nothing."

Did he really mean that? Clint held back a groan. Because it had meant something to him. Got him thinking about possibilities he'd never considered before. Had him wondering what it would be like to share a woman with another guy. How they would end up with incidental junk-touching…and maybe more.

It seemed odd to think they could explore so much yet stop short. Would they?

"Is that what you're going with? Really? From my perspective it looks like it had a pretty big impact." Their girl pushed her eggs around her plate with her fork. At first she seemed upset. Then she turned cranky in a flash. And she lashed out, for which he didn't blame her at all. They deserved it. "It made you two fools run away from me. From *us*. From what we'd shared the night Mason and Tyler busted down my door. I may have hardly any experience but I'm not a moron. What happened that night was special. I'm guessing your *nothing* kiss was too."

"Well, yeah." Clint paused shoveling hash browns into his mouth long enough to scrub his knuckles over his eyes. "So I think we freaked a little. At least I did. It's a lot to ask of a guy. You know, to first think he might not have the girl of his dreams to himself like he'd always imagined. And, on top, to learn that maybe he's not entirely straight. Or at least open to the possibility of some variety. Right?"

Matt swallowed hard. Probably not only because orange juice gave him heartburn either. As much as he enjoyed the treat, the dumbass would pay for that later. Clint made a mental note to pick up some antacids from the gift shop in the lobby.

Neither he nor Jambi let his partner off the hook, though. They waited patiently until he agreed, "Right. And it didn't feel like we should tangle you up in our mess when we couldn't seem to get our shit together."

"Exactly." Clint slid a piece of his cinnamon toast onto Jambi's plate when he noticed how quickly she devoured her own sweet side dish. Anything he could do to care for her, to show her how he felt, he would. From now on. The last twenty-four hours had reminded him how important it was to make the most of each moment. They'd wasted too much time on misunderstandings and misery.

"So what are you going to do about that?" Jambrea pouted a little. "If you haven't made any progress, then nothing's changed. I want you to know I support your self-discovery. I think it's great if you're happy with each other. I'm just..."

Moisture gathered at the corner of her pretty eyes. Clint would rather Matt have kicked him in the ribs than see the evidence of her pain. Which they'd caused.

"What, wild thing?" Matt wiped away a tear with the pad of his thumb.

"I'm not sure I can survive being the lubrication that makes it easier for you two to be together, only to be ditched afterward, when you're strong enough to admit it's really each other you want." She blinked a few times, getting herself together, proving again exactly how tough she was. "I care for you both. And, clearly, I'm not the kind of woman who can walk away once my feelings get involved."

"Are you trying to tell me they're not already?" Clint prided himself on his maturity when he didn't even crack a smile at Jambi's lube reference. Maybe because he thought he might weep too if she said she didn't feel the same way he did—jumbled up inside and sick at the idea that they might never figure this shit out. It'd been hard enough to deal with the fact that Matt didn't seem like he planned to make their one-time indiscretion a habit.

For a long time, Jambrea didn't answer. Instead, she let Matt fork up a strawberry from his pancakes and slip it between her lips. Clint had never been so jealous of a utensil in his life as he was when she licked the last bit of whipped cream from its tines.

"Jambi, I think you *can't* say you're unaffected." Matt paused his breakfast long enough to finger-comb some of the tangles from her hair. To see his big hands work so skillfully, with a delicate touch, impressed Clint and inspired wicked thoughts. "For the record, I can't either."

"If none of us gave a shit, the last six months wouldn't have sucked so bad, right?" Clint hoped his rationale panned out. He'd spent a lot of nights repeating this mantra to himself. "We'd have given up and gone our separate ways by now if we felt nothing. Who needs all this bull if you're not invested, right? Hell, Matt could have handed in the request for a new partner that's been sitting in his desk drawer for at least the last six weeks."

His insides twisted and he pushed his plate away.

"Oh, fuck. You saw that?" Matt's face drained of its usual tan, leaving him pale. Like he'd looked the last couple times he'd had a massive hangover, which had happened more in the past few months than it had in the five years before that.

Jambrea wiped her mouth with her napkin, temporarily distracting Clint from the hot coals eviscerating him. She set the cloth down then reached out, taking one of their hands in each of hers. "That's crazy talk. You two are a perfect match on

Spread Your Wings

the force. You'd never be as good with other cops as you are together. I love watching you team up—like at the annual barbecue. How many years in a row have you won the partner games trophy? It's seamless."

"Mason and Tyler broke our streak, one of those years in the middle, but...yeah." Matt spoke directly to Clint. "I couldn't do it. Even though I thought it was best for you. I'm a selfish prick. I'm sorry. I couldn't let go."

"I would never give up on you." Clint hated the rasp in his voice. The horror that had sat like slime in his guts since he'd spied the paper while hunting for a pack of gum bubbled to the surface. "I'd never even think about it. You're stuck with me, asshole."

"Same goes." The big guy reached across Jambrea to chuck him on the shoulder. "No matter what happens here today, or in the long run with wild thing, you're my partner. If that means I have to back away from this, I will. You deserve her."

Jambi seemed like she might protest, but Clint didn't plan to let it come to that.

"I'd do the same. Give her up for you. I know you'd take good care of her." He squeezed Jambrea's fingers, which trembled in his. "But I'm starting to think neither one of us is going to have to make that sacrifice after all."

"Would you give us another chance, Jambs?" Matt's chest didn't so much as move. He must have held his breath as he waited for an answer from the wild thing they'd nearly scared away with their stupidity. Maybe he simply hadn't been able to believe he could get that lucky. "Please?"

When was the last time Matt Ludwig had begged for anything?

Clint sat forward, as strung out as his partner, waiting for the answer that could change their lives forever. In reality, she'd already done that. In an amazing way. Would her renowned bedside manner extend to them, even after all they'd fucked up?

He crossed the fingers of his free hand behind his back.

Jambrea nodded then whispered, "Yes, of course. But try not to screw it up this time, huh?"

Clint practically dove for the tray. He shoved it off the mattress, onto the ground, only vaguely aware of it landing right-side up. Their cleared-off dishes clattered before the racket was muffled by the plush carpet. There'd be plenty of time to worry about cleaning up the mess later. After he finished devouring the sweet treats in front of him.

Freedom—to display his lust for Jambrea, and his curiosity about Matt—rioted inside him, transforming him into a beast he didn't know existed. He scooped his arms beneath their wild thing and lifted her enough for Matt to peel her robe off. If his partner's hum was any indication, they could get used to her wearing such easy access garments around the house.

Clint knew it'd be a hell of a long time before he forgot this unveiling.

A willing exposure. So different from the sneak attack of the night before. While he'd thoroughly enjoyed every ounce of pleasure they'd infused her with, something about being certain she accepted him—them—made every glancing touch of his skin on hers that much more potent.

Jambrea shivered when he trailed his fingers along the pale column of her neck to toy with her collarbones. He glanced sideways at Matt, who smiled softly as he witnessed the interaction.

"It's weird to see how you are with her. In a good way, I mean." Matt cleared his throat. "It's like I know you so well, but never really thought about how you get it on. It's fascinating to see this side of you. Familiar. Not."

"I noticed you staring last night." Clint tried not to betray how much Matt's intense watching had contributed to his massive hard-on and the ride he'd given Jambrea, and himself by default. He couldn't wait to do it again.

Jambrea let her head drop onto the pillows and kicked her feet in a mini tantrum that set all the best parts of her to jiggling. "That's so unfair."

"Don't worry." A chuckle escaped him before he settled low enough to buss her forehead. "We'll give you plenty to look at. If you can keep your pretty eyes open, that is."

For once she didn't object. Instead she reached up and cupped his cheeks in her soft hands, making him wish he'd taken the time to shave. His five o'clock shadow could get kind of scruffy if he wasn't careful. It'd been a while since he had to worry about a woman's delicate skin.

Or maybe it'd be best if she allowed him to mark her. Stake a claim. After this, there would be no turning back. If they proved to each other that this triangular bond was possible, he had a feeling their joining would become permanent. Quickly. At least he knew he would fight to the bitter end to reach that goal.

If he and Matt could figure something out between them...even better.

But he'd take what he could get.

Jambrea tilted his face down so she could stare into his eyes. The focus in her gaze had him stalling for a moment. He could look at her like this forever and die happy. "Would you please kiss me already? For real. Like that night... I've missed you."

Matt groaned and dropped his hand to her shoulder. He massaged her beside Clint's torso, not caring that his knuckles skimmed Clint's ribs on the backstroke. Or, hell, maybe he did it intentionally. "Same goes, wild thing. I've DVR'd half a season of that murder mystery show you like just so we can cuddle at the scary parts again. More than anything, I miss the friend I found in you."

Matt stretched out on his side and propped his head in his hand for a front row seat to the show Jambrea put on with

Clint. "You know, I think Rob would be pleased that so many beautiful things have come from his case. I'm not saying I'm glad it happened, that we lost him, but if we had to, at least he's looking out for us, wherever he is now."

Clint groaned as he thought of their fallen man in blue. Lacey's brother had been murdered not so long ago. In finding his killer, Lacey's, Mason's and Tyler's relationship had morphed from friendship into...this. The more the guys hung out with Jambrea's co-worker, Lacey, the more excuses they'd had to get to know their wild thing better. He kissed Jambrea deeply, hoping she wouldn't mind if he used the bliss they generated together to salve his still-bruised heart.

"Tragedy might have kick-started this chain reaction, but we're doing our best to make up for it. To carry on like he would have wanted us to. He'd be happy to see this, I think." Matt squeezed Clint's shoulder, giving him courage to sample Jambrea's sad smile.

"Of course, then I'd have had to kick his ass for checking out our girl when she's naked." Matt shook the bed with his laughter. The sound turned Clint on even more. It'd been so long since he'd heard it.

Jambi arched beneath him and spread her legs, giving him room to settle between the long, strong limbs. He admired her statuesque form and the confidence she gave him to unleash all of his passion. For Matt, those concerns and her mitigation of them would be twice as important. He was huge, but Jambrea had accepted him with minor difficulty last night.

Even though she hadn't slept with a man in fucking forever.

Clint was both humbled and sobered by that thought. He separated them just enough to nuzzle their noses and take another peek at the bemused look in her eyes. "You'll tell me if we're going too fast for you, right?"

"If you go any slower, I'll die of old age before I get my fill."

She entwined her fingers in his hair and tugged, mashing his mouth onto hers. Ravenous, she devoured him. All he could do was keep up. He stroked her everywhere he could reach, his hands equal parts greedy and restless. And when he collided with Matt's roving fingers he realized his partner did the same.

The electric jolt caused by their incidental contact had him grinding his hips against the softness between Jambrea's thighs. In response, she arched up, pressing them more tightly together. Since he hadn't bothered with anything other than a towel wrapped around his waist for coverage, there wasn't much left to the imagination.

Especially when the knot at his hip began to unwind.

"You want that off?" Matt paused with his fingers hovering over the terrycloth.

"As long as Jambi's okay with it." He nodded.

"Stop treating me like I'm delicate. Almost innocent doesn't count for shit." She flexed her fingers on his shoulders, impressing his muscles with the sharp crescents of her nails. The small prick of pain turned him on more.

"Fine. Take it away." He stiffened his spine and threw restraint to the wind.

Matt tugged on the towel. It slithered between him and Jambrea, rubbing his cock with softness along the way. That sure as hell didn't help his self-control any.

When it was gone, his first impression was of warmth. Jambrea's skin and his pressed together, encouraging him to redouble his seduction. This time he concentrated on licking and sucking a path along her jaw, then below her ear and onward down her neck.

With her mouth free, small pants escaped her parted lips. They kept time with the rhythm he set for them with the press of his hips, which dragged his cock along the furrow of her pussy. Soaked, she allowed him to glide through the succulent flesh and teased him with a hint of what it would be like to find his way home again. Buried inside her, he'd felt...perfect.

And he couldn't wait to do it again.

He might have adjusted the angle of his hips, introducing the head of his cock to her opening if Matt hadn't taken the opportunity to tip Jambrea's face toward him and pick up where Clint had left off. His partner bestowed one hell of a kiss while Clint stole glimpses from his post.

In the meantime, he encouraged Jambrea's surrender to their combined advances by shifting lower to lave her right breast while his hands plumped the other. Once her nipple stood tight and tall, he switched to the opposite side and repeated his treatment.

"Mmm." She couldn't do more than moan with Matt's firm mouth caressing hers. If Clint wasn't mistaken, the man had insinuated his tongue between her lips and teased her from the inside.

When Clint allowed his hand to wander down her side, something hot, hard and heavy nudged his forearm. Matt's monster cock. He lifted his head long enough to tease his friend, "Keep that thing to yourself, would you?"

When his partner glanced at the damp spot he'd left glistening in Clint's arm hair, he seemed to shudder, though not necessarily in repulsion. "I don't think so. If you were a good friend, you'd jerk me a little while you're messing around down there."

Jambrea quaked in Clint's hold. Had she orgasmed from the thought alone? Or maybe a shockwave of pleasure, a precursor to the real deal, had zapped her nervous system. Either way, that was all the encouragement he needed.

While the two lovers in his bed toyed with each other, he tested out the heft of another man's cock for the first time. Strange yet familiar, the weight and soft-covered hardness impressed him. He'd never make quite the handful his partner did, even with Jambrea there to beef him up. After measuring the length a few times with his shaking fingers, he felt confident his shaft was a bit longer, which helped salve his pride.

A squeeze around the fat shaft had Matt groaning into Jambi's mouth.

Clint's penchant for pranks and practical jokes had him pumping away in no time. While he set a steady pace with his left hand, he continued his trek down Jambrea's torso. The softly rounded curve of her stomach made a comfy pillow when he issued himself a time out to circle her belly button with his tongue. She was his ideal woman. Lush, curvy and genuine.

Nothing artificial ruined the flavor of her on his palate.

"Hey," Matt grumbled after a minute. "Quit that. I'm not freaking made of stone, you know. I'll come all over her if you keep that up."

Jambrea whimpered as if she might not mind.

"You feel hard enough to me." Clint relinquished his hold with one final swirl of his finger through the divot at the peak of the head. The puddle of precome there ensured he'd done a decent job for his first time out of the gate.

He heaved a sigh of relief when things didn't seem any weirder than they had been lately between him and Matt. Actually, they both relaxed a bit. Maybe he should have accosted the dude one night while they played videogames and offered to give him a BJ. He'd have been willing to go down on Matt to shatter the barriers the other man had flung in their path after that one not-worth-the-trouble kiss.

Now this, *this* could be worth something.

As if they hadn't crossed some major lines, they returned their attention to the woman between them. Because today, maybe always, she was most important.

After years of waiting, she deserved to have the time of her life. He wanted to be the man—well, one of them—to give it to her.

No secrets, no remorse, no limits.

"Go ahead," Matt ordered. "If you don't taste her soon, I'm going to steal your treat. Lucky bastard."

"There's plenty to go around." She clammed up, as if she couldn't believe she'd said that out loud. Even in the company of her closest friends, she'd always talked the least. Clint guessed she'd gotten in the habit of screening her thoughts, filtering the crazy things she wanted to blurt. His goal was to make her lose those inhibitions. With him and Matt, she was safe to be herself. He hoped she'd see that they didn't mind at all. In fact, they adored her.

"That's the spirit." Clint trailed his fingers down her arm to her wrist. He knew which one held her *no regrets* tattoo without looking. When he rubbed it, she hummed. Maybe she'd start to see they really had been paying more attention to her than she'd realized.

Lacey, Izzy, Lily...hell, any number of the rest of their friends had assured him and Matt that she didn't believe, during all those tense times, that he and his partner had been fighting over her.

And here they were, willing to share and be shared. Finally all riding the same wave.

Damn, they'd each come a long way.

This hadn't been possible a few months ago. Today, they were trying their best to make her believe it could be real. Sustainable. A healthy, lasting relationship.

Because a few smoking romps through the sheets weren't going to satisfy him.

He prayed she knew that.

"Clint." His partner snapped him from the initial phases of the worry cycle that'd had them spinning around until dizzy lately.

"I'm on it." He slithered lower on the silky sheets, which

were no match for the smoothness of Jambrea's skin. He breathed deep of her musk, more potent as he neared her core. The scent of her imprinted on him. Forgetting the sweet tang would be impossible.

Inhaling, he nuzzled her mound.

She yelped and flinched at the barest contact.

Matt soothed her from above, leaving Clint to concentrate on the task at hand. The reassuring tone of his partner's calming litany settled him as well. Despite his size, the big guy was the one who always talked people out of fights, convinced them to drop weapons or to step away from the ledge. This time, he simultaneously relaxed Jambrea while leaving her ready to get all riled up.

Clint extended his tongue, using the tip to initiate the slightest pressure on her lips and the top of her slit where her clit barely peeked from between the folds of engorged flesh. Super sensitive, she lurched above him. Fortunately, Matt squelched any chance of her wriggling away with one massive arm across her abdomen and the press of his leg over hers.

The furry length of his muscled thigh brushed Clint's side. Instead of gritting his teeth and bearing the connection, it reassured Clint. They were in this together. The heat and strength of his best friend bolstered his confidence and his drive to please the woman they held between them.

This time when he encountered her juicy pussy, he didn't stop at introductory touches. Instead he sealed his mouth over her and began to suckle, cleaning the spilled arousal from her lips and ringing her entrance with his tongue. He lapped her slit from the bottom of her opening to her clit.

And when she whimpered, he raised his head for a moment.

Long enough to spy Matt expertly manipulating her breasts while he devoured her desperate cries of awakening excitement. Their passion fueled Clint's. He curled his hands beneath her legs and splayed them on the lower swell of her belly. The tops of his fingers met with Matt's arm. They both adjusted subtly, making the most of the luscious area of her body while stimulating as much of her as they could.

Hopefully that included her mind and soul.

Matt would probably bust a gut if he could hear Clint's lofty thoughts. The guy was much more primal—raw and instinctual—than philosophical. Their balance served them well. In this too, he imagined.

When he prodded the tight ring of muscles at Jambrea's entrance, she sucked at his index finger with rapid clenches that pulled him a bit deeper inside her. Combining the swirl of his tongue on her clit with the probing of first that one digit then another and, finally, three had her mewling.

The ripples of her channel made his cock jealous of his hand. He explored, testing a few different motions and places within her to see how they made her react. When he pressed against the forward wall of her pussy, just above her pubic bone, she gasped.

Matt had his back, even if her delight hadn't been obvious. "Right there. Do that some more. She'll come all over your face."

As if the dirty talk turned Jambi on as much as it did Clint, she practically vibrated in his arms. Her fingers locked in his hair and dragged him into position. Her free leg snaked around his even as she spread wider, opening herself to him completely.

Triumph made her sweeter to his taste buds.

Clint repeated the spiral of his middle finger over her most sensitive zone. He suckled on her clit, flicking the hood with the tip of his tongue. Within seconds, he was rewarded with the complete tensing of her body, followed rapidly by a gush of moisture, which he eagerly consumed.

It was the tap of Matt's hand on his shoulder that alerted him to her slide into the afterglow phase of her climax. He helped her milk the last of the rapture from her orgasm with slow, gentle strokes, then withdrew completely, placing one last kiss on her flushed pussy.

When he settled beside her, opposite from Matt, she turned her head to face him.

"Thank you," she whispered. "That was fantastic."

"Anytime." Clint swiped his hand over his glistening lips and chin before leaning in to kiss her. She didn't seem to mind the lingering taste of herself on him.

"Well, not anytime. Next time is my turn." Matt surprised them both, maybe even himself, when he lifted Clint's wrist and licked the glossy length of his finger. "Fuck. She's delicious."

"Uh huh." Saying more would have been impossible as he stared at Matt, who savored the delicacy he'd ingested.

Clint's cock pulsed where it nestled against Jambrea's side, most likely leaving a trail of precome in its wake. He had to have her soon or he'd embarrass himself in front of both his best friend and the woman they hoped to impress.

"Matt," he called out, urgent.

"Yeah, you'd better go first anyway." The guy smiled wryly. "I'm even more skeptical about you taking me, wild thing, now that I know about your history. Please tell me I didn't hurt you last night."

Clint's need went on hold as he observed the authentic concern in his partner's gaze. "I was there. She loved every minute."

"True story. I did." Jambrea blinked. Her pupils were huge, though her eyes were clear and focused. "And I can't wait to do it again. But yeah, Clint made a very nice appetizer."

"Hey." He wasn't sure he liked being the opening act, well, except for the whole about to blow factor.

"But guys..." Matt glanced away before meeting their stares. "She didn't take all of my cock last night. I held her up. I know I'm a lot to ask of my partners. Hell, I've been dumped twice because I was too much of a chore. 'Unpleasant', I think was the word."

"Do you mean that bitch, Tiffany? 'Cause she did you a monumental favor." Clint shook his head. "I never understood what you liked about her. She treated you like shit."

"I can't wait to have all of you." Jambrea came to the rescue as usual. Her kindness outstripped everything else. No way would she ever belittle them, whether they were hung or pencil-dicked. "I'm sorry I couldn't do it right away."

"Jesus." Matt zoomed in for a kiss. "Are you apologizing for yesterday? Because I swear to God it was the best sex of my life. It wouldn't even have mattered if I didn't get to be inside you at all. Just sharing the moment, bringing you pleasure, that would have been enough."

"Well, this is about more than getting by." Their wild thing flashed a wicked smile. "This is about everything. All you've hoped for. It might not be today, but I will accommodate you. Even if it takes some practicing."

The ease with which she put Matt's doubts to rest, when Clint had been unable to do the very same thing for months on end now, turned him on beyond belief. He wanted to hug her with the force of an anaconda. Except that he'd never harm her. At least not on purpose.

Regret had no place in their bed.

So he dedicated himself to making it up to her instead.

"Jambi, you know we're safe from Lily's files. And we read that you're on birth control. Unless you have some condoms in those boxes of yours…"

"Who would I have used them with?" She rolled her eyes. "I'm a nurse. I'm clean and I know how strenuous Lily's screening is. I made sure of it when I went to her with my request. Go ahead, Clint. I want to feel you in me bare."

"Oh fuck." Matt dropped his forehead to her good shoulder.

"I'm hoping you will. Some time before I die." She stuck her tongue out when Clint growled at her. Then she surprised him by rolling onto her side. A wince reminded him of her injured arm, but she situated herself until it was apparently comfortable. "One request..."

"Anything," both he and Matt answered in unison.

"Let Matt hold me while you make love to me?" Her almond eyes begged him. There was no way to say no, not that he wanted to.

"Of course." Clint reached for his partner's arm and drew it over the woman pinned between them. He guided Matt to Jambrea's thigh. The guy caught on quick and curled his fingers around her leg, lifting until she was open and ready for Clint to fit himself to her.

He didn't waste any time in doing exactly that.

Slippery and hot, her pussy felt like heaven on his aching cock. He tried to go slow, but found himself on the cusp of penetrating her in the span of a few heartbeats.

"Yes," she hissed as she craned her neck forward enough to nip his bottom lip. "Do it."

For some reason, he felt the need to check with Matt first. His partner was staring at him when he glanced over. "Give her what she wants."

And Clint didn't need more encouragement than that.

She took him inside for the first time, knowingly, as if they'd been made for each other. His cock tunneled deeper with every rock of his hips. Not to mention the answering flex and release of her pelvis. A natural oscillation brought them together tighter and tighter with every pass. Soon she did have his entire length.

He'd never been so happy in all of his life. Content yet exhilarated. Steeped in ecstasy still certain there were better things ahead. Reaching for impossible heights, he tried to share the experience with his partner.

"She's tight, and hot, and wet. So wet." He filled Matt in. "I have to fuck. It feels too good. Killing me."

"Me too." Their wild thing thrashed. Her head rocked on the pillow even as Matt held her still. "And I can feel him so hard on my ass. I want you both. Together."

"Someday." Matt's placating didn't do much good.

"No, now," she insisted.

"There's no way." Matt shut her down, for her own safety. "Trust me, I'll give you anything I can, but that's just not possible. Especially not with me in your ass. I'll hurt you. Tear you. You're not ready."

The disappointment on her face cut both men sheltering her.

An idea came to Clint. "What if you take him in your mouth? Then you'll have us both at the same time. We'll all be connected."

Because suddenly the idea held a hell of a lot of appeal to him too. Linked in desire and passion, they'd left the nest of possibilities and ventured into reality.

They would spread their wings and learn to fly as one.

"Gimme."

It might have been wrong of him, but some primeval part stood up and roared when he realized they'd broken her down to her essence. Here and now, all that mattered were their base requirements. And it meant the world to him that all their desires were complementary. No one had to hold back. No one had to sacrifice to fulfill the wishes of the others.

They all needed the same thing.

Clint blanketed Jambrea as he began to propel into her with even strokes that picked up steam and travel as he found his groove. Less than a foot away, Matt's thick body came to

Spread Your Wings

rest as he knelt over Jambrea's head.

She reached up and tugged him to her, opening her mouth to suck on as much of his thick cock as she could shove in her mouth. Though it wasn't a whole lot, really, it was enough. The feral gleam in Matt's eyes as his gaze met Clint's was enough to sear him.

He trusted Jambrea to shut him down if he pushed her too hard, though he was sure the wild thing loved each pummel of his hips into hers. Hell, he could tell by the ever-increasing clamp of her pussy over his cock that she loved every minute.

And as she pleased Matt, her responses grew bolder. Her vocalizations louder and less intelligible, except by the barbaric part of his brain, which knew exactly what she craved. He rode her hard, fast and furious, giving her everything he had and then some.

The shockwaves instigated by their connections had her taking more of Matt's cock each time Clint buried himself completely. And before long, she hovered on the edge of another climax.

"Fuck. Yes." He gritted his teeth and kept up his pace despite the compression of her pussy on him, which made it more and more difficult to penetrate her channel. "Go ahead. Let go. Fly, Jambrea. We're with you."

"Yes! Now!" Matt shouted into the charged air between them.

It was hard to say who caved first, but Clint was pretty sure it was him. He flooded their wild thing with all of his pent up desire and lust. All the while, he smothered her with kisses—on her cheek, beside Matt's cock or anywhere else he could land one—and praise, hoping she could comprehend even a sliver of his admiration.

She shattered around him even as Matt's cock twitched repeatedly. A trickle of pearly fluid escaped Jambrea's parted lips and ran along her chin as the huge guy pumped the contents of his proportional balls into her eager, waiting mouth.

Clint couldn't say what urged him to do it, but he reached up and swiped the excess from Jambrea and sampled the proof of his best friend's passion before he could think better of it.

Gasping, they fell apart, yet rearranged themselves to fit back together as soon as they were able to move. They settled into a tangle of limbs on the heavenly bed in the lush room. Jambrea didn't resist when Clint lowered his head and brushed a kiss over her lips. Matt followed suit as soon as his partner vacated the prime real estate around her mouth.

The guys met each other's stares over her relaxed body even as the mingled taste of Jambi and Matt activated Clint's taste buds. Relief infiltrated every cell of his body when he didn't sense any of their recent awkwardness lingering in the aftermath of their epic release. The man looking back at him was his best friend. The one person he regularly trusted with his life. This time was no different.

Clint nodded. They could make this work.

One step closer to his goal, he did an internal victory dance.

Chapter Ten

"Guys," Jambrea practically purred.

"Yeah, wild thing." Matt huffed as though he'd chased a burglar a dozen blocks, hopping fences along the way, even though they'd probably been lying in silence for a solid ten minutes.

"You know how when you don't eat for a while you get really hungry and even a full meal leaves you wanting dessert?" She licked her lips.

"Are you serious?" Clint picked his head up to stare at her, one brow raised.

"Well, yeah." She couldn't believe she still had the capacity to blush in front of them. "I've been starving for ten years."

"Yo, Matt, can you get it up again yet?" A warm hand snuck across her belly from Clint's side of the bed to Matt's. She grinned when he fished around between his partner's legs to test the firmness of his cock. "You're halfway there. Come on. Give me a minute and I'll be right behind you."

"If not, I can take care of myself. I'm kind of an expert at this point. And well, my toy collection *is* in one of those boxes right over there." She cleared her throat. As a nurse, there weren't many bodily functions that put her off anymore. A fact of nature, lust could be sated in any number of ways.

"Not gonna happen." Matt's vehemence surprised her. He usually was super laidback. Unless someone threatened his fellow cops. Or her, she supposed. "You're not going to depend on some battery operated boyfriend when you've got us around. We'll take care of you. Satisfy you. Always."

"Shut up, dumbass. Let the lady give us a show. We can help her along the way. Add our own special touches. But don't stop her." Clint shoved to his elbows. "Tell me what I'm looking for and I'll be right back. I'd love to play with you and your *toys.*"

Matt shifted. "Damn, you're right. Actually, I might be up for round two after all."

"No, no. Too late. So sorry. I want to see this more than your nerdy ass wanted to see the last Lord of the Rings movie. I stood in line forever for that midnight show with hobbits and orcs and who knows what else circling around us. I even wore that damn costume you promised would be cool. You owe me." Clint shushed his partner. "After we watch her come a few more times, I bet we'll both have our second wind."

"No kidding." Matt traced Jambrea's spreading smile with his fingers as she imagined them dressed as knights of Gondor. She'd seen the pictures. They'd looked sexy in plastic armor. And noble. Nothing different there, really. She thought the same thing when she spotted them in their more contemporary uniforms. Matt drew her back to the present. "Peeping on you touching yourself will be like a fantasy I've had a lot of nights. Imagining you while I rubbed myself. You're not the only one flying solo lately, wild thing. No one could live up to you. I don't think I've even checked out another woman since you took care of Razor after he got shot. Never been jealous of a victim before."

She wished she could say all she felt. Emotion clogged her throat.

So Clint saved her from her temporary muteness.

"That's sweet." He tapped his bare foot. "Now where's your stash, Jambi?"

She chewed her lip until Matt flicked the pad of his thumb over the resulting sore spot with butterfly brushes. "Um, there's a black velvet bag in there. It has my favorite vibrator in it. It's in the box labeled *Stuff.*"

"Very clever." Clint chuckled as he rolled from bed with the grace of a ballroom dancer. "No one would ever suspect your naughty *stuff* was in there."

He located the box in less than thirty seconds, then began playing moving Tetris to unearth his prize. No more than a minute had passed before he flipped the lid off and rummaged inside. Oops. She winced as she remembered what else she'd packed in there.

"Don't mind the porn collection." She swallowed a laugh at Matt's wide-eyed stare. "What? Girls like dirty movies too. If they're good ones. Hell, Lacey sends me links to the raunchiest *stuff* all the time. She's like the queen of awesome porn. Only a few of them were keepers, though. We give each other our favorites on DVD for our birthdays every year. This year Izzy and Lily played too."

Rambling or not, she couldn't help defending herself. Not that she needed to.

"You're shattering all my illusions." The wide grin on Clint's face proved he didn't mind. "Here I thought you were such a good girl."

"I was celibate, not a saint." She smiled as she snuggled into Matt's broad chest. With him, she felt like nothing could hurt her. All their troubles seemed like a horrible nightmare that faded with each minute of sunshine they shared.

The attraction between them had never burned so bright before. They'd tarnished it with their doubts and insecurities. She refused to do that ever again. From now on, they'd see the real her. All of her.

Vast vibrator collection, bisexual BDSM porn library, unnatural attachment to her pet fish and all.

"What're you so happy about, huh?" Matt tickled her as he took in the pure bliss that had to have been written all over her face.

"I can't believe this is finally real. That you're here, with me, and not planning on running away anytime soon." She touched his cheek, tracing the slight scar he had above the peak of his eyebrow. He'd gotten the ding from a wayward piece of shrapnel during a raid of The Scientist's original laboratory, on the day they attempted to prevent the dissemination of the Sex Offender formula.

Izzy had told her how he'd jumped in front of her and Razor, protecting the duo when the shit really hit the fan and a firefight broke out. He'd used his bulk as a human shield. "Sorry this left a mark."

"You stitched it as best you could." He kissed her fingers. "We'd waited forever, finishing the manhunt before Clint dragged my ass to the ER. Don't chicks dig scars anyway?"

She rolled her eyes. "I prefer you in one piece, thanks."

"Speaking of...how's your arm?" He peered at the bandage as if he could see through the gauze and tape.

"It's fine."

"No fibbing or we won't play with you." Clint shook her purple metallic vibrator at her as he returned to bed. "This is the new us, remember? We won't sideline you if we know you're being honest about your condition. Otherwise, I'll wrap you up in all the bubble wrap you had this thing surrounded in. Afraid it might break? Taking no chances, huh?"

"Ugh." He had her there. On the serious points anyway. Fine, she could admit it. "It's sore and aching a little, but it's nothing the endorphins of a good orgasm or three more won't mask."

"Okay." Matt kissed her lightly, with a tenderness that shot straight to her heart. "But you'll let us know if it gets to be too much, right?"

"I promise."

"Good." Clint's voice sounded deeper when he said, "I might

have threatened to spank you for misbehaving, except your movies would seem to indicate that would be an ineffective punishment."

"Kind of." She laughed. "Not that I would know firsthand. Still, the idea has always appealed. And after watching Lily in the club. Well, yeah... You're probably right."

"We'll find out soon enough." Matt guaranteed her fantasy would come to life eventually.

"And it seems you have a thing for guy-on-guy action." This time he looked to Matt, not her, when he fanned out several of her most pussy-tingling titles. She'd never realized quite how many of them featured bisexual couples. To her, pleasure was pleasure—no matter who delivered it to their mate. "Guess I shouldn't have worried you'd be grossed out or some shit."

Yet clearly they had thought she could be so closed-minded. The hope and relief spreading across Matt's face as he sat up for a better look made it obvious to her. She patted his back.

"Wow. We were really dumb." He drew her into his lap, tightening his arms around her midriff. "I was so afraid of losing you. Of scaring you off or hoping for more than you could handle. From now on I'll ask you first before I flip out."

"Probably not a bad plan." She reached behind her to ruffle his hair. "Maybe we should all do a little less thinking and trust our instincts a ton more."

"All right." Clint hopped onto the bed and shuffled closer on his knees. "Then what are your primeval urges telling you, cave dude?"

"That we shouldn't make her responsible for getting herself off when we're more than capable, stiffies or not." He rumbled the bold statement near her ear.

"I totally agree." Clint winked at her. "Unless you object, wild thing?"

"Uh, no. Go right ahead." She squirmed a little, getting comfortable in the seat Matt made for her. His rejuvenating erection settled in the small of her back. How the hell would she ever be able to take all of his girth? He put her vibrator to shame, even half-hard.

"Don't mind if I do." Worming his way between Matt's legs, plus hers, Clint settled with his head on her thigh.

Matt searched behind them with one hand, snagging a few pillows to stack. He leaned back on the fluffy wedge, inclining her torso and leaving her even more open to the probing of his partner. His hands wandered from her upper thighs to her abdomen, then higher as far as her breasts. He cupped them, weighing them in his palms.

"You two fit together," Clint murmured as he dragged the blunt tip of her vibrator up and down her pussy. He used the moisture seeping from her, his own release mingled with hers, to slick the hard plastic.

As if to test the seam between her and Matt, Clint then trailed the instrument down her ass to where she sat on his partner. He prodded the place where they came together, finding no gaps. If Matt's sharp inhalation was any indication, she'd guess Clint had accidentally—or maybe deliberately—nudged his balls or the base of his cock with her toy.

Now she loved it even more.

She whimpered, unashamed by her overwhelming desire for them.

Matt rewarded her, rolling her nipples between his fingertips. At first, the pressure he applied was too light. He increased his hold little by little until she cried out. Finding the sweet spot that maximized her enjoyment, he pulsed tiny pinches of ideal tension on the tips of her breasts.

"You're making her wetter." Clint gave a status report from between her legs. "Do that some more. And kiss her. Did you see how much it turned her on before?"

Matt hesitated and his body went stiff beneath her, not necessarily in a good way either.

"She's not like Tiffany, Matt." Clint spoke softly now, enough to ensnare her attention despite the burgeoning passion he stoked with swirls and dots of the tool over her lips. *What a tease!*

"W-wait." She tried to concentrate on what they were saying. "Who is that? Why do I hate her already?"

Clint laughed. "Because you're smart. She was a girl Matt dated for a while. I swear that bitch only used him for his fat cock. Never wanted to hang out with the rest of the guys and their dates, never gave a shit about anything going on his life, never cared for him to kiss her or show any affection when they were fucking."

"It wasn't as bad as all that." The defensiveness in Matt's tone made Jambrea believe it had been. Probably worse than he let on.

"The hell it wasn't." Fire burned in Clint's gaze on his partner's behalf. It stirred something in Jambrea. "She used you. For sex. For your body. If a guy did that, he'd be a major prick. It's no different for a chick. I feel sorry for that rich bastard she conned into marrying her."

While she couldn't hug Matt from this position, Jambrea found his hands and squeezed. He returned her gesture.

"And if there was any doubt, the fact that she tried to bribe you into boning her even after she was hitched—with fancy watches or season baseball tickets or even a car—sure as shit should have clued you in." Clint slapped Matt's thigh. "Don't let the past fuck this up for us both. Kiss her. Like you mean it. Like you want to. Now."

Jambrea didn't even have time to take a breath before Matt cupped her jaw in his hand and rotated her head less gently than she expected from him. He drew her face to the side then swooped in over her shoulder to fuse their mouths.

The blended flavor of him and fresh fruit encouraged her to sip from his lips time after time. Their mouths glided back and forth, and when he pressed his tongue against her, she parted, welcoming him.

Lost in their interaction, she went limp, allowing him to simultaneously cradle her and present her to his partner. Her teeth scraped along the firmed muscle of his tongue when Clint reapplied the cool plastic vibrator to her pussy.

This time he didn't stop with doodling on her sensitive flesh with the tip. No, he pressed the shaft to her opening then inserted an inch or two. Her instructions came out completely garbled when she didn't bother to stop playing tonsil hockey with Matt long enough to articulate her preferences.

"What?" He paused despite her pelvis lifting to keep the device inside.

Matt backed away enough for her to try again. Jambrea said, "I like it deep, and toward the back."

"Oh, a challenge. I love those." Clint pressed a kiss to her clit, making her coo. "You go back to what you were doing. Leave me to this. I'll keep exploring until I get where you want me. Let me know when I find the best spot."

She didn't think she'd mind being his test subject.

Even getting it wrong with these two felt better than anything else she'd experienced.

A soft touch on her cheek brought her attention back to Matt. "Was that enough?"

"Are you crazy?" Jambrea craned her neck until she consumed Matt again. The moment their lips locked, Clint pressed onward, feeding more of the vibrator. The increasing thickness spread her taut muscles farther apart with every bit he introduced.

Nothing could compare to having them inside her. Still, she figured the warm-up would serve her well when they caught up to her. Having Clint's hand guide the toy somehow made its effect more potent. Elusive pleasure sparkled over her in glints as he skimmed the spots she would have zeroed in on, ending her fun too soon.

Matt broke their never-ending kiss to suck in a few breaths. Before he dove back in, he peeked over her shoulder. "Shit, that's hot."

"She's almost burning my fingers." Clint smiled up at them. A touch of tightness around his mouth caught her attention. She was starting to associate it with his arousal. When she skimmed her gaze down the sleek expanse of his back to his ass, she noticed the clench and release of his muscles there as he rubbed himself on the silky soft sheets.

"I'm pretty sure you can turn the darker part at the top there to make it buzz." Matt bounced beneath her as he teased his partner. "You know, if you want to fast forward a bit. My cock would appreciate it."

"You and your cock can kiss my ass." Though Clint rolled his eyes at Matt, he didn't argue.

Jambrea braced herself, but the vibrations from her toy added another layer of ecstasy she wasn't sure she could resist for long.

Turning the dial slowly, Clint ramped up the intensity.

"That's right, wild thing." Matt held her steady when her spine arched and her head landed on his shoulder. "I've got you."

Good thing, too. Because just then, Clint angled his wrist a few degrees differently. The tip of the vibrator rumbled against her favorite spot. She called out his name even as her fingers clawed at Matt's forearms and her toes curled against his shins.

"Right there." Matt sounded nearly as affected as she was. He bundled her against his chest as she attempted to writhe. Shockwaves emanating from the powerful wand radiated along her tensed channel. The base tucked upward, quaking through her outer lips until even her clit could sense the reverberations deep inside.

And then she was lost.

"Yeah, that's it." The warm croon in her ear only enhanced the riot of pleasure between her legs. "Come apart for us. Let us see how beautiful you are when you give in to it. To whatever this is between us."

How could she deny him?

Clint cursed as the first spasm of her pussy tried to snatch the vibrator from his hand. He kept hold of it even as she bucked. If it hadn't been for Matt grounding her or Clint easing her eruption of rapture with soothing kisses on her thigh, she feared she might have shattered.

When the orgasm began to wane, Clint gradually damped the tremors until her vibrator was silent once more. The stillness in the room, except for her ragged breathing, made her a little nervous. What would they think of her abandon?

The hard plastic slipped from her as Clint withdrew. It made her yelp and jerk when it grazed oversensitive tissue. Her sudden movement caused it to dip and Clint's aim erred.

Maybe.

"Watch what you're poking with that thing." Matt growled from beneath her. She might have believed his offense if his cock hadn't pulsed at her back.

"What are you talking about?" A wily smile stretched Clint's mouth. "This?"

Jambrea peered between her legs in time to see the tip of the vibrator nudge Matt's asshole. He groaned as his whole body flexed, lifting her an inch or two higher.

The sight had the embers of her climax flaring to life.

More, she could take more.

Especially if it meant traveling farther down this road.

She turned her head as much as she could so she could

read the expression on Matt's face when she said, "If you're a good boy and let him amuse himself with you, I'll fuck you right now. Take as much of that fat cock as I can while he opens up your virgin ass."

Jambrea had an out of body experience, watching some bolder version of herself say these naughty things to the incredible man beneath her.

"We're screwed. You've been hanging out with Lily too much," he griped even as he choked out a laugh. A twinkle in his eye made her sure his faux annoyance hadn't damped the arousal raging between them all.

His chuckle mixed with a groan when Clint flipped the vibrator on then off a couple times in rapid succession. No gentle crescendos for Matt.

"Shit, yeah." Clint groaned. "Take her up on it or I'm going to fuck her instead. I'm hard enough to use my cock as a nightstick right now."

"You already had her pussy today." The press of Matt's cock intensified behind her. She couldn't believe how thick it had gotten. It twitched as he and Clint jockeyed for position. Learning how to manage all three of their desires might take a little time. "My turn. If you're serious, wild thing?"

"You'd really let me...you know?" Clint's eyes were wide when Jambrea switched her gaze to him.

"If it means I can feel her sweet pussy hugging me again." After taking a deep breath then letting it out slowly, Matt made his decision. "Yes."

"I would be honored to have you inside me under any circumstances." She couldn't let him think her ultimatum held any water. "There are no conditions. It's up to you."

"Stick to being bossy. At least for now." He smiled before he sank his teeth lightly into her shoulder, then whispered, "You're making this easy for me."

"In that case..." She rubbed his arm, where it wrapped around her. "What are you waiting for, Clint? Give the man what he asked for."

Clint glanced up at them both, long enough to verify for himself that Matt was serious. Then he bit his lip and tucked the vibrator against Matt's puckered muscles once more. "Take a deep breath and push out when you feel the toy—"

"Dude, I know how anal sex works even if I've never found a woman who can take me." Matt laughed.

"Fine, then. You don't need any coaching." His partner didn't hesitate.

Jambrea moaned along with Matt when Clint pressed the vibrator beyond the sphincter guarding his entrance. Once he'd penetrated a couple inches, the rest of the incursion went smoothly. She might have asked how it felt if she couldn't already tell by the bulge of Matt's cock, which now throbbed behind her.

"You did so good." She used her best nurse voice to praise Matt as Clint rotated the embedded vibrator, getting Matt used to the moderate girth and the way it felt moving inside his ass. "I think you deserve your reward. Don't you?"

"Fuck yeah." He shifted his hands so that they circled most of her waist. Impressive since she was no sprite like Izzy or her half-sister Lily. Next thing she knew, he'd lifted her a foot or so in the air without her assistance.

Damn, he *was* as strong as he looked.

It only took a second to regain the ability to speak when she caught the hunger in Clint's stare.

"Now help work him inside me." Ordering Clint to assist thrilled her. Maybe she had learned more than she'd thought from her Mistress ally.

Matt groaned when Clint took hold of his cock and aimed it upward, toward her pussy. He guided his friend, who was flying blind. "Let her down. Slowly. A little to the left."

When the hot, wide head of Matt's erection settled against her pussy, Jambrea's delight turned to something more ferocious. She wiggled a bit, speared on the tip of his cock. The spiral she rocked her hips in helped to insinuate him in her like a corkscrew. Clint spread the lips of her pussy then, with his free hand, smoothed some of her obvious arousal over the thick shaft burrowing inside her.

The other kept the vibrator firmly embedded in Matt's ass.

The big guy groaned from beneath her.

"Everything okay?" Clint asked his partner, who'd let his head drop back onto the pillows, breaking eye contact.

"Amazing. Don't stop now." He grunted. "In fact, why don't you turn that thing on?"

"Are you sure you don't want to wait until our wild thing has all of you? Don't want to bounce her off and have to start all over again." Clint's advice made sense.

Jambrea could hardly hear them, though. All she could focus on was the slight burn and the stretch of her pussy around Matt. He really hadn't given her much of himself the day before judging by what she felt now. Even still it had been plenty to satisfy her.

Today was about pleasing him. She never wanted him to feel left out or self-conscious about his body. Not after all the times she'd been the one to skip dress shopping with gal pals when she knew her friends didn't need to frequent the big and tall specialty shops she did.

They were made for each other.

She would prove it to him.

"Just do it." Matt sounded as if he spoke through gritted teeth. "Please. Help me out. I need more."

Right when Clint flicked on the mechanical motion, Jambrea sank in his grip as best she could. Combined with the instinctive upward arc of his hips in response to the new sensations bombarding his prostate, he tunneled deeper inside her. Much farther than he'd been yesterday.

He attempted to lift her, but she cried out. "No. Don't."

Clint saw her struggling and distracted Matt by beginning a slow, long pattern of in and out thrusts with the toy. The helpless man beneath her relinquished his grip and let her have her way with him. He fisted the sheets and drew his feet up until they rested flat beside Clint's hips. His knees bent, he relied on the leverage to drive upward each time Jambrea used more of her weight and gravity to her best advantage.

When they collaborated instead of hindering each other, they made quick progress.

"Almost there, you two." Clint continued to pulse the vibrator in and out while he measured the gap between Jambrea and Matt. "Less than an inch now and he'll be completely inside you, wild thing."

"Oh God." Matt couldn't seem to form coherent sentences anymore. She didn't blame him. Soon she wouldn't be able to remember so much as her name. "Wish I could see."

"Just open your eyes." His partner laughed. "You haven't actually died and gone to heaven. It only feels like paradise."

"Face. Her face," Matt stuttered as Jambrea relaxed her thigh muscles, taking another bit of him. Filled to capacity, she knew that as soon as she moved she was likely to come. She braced herself on his knees, loving how he supported her, even in this.

"Can you turn around, wild thing?" Clint asked.

"Huh?" She didn't understand at first.

"He wants to watch you come. See what it does to you to hold him deep inside. Maybe even to kiss you again while you both surrender. Would you give him that?" Clint's plea on behalf of his friend inspired Jambrea.

"Of course. I want it too." She started by bracing herself on straight-locked arms with her palms planted on his washboard abs. But the pressure on her injured muscle had her hissing and nearly tipping backwards, ungracefully.

"Careful." Clint kissed her belly. "Go slow, and watch out for his nuts. Nothing else you do will hurt this big lug."

With their help, she rotated like a chicken on a spit. A big skewer at that. The motion completed their joining. She came to rest on his pelvis, fully impaled, with her knees on either side of his hips. This time she faced him.

When she opened her eyes and met Matt's stare, her pussy contracted around him. "Hi."

"Hi." He seemed equally as devastated by the perfection of their linkage, or maybe because of the foreign object Clint wielded like a pro. "This isn't going to be a very long ride, I'm afraid."

"Good. Because I'm dying over here." Clint pinched her ass.

"Sorry, but I usually can't come without rubbing my clit." She blushed as she admitted how well she knew her own body. "Do you mind?"

Clint rounded on them so fast she wondered how he'd managed to scramble to his knees instantly. He flopped onto his side with his head resting half on her thigh and half on Matt's ripped abs. His arm still reached up and behind her, doing whatever he was doing to his partner.

With her straddling Matt and Clint lying beside them, his cock landed somewhere in the neighborhood of Matt's armpit. Neither of them seemed to mind, though. Clint rasped, "No way are we letting you take care of yourself again."

Before she knew what he planned, he'd leaned over and extended his tongue, licking her clit with a steady flicking of his talented muscle.

A flash of arousal lit up every nerve ending in her body. As if on autopilot, she sought completion along with the man she rode. Men, if you counted the addition of Clint's wriggling tongue.

And she did. God, she did.

She posted up and down on Matt as if riding a horse. He felt as sturdy as one beneath her, his thick muscles bunching and flexing as he fucked into her and accepted the vibrator plumbing him with help from his partner.

Each trip didn't move her very far. There wasn't much room to maneuver either with Clint's face buried at the junction of her thighs or because of the way Matt's cock filled her, his head locking deep within her core. Still, the slight grinding motion was enough to ensure Matt's veiny shaft caressed every bit of her pussy.

"Matt! Clint!" She tried to withstand the tsunami of delight they conjured. Resisting proved impossible.

"Yes, wild thing." Matt lifted his hands to her chest, flicking his thumbs over her gathered nipples. "Come for us. With me. Now."

She couldn't have said no.

Wouldn't have.

Clint's tongue lashed her even as Matt's cock bulged. She threw her head back and screamed as she came. The jets of superheated liquid that splashed inside her as Matt joined her in simultaneous release only amplified her reaction to her new lovers.

Squeezed from the barest room left inside her, Matt's come leaked from her pussy and onto the tip of Clint's tongue, which never stopped triggering wave after wave of her climax.

Until he surprised them all by shouting, humping Matt's side with two quick jerks and launching several lines of his own come across Matt's pecs and ribs. Jambrea couldn't help herself. She came again, starting another cycle of pleasure that echoed through them all.

At the height of his orgasm, Clint must have let go of her lucky vibrator. The buzzing sounded louder between Matt's thighs on the mattress. When Clint adjusted his position to reach it, Jambrea leaned forward.

"Sorry I couldn't do this before." She stared into Matt's hazy eyes as she lowered her torso and kissed him, gently yet thoroughly. Their heaving chests smeared Clint's ejaculate between them. Neither of them minded. Actually, it felt right to have him gluing their skin together.

They were still feasting on each other's lips in between whispered compliments when Clint returned from the bathroom, where he'd likely cleaned her toy and left it to dry.

"Holy shit." He crashed to the mattress. "Jambi, if you need more, I'm good for it. Just give me a second to keep my heart from exploding first. I swear I've never come that hard in my life."

She ran her fingers through his hair, adoring the damp softness that painted the V between them. "Nah. I'm good now. So good."

"Yes. Yes, you are." Matt grinned up at her with enough affection infusing his lurid stare to have her reeling at the potent combination.

A few minutes later, they'd recovered some of their wits and a little nervous energy.

Though they'd nearly fucked each other senseless, it was the middle of the day and none of them seemed likely to fall asleep any time soon.

All three of them perched cross-legged on the bed, their knees touching so that the area between them was an equilateral triangle. Jambrea let her hands wander until her right palm rested on Matt's knee while the other was filled with Clint's. The center of Matt's chest glistened with the messy trail of Clint's release. She probably matched. A shiver ran through her at their nearness, not to mention the leaps and bounds they'd taken in the past hour or two.

Soon Clint and Matt put their hands up. They each meshed their fingers with hers, then each other too.

"Is this weird?" Clint's cheeks were adorned with twin red spots when he asked his partner for feedback.

"For you? Or for me?" Matt didn't seem fazed.

"Either. Both, I guess." As if he were reading an awkward-o-meter, Clint squinted at his best friend.

"If it is, it's about to get a whole hell of a lot worse," Matt answered.

Jambrea's heart grew three sizes when Matt let go of Clint. He wrapped his meaty hand around Clint's neck and drew the guy closer. They hovered no more than a millimeter apart, staring into each other's eyes.

She held her breath.

And when they surrendered, coming together—mouth on mouth—she couldn't stop tears from running down her cheeks. They were beautiful. Powerful, and perfectly balanced.

The connection they had as longtime friends, who'd literally learned to entrust each other with their lives, spilled over into this exchange. Privileged to observe their bond growing and morphing in front of her, she leaned forward and tried not to blink.

While they might have suffered one or two clashes of their teeth as they wrestled for control, they quickly developed their own pattern of thrusts, parries and dodges that enthralled her. Through it all, affection and a level of comfort—which she hadn't yet quite developed with them—escalated into something amazing that transcended physical expression.

When she thought they might have forgotten about her existence, Matt lifted his hand to Clint's face, held him still, and withdrew just far enough to nip the other man's slightly swollen bottom lip. Clint grinned as he shook his head, breaking free.

"Who knew? You're actually a pretty good kisser, Ludwig." Clint hopped up, giving Matt ample opportunity to slap his ass with a resounding smack that echoed through their oasis.

The crack was almost as loud as the guy's whistling as he headed for the bathroom to clean up.

Matt crashed to the mattress, his arms and legs splayed as if he couldn't hold himself up a moment longer. He laughed and laughed. The ringing of his delight melted her from the inside out.

Jambrea crawled to his side and snuggled against his chest as he wrapped his arms around her, sheltering her. With these two men in her life, she knew nothing could hurt her again. Loneliness and doubt were things of the past.

"Thank you for being so brave." She kissed the spot over his heart.

"Thank *you* for refusing to let us run. You gave me the courage I couldn't find myself. To take a risk. To jump." He squeezed her so tight her eyeballs nearly popped out, but she didn't care.

Never would she prefer him to let go.

For the first time, she believed he wouldn't.

None of them would.

Chapter Eleven

An hour or two later, they'd recovered enough to start eying each other like a tasty mid-day snack. Jambrea crossed and recrossed her legs where she lounged on the couch with Clint, her head on his shoulder. Her fingers walked up and down the tail of his dragon tattoo, which peeked from beneath the sleeve of his T-shirt.

It made her smile to feel like she had the right to touch him. No more keeping her hands in her pockets when she was around the guys for fear of offending one or the other, or both.

On the TV, the anchorman droned on about the positive identification of a mutilated heart that had been mailed to the White House. DNA testing confirmed it belonged to Rudolph Small, the presidential hopeful who'd gone missing almost a full month ago. She shuddered.

"Is this too gross for you?" Clint pointed the remote at the screen, which flashed blurred out images of what could only be gruesome shots of the decomposed organ, maggots and all. "I can change it."

"Nah. I've seen a lot worse at work." She still didn't have to like it though. "I'm more disgusted by that wax-lip grin on the opposing candidate's face. That's Bertrand Rice, right?"

"Yeah." Clint wrinkled his lip. "And I agree with you. What kind of idiots does he think we are to be droning on about remorse for the victim's family when last week he attempted to smear good ol' Rudy from Virginia to Hawaii and back? It's pretty convenient timing if you ask me."

"No kidding. He'll probably tap dance on Mr. Small's grave

before long. I have to admit, I'm not a huge fan of politics." She sighed. "Or violence. It makes you wonder about what kind of person could do that to another human being. That's not the product of self defense. It's cold, calculated and intended to terrorize someone other than the victim, right? The poor guy would have died before he knew what was happening if such a traumatic chest wound was the fatal strike. Probably they didn't butcher him until long after he'd already croaked. If they'd wanted to make him suffer, they'd have opted for something a lot more...survivable. At least for a while."

"You'd make a fine cop, Jambs." Matt smiled at her. "I was trying to figure out who that was actually a message to. The president seems like a stretch. He's already in his second term and wasn't supporting this candidate anyway. More likely they pulled that stunt to make sure it was broadcast to the intended audience, whoever that might be. The media should know better than to air that shit."

"Except it makes for good ratings. More money from advertisers. I hate when I click on a news story online and some cheery jingle for dishwasher detergent plays before a clip of tornado destruction or war updates. It doesn't make sense to me that they smear their products with such vile atrocities. But I guess a captive audience is a captive audience, so why not exploit it?" She sighed. "I spend a lot of my time patching up wounds inflicted intentionally. It's been getting kind of hard lately to remember the majority of people hold life in higher regard than that."

"Tell us about it." Clint rested his chin on the crown of her head. "It's one reason I love spending time with you. Compared to most jerkoffs we deal with on the job, you're a welcome relief. Kind, sweet and innocent."

"Less naive now than I was a few days ago." She smiled up at him with equal parts minx and maiden.

"We'll have to work on that some more soon." Clint

laughed. "But no matter how many new and inventive positions we contort you into, you'll still be a damn fine person. And that's what I appreciate most about you."

"Thanks." She beamed up at him.

Matt paced the floor beside them a few more times before he ran his hands through his hair. None of them did well with being cooped up. Even Parker swam laps in his travel bowl, which had a place of honor on the coffee table, instead of residing over his aquatic kingdom from the comfort of his pink porcelain castle.

Fortunately, she had some ideas about how to burn off their excess energy.

Apparently so did Matt, and their solutions had nothing in common.

"I'd better take a walk," he said in a rush, ruining her daydreams with a reminder of the world—and danger—outside the walls of their refuge. "The library is about six blocks away. That'll be the best place for me to contact the rest of the guys. I'll check in and see what's up."

Clint looked between his partner and Jambrea three times before Matt made up his mind for him. "You can't come. We're not going to leave her alone. And all three of us out in the open is too much of a risk."

"Then let me go." Clint presented his arguments. "You're more conspicuous than me. Even random people remember someone as big as you strutting past."

"I do *not* strut." He crossed his arms, doing nothing to invalidate Clint's concerns.

Matt impressed her, especially now that she knew more of the man behind the muscles. Broad shoulders tapered to a trim waist and his tight ass filled his jeans to perfection. The gun strapped to his hip added just the right hint of no-nonsense.

Jambrea remembered the first time she'd seen him,

Spread Your Wings

dwarfing one of the waiting room chairs in the ER as he hung around for a suspect who'd gotten knifed a couple times in a drug deal gone bad. It hadn't taken her more than five minutes to find Lacey and ferret out his and his partner's identities, though they hadn't known she existed for another couple of months at least.

Once the shit hit the fan with Razor and he'd been assigned to her ward, they'd gradually taken notice of her too. At first she hadn't believed either of the pair could possibly be as interested in her as their mutual friends believed. Finally, she was starting to think Lacey, Lily and the rest might not be totally insane.

Still, yeah, *her* guys would stand out anywhere.

"Hate to break it to you, but neither of you are wallflower material." She shrugged. "If you wanted to be smartest, you'd send me."

"Hell no." They shut her down as one.

Clint gained his feet. "No fucking way. Are you nuts? You already got shot once. Did you forget about the stairway incident too? Whoever we pissed off knows how much you mean to us. They know you're special. I refuse to give them another opportunity to steal you. Not happening."

They were saved from a full out argument—one where she would try to get it through their thick skulls that she would rather die than be left behind again—by an odd knock on the door. One tap, a pause, then two more quick bangs.

The pattern repeated a second time, followed by a familiar voice. Lucas. "Hey kids, put some pants on and let me in."

Jambrea couldn't help it—she blushed. Because despite the regular teasing of their friends, this time the sly insinuations were true. And the whole group of Men in Blue knew it. Nothing was kept secret in their pack. Even if she hadn't scored her bullet wound running from Gunther's Playground—scantily clad, with the pair of cops hot on her heels—they would have somehow known by now.

At least the hotel staff had left their clean and dry clothes outside the door at some point.

Matt checked the peephole. Then he slid the chain off the door and flipped the lock. When he admitted their ex-military pal, Jambrea was surprised to see he wasn't alone. Though it took several seconds for him to hobble all the way into the room—as he'd switched from his cane back to his crutch—he eventually revealed the woman following close behind him, as if to catch him in case he fell.

Ellie's wavy gold hair didn't do much to brighten her expression. Jambrea hated the taut lines at the corners of her blue eyes. So she got up and circled around the guys, who all started to talk at once, to give the woman a hug.

"Thanks," Ellie whispered. "It's his leg. It's worse. Killing him. But he won't let anyone help. He keeps taking more pain pills, though they're not helping anymore."

"I'll try to talk to him." She squeezed Ellie, then moved away before Lucas could catch on. Their concern would be mistaken for pity. His pride would rebel, she was sure of it. After all, she'd treated a shitload of patients with the same mentality. The only ones worse were the dirty old men who thought they were entitled to a dozen sponge baths a day.

"Have a seat." Matt didn't give Lucas an option. He clapped the guy on the shoulder hard enough to unbalance him. His choices were sit or fall on his ass.

Jambrea flashed her lover a thumbs-up from behind Ellie's back.

The skittish young woman waited for Clint to slide all the way to the other end of the couch before she took a place near Lucas, giving them a glimpse of her own battle scars. Despite the closeness they all shared, she never allowed herself to be penned in or get too close to a man. Other than the one she now held hands with.

That Lucas didn't shake her off shocked Jambrea.

"You two might want to do the same." Lucas looked tired when he glanced between Matt and Clint. "I have some info for you. None of the other guys wanted to jeopardize your cover by meeting in person. But Ellie and I don't have any ties, really, to your bunch of cops."

"So spit it out." Matt's patience had worn thin. It had to be important or the Men in Blue would have emailed, sticking to their plan.

"Seriously, get your girl a chair. It's not good news." Lucas rubbed his forehead.

In a flash, Matt whipped a leather seat on wheels from the desk on the side of the room. Jambrea lowered herself when her jellified knees wouldn't support her anyway. Matt laid his hands on her shoulders, never leaving her side.

"We've ruled out a lot of suspects on our initial list." Lucas began.

"That's great. A narrow field should help." A sigh of relief came from Clint, who never took his gaze off her face.

"Actually, we think we're going at it wrong." Lucas paused when he caught Jambrea's riveted stare. Intuition, or something else, stirred in her gut. He couldn't be about to say what she thought. "After investigating the scene at Jambrea's apartment, JRad and Razor went back for some more pictures. Someone's been through every inch of her place. They upended the furniture, tore out the carpet, hacked her mattress to shreds, and emptied the kitchen cabinets. No stone was left unturned."

"What?" Jambrea swallowed hard. There went her deposit. Who would do this to her? Why? "I don't have anything valuable. No real jewelry or fancy electronics, and I don't keep money in my apartment. Hell, I use my credit card for everything so I can get fuel perks and cash back and crap."

"It's not us they're targeting, is it?" Matt's deadpan tone scared her.

"No. Someone's after her. Either she has something she

doesn't know she has or they think she has something she doesn't." Lucas shifted his gaze to the pile of boxes in the corner.

"I-I have no idea what it could be." She shrugged. "You guys saw the best *stuff* already."

Despite the tension, Clint released a strained snigger. "I don't think they're interested in your pornos, wild thing."

"I might be." Ellie tried to defuse the tension. "Have anything good I can borrow?"

Lucas swiveled to face his decoy companion so fast it might have been funny under different circumstances. When he caught her devilish smile, he shook his head.

Back on track, he cleared his throat. "I hope you don't mind, Jambrea. But I was curious. I looked into your military history. Did she tell you guys what she got that Silver Star for?"

He looked between Clint and Matt.

"Uh, we hadn't gotten around to that yet." Clint shifted in his seat.

"Well, your girl is hella courageous. Turns out she dragged nine wounded men and women from a hospital under direct enemy fire and hid them in a storm shelter, watching over them until a rescue team infiltrated the hot zone." Respect oozed from his retelling, which sounded a lot more grand than she recalled it being.

"Are you crazy?" Matt glared down at her as if he took her risking her life personally. Maybe he did.

"You would have done the same." And it was one of the reasons she lov—*liked* him so much.

"But what her official record doesn't say, is that she also freed a valuable asset. A ghost fighter. A super spy. Whatever you want to call it. *That's* the reason they awarded her such an honor." Lucas shocked the hell out of her with that little tidbit.

"How do you know about John?" No sense in denying it

now.

"He and I ran in some of the same circles. Well, kind of. He was a lot higher up than me. Our paths intersected a couple times when I provided distractions or cover." Lucas's face was unreadable. He masked everything about his own experience and only relayed facts. "He was the absolute best in our field. No one crossed him and lived to regret it. He took whatever *jobs* he believed were right regardless of who that made his bosses. He was a wild cannon, which sometimes had him fall out of favor, though that never lasted long. Too useful for his own good, he was the most reliable sniper in the history of our service."

"Someone had him locked up in solitary in my hospital." Jambrea drew a deep breath. "He'd pissed someone off, right?"

"I'm sure of it." Lucas didn't elaborate.

"All I did was give him a chance. Caged like some animal, he was a sitting duck. And in return he helped me escape when I'd stayed too long. But...wait." Jambrea swallowed hard. "You said *was*. Is he retired now?"

Why did she care? He hadn't come back for her and now she wouldn't want him to. Not if it meant ruining this budding relationship, or whatever she had with Clint and Matt. Her heart had moved on, finally. Still, she had to know.

"You can't walk from those kinds of jobs, Jambi." Lucas spoke softer now, his face compassionate. "John David's body turned up last week. He had a great run. Longest of anyone I can think of. But you can't keep that going forever. I'm sorry, honey. He's finally getting the rest he deserved."

"No!" She couldn't believe it. Not after all this time. She'd expected that news to reach her somehow, years ago, yet it never had. And part of her felt like she would have known if his spark was extinguished from the universe.

But she hadn't. He was simply no more.

Burying her face against Matt's stomach when he rounded

the chair, she bawled. For a long while he rubbed her back in soothing circles. And when she finally realized how quiet the room was, she sniffled and peeked from beneath his sheltering arm.

"Was he the guy?" Clint asked. "The one-night-stand you waited ten fucking years for? Some douchenozzle who knew he could never give you more, but stole your virginity anyway?"

"Calm down and have a little respect for her privacy, would you?" Matt glared at Clint before flicking his glance to their guests. Then he tipped her face toward him, capturing her attention. "You don't have to answer him."

She didn't have to because they already knew. But she nodded anyway. "It's okay. He's not wrong. Yes. John was the guy I told you about. He wasn't a monster, though. Not like you're making him out to be. He was decent. Kind."

Clint swore viciously, inventing a few really nasty phrases. "Are you serious? How dare he give you hope there could be more when he *knew* what his life would be like?"

Quick to defend the quiet man, she held up her hands, separating from Matt enough that Clint could see her sincerity. "I swear, it wasn't like that. I'm the dumb one. He told me we'd never meet again. That he was never coming home. I'm just stubborn, I guess."

This time she smiled through her watery gaze.

"When I feel...strongly...about someone, I don't give up easy." She stared at Clint, hoping he understood she included him among the select few forever-people in her life.

Matt too.

"Hang on. *You* were John's girl?" Lucas put his head in his hands. "This is getting crazier by the second. We all thought you were a myth. Some kind of bedtime story you tell green soldiers to give them comfort and keep them from blowing their brains out once they realized what a huge fucking mess they'd gotten themselves into. I heard him talk about you. More than once. About your open arms and kindness. Jambi, he never forgot you."

And that was all she could ask for.

A part of her settled for the first time in forever. Some splinter of her subconscious accepted that she wasn't cheating on John. They'd had something beautiful and timeless, though brief. It had impacted them both profoundly.

What more could she have asked of her first attempt at love?

"Thank you," she whispered to Lucas.

"I'm so sorry for your loss," he murmured in response.

She nodded and swallowed hard. There would be time to mourn later. "But I don't understand how any of that matters now. It's long over. I hadn't seen him in forever."

The three men exchanged glances.

"Someone else figured out who John's girl was." Matt puffed up beside her. "I might have thought they wanted revenge if they hadn't searched your apartment so thoroughly. Think, Jambi, did he give you anything?"

"Only himself." She peeked up at Ellie, finding the girl riveted on her every word. "Trust me, I would remember. There was nothing like that. No tokens or mementos."

"When did he come to you?" Lucas got slapped in the shoulder by Ellie for violating Jambrea's personal space, but privacy was a luxury they couldn't afford. If it was important to figuring out what the hell was going on, she didn't mind embarrassing herself. She couldn't sink much lower at this point. They all knew what a fool she'd been.

"The night of the award ceremony." She rubbed her tattoos. The mental movie she replayed was as vivid as if it had happened yesterday. "I was flattered. For someone like him to sneak in to the service, then find me later, wait for hours while I went out afterward before going home...well, it meant a lot.

Made an impression."

"And he stayed the whole night?" Lucas leaned forward.

"Jesus, do you want to know what positions they did it in too?" Matt glared at the other guy, making her wonder if he'd stoop to beating up a wounded warrior.

"No. But I wonder if you were in his company the entire time. Did you leave him alone? At all? Even for a minute or two?" Lucas didn't relent.

"Just while I took a shower, that's all." She shrugged. "I thought I'd give him an out in case he wanted to slip away before things got uncomfortable."

"Jambi." Clint reached for her. Too far away to touch her, he abandoned the couch and sat on the floor beside her instead. His hand wrapped around her ankle. "I think he used you. That bastard planted something in your apartment."

She'd gotten the same vibe from Lucas's line of questioning. No, it couldn't have been fake. What they'd shared had been profound.

Lucas came to John's defense. "Don't stain the reputation of a dead man. I knew him well enough. He wouldn't have screwed with her head like that. Though, yeah, he obviously left something behind. I think he did it for safekeeping. He trusted Jambi. Like no one else. She touched him. Reminded him that there were pure people in the world. Different from the game of deception and constant vigilance we played. He gave her something. To protect."

"I swear he didn't." She hated to disappoint them. They could dissemble every bit of the contents of her boxes and they'd find as much big fat nothing as the criminals who'd destroyed her house. She should know, she'd packed them herself. If there was something extra, she'd have discovered it then.

"Can I see it? Your medal, I mean." Clint's soft request made her curious.

"Sure. It's been on my shelf for years. That whole time. Nothing different about it. Hell, you saw it yourself earlier this morning and I think one of you was looking at it that night you came to my place during the Sex Offender investigation." She shrugged as if she didn't remember every moment of that experience too. Climbing to her feet, suddenly exhausted, she hunted for the box she'd jammed her spilled belongings in. With the crumpled sides, it was easy to spot the couple that had broken Matt's fall.

She couldn't believe they'd almost gotten hurt, maybe worse, because of her.

It'd been much better, less guilt inducing, when she'd assumed it was the other way around. *Damn.*

The sooner they sorted this out the better off they'd all be. Not that she was sure she wanted her life to go back to normal if that meant she'd no longer share close quarters with Matt and Clint.

"Don't lift that with your bad arm." Matt shooed her from the crates and picked up the one she'd gone for. "Tell me what you need done and I'll get it for you."

"Thanks." She peeked inside the first one he held open then shook her head. "Let's try that one."

He rearranged them again and pulled out the next candidate. *Bingo!*

Jambrea plucked the black case from the top of the jumbled contents. She looked at every surface of the box then flipped it open. Same old Silver Star.

"Here you go." She held it out to Matt.

The warm brush of his fingers as they transferred her award had her drawing in a breath. He smiled and dropped a kiss on her forehead.

"About damn time," Lucas muttered.

Matt peered at the front then the back of the Silver Star

before shrugging. "It seems like a medal to me."

He handed the box to Lucas, who did the same while Ellie looked on. Then Lucas tossed it to Clint. Except the other man seemed to be too busy—watching Jambrea and Matt trying to keep their hands off each other—to catch the damn thing.

It bounced off the edge of his hand and skittered on the floor.

"Guess we know who's getting cut from the Men in Blue baseball team this year." Lucas laughed, though the gesture held no real humor. "You can keep me company in the stands."

Clint flashed him the middle finger before snagging the box from the ground. "Sorry about that Jambi. Shit, I think I messed it up a little."

She peeked over his shoulder to see him trying to flatten down a piece of the velvet cushion. "Wait. Don't."

Then he froze before glancing around at them all. "Are you thinking what I'm thinking?"

"Rip it out." Jambrea didn't hesitate.

All five of them seemed to creep closer together in their circle. They stared as Clint tugged and the interior popped out in one piece.

"Son of a bitch," he murmured.

"What is it?" Matt peered over his shoulder. Nothing fell out of the box.

Clint held it up, facing the group so they could see.

Three numbers were scrawled inside.

4-14-50

"Oh, shit." Matt closed his eyes briefly. "And what business did he have drawing that lopsided heart next to his secret message when he was putting you in so much danger? I'm liking this guy less and less."

"This is bad, right?" She ignored his tirade and looked to Clint, who remained calm, or at least kept his seething inside where it couldn't upset her more.

"Come here, wild thing." He held his arms open and she sank into them. "We'll figure out how to make this right together. You're not in this alone, okay?"

Ellie spoke up, quietly. "These are the best guys around. They'll help you like they helped me. No matter the cost."

When Lucas looked at her they both paused. She hadn't said it aloud, but they all thought about how he'd been injured rescuing her. "I'd do it again in a heartbeat, E."

"I know you would." The frown she wore disfigured her pretty features.

"So what the hell is this shit?" Oblivious to the scene playing out before him, Matt squinted at the writing in the medal case. "A date?"

"Or some kind of combination," Clint suggested. "Maybe to a safe or a security deposit box or who the fuck knows what."

"I bet the bad guys have some clue." Lucas cleared his throat. "Why don't you let me take it to JRad? I've never seen a computer whiz like him before. Not even in my old agency. Between the rest of the Men in Blue and him, I bet we can figure something out."

"And in the meantime..." Clint looked over her head to Matt.

"No, uh-uh, none of that secret talking-without-talking crap." Jambrea pushed away from the warmth of his chest for a moment. "Keep me in the loop. I'm part of this now, aren't I?"

"Shit. Of course." Matt crouched beside her and Clint. "We're thinking we can't stay here. This is worse than we thought. These people are experts. It'll be wise to change location. Somewhere farther out this time."

"I have a suggestion," Lucas paused before dropping the last bomb. "We need someone to check this out anyway. We don't have many leads. Wasting major intel isn't a possibility.

195

And I think only one of us has any shot at getting through on this..."

Irritatingly, he looked for permission from her guys before continuing. When Clint and Matt nodded simultaneously, Lucas said, "We have an address that came from a supporter. Someone who wouldn't crack to unfriendlies for anything. Mason worked some magic to get us close, then I got us the connection through my old pals. There's always been a rumor. Even more vague than the one about John's girl. About his little sister. I have an address. It's way the fuck in the middle of nowhere. JRad's satellite images show over a thousand acres walled off in the mountains. A whole compound, really. Looks like John taught his kid sis a thing or two about protecting herself."

"So we're likely to get our heads blown off when we approach?" Clint raised one brow.

"Probably more likely to run over a landmine or something. I doubt she'll let you get close enough for a decent shot." Lucas shrugged. "But it's worth a try."

"You think she knows about me?" Jambrea winced.

"I think it's probably the best chance we have at another piece of the puzzle." He looked to Matt and Clint. "Agree?"

"I don't like it. But..." Matt grimaced, then nodded. "Yep."

"I guess it's time to hit the road, then." She stood, dusting imaginary lint from her pants, mentally preparing herself for another move. The change of scenery would do her good, she tried to convince herself. "Ellie, would you mind taking Parker, watching him until this is all finished?"

"Sure, no problem." The younger woman smiled and wiggled her finger near Parker's bowl. He splashed at the surface as if saying hello right back. "I'll have the Men in Blue work with the hotel to get your things too."

"Thank you." Jambrea hugged Ellie. "I guess that's everything."

"Mind if I use your bathroom first? Then I'll cover you as best I can on exit." Lucas grimaced as he shook his crutches. Discreetly, he tapped his pocket.

Attuned to the sound, Jambrea caught the rattle of pills in a prescription bottle. This was no potty break. It was a chemical stop, she was sure. The fact that he was hiding it, probably from Ellie, couldn't be good. She'd seen this pattern far too many times to let one of her friends spiral that drain.

"Whatever, man." Matt waved toward the lavish restroom.

Jambrea pretended to gather her belongings near the doorway, then ducked into the tiled space behind the slow-moving guy. She locked the door at the last second.

"Uh. Thanks, Jambi. I know you're a nurse and all, but I've got this." He rolled his eyes, which might have been funny if she couldn't see how bloodshot they were or how his jaw trembled beneath the force he clenched it with. The evidence of his agony was blatant. Unfortunately, she witnessed similar cases every single day.

"Take your pants off." When he didn't budge, she repeated herself, then added, "Drop your drawers or I'll do it for you and flush those pills in your pocket down the toilet while I'm at it."

"I don't think Matt and Clint will approve." Still he didn't flinch.

So she reached forward, her fingers curling in his extra-loose waistband. How much weight had he lost? Too much.

"Jesus. Fine." He unbuckled his belt, on the tightest setting, ripped open the button fly of his cargos and let the canvas pool around his ankles. As if the simple act had drained all his energy, he plopped onto the closed toilet lid and hung his head. "Go ahead. Tell me how fucked up it is."

Jambrea swallowed hard, completely ignoring the beautiful frame that didn't quite support his injured limb. She honed in on the urgent issue. Black splotches screaming of infection and necrosis smeared the already scarred tissue of his mangled leg.

She'd bet his toes were a telltale shade of purple. That he hadn't yet collapsed from the toll on his system bewildered her. After thousands of traumatic injury patients, she had a pretty good idea of where this was heading. It wasn't a utopian place. "Lucas, you need a doctor. The hospital. *Immediately.* I'm texting Lacey, Mason and Tyler to pick you up and take you over to St. Joseph's."

"No more." He tried to snatch her phone from her grasp, but she danced out of his reach. His face crumpled. Bitterness or despair, maybe both, marred his handsome face. "I can't take it. I'm all shriveled up. I used to be a soldier. A man. Now look at me!"

"I am." She clicked send on her message, set her phone down, then approached as she would a wild animal, though he didn't shift. When she stooped to his level, she took his face between her hands and stared straight into his eyes. "I see one of the bravest men I've ever known. One of the strongest too."

"Bullshit." He slammed his lids closed, and for a terrifying moment she thought he might cry.

Jambrea would have held him if he had, but she figured only one woman would have that privilege. He shook off the raincloud hovering over him, gathered himself with several deep breaths then blinked away his emotions. It surprised the hell out of her when he tapped the tattoo on her wrist.

"'I never saw a wild thing sorry for itself', right?" He cleared his throat.

"Damn straight." She swooped in for a sneak-attack hug, whether he liked it or not.

"They told me if this last round of drugs didn't clear up the problems, I might not have a choice anymore. Fighting isn't an option. I'm gonna lose my leg, Jambi." His gaze dropped to the tiled floor and stayed glued there. "I've lost the war. It's over."

"Oh, Lucas." This time she couldn't stay upright. She knelt between his knees and clasped his hand tight. "Yes, I believe that's true. About your leg, not the rest. Can you smell it? The flesh is already lifeless in places. It can't be undone. I'm so sorry. But..."

Maybe it was too soon for him to hear the truth.

"What? Don't hold back now. Lay it on the line. I'd rather wrestle an enemy I know." He swallowed hard.

"Honestly, I've wondered for some time if your quality of life would have been better with a prosthetic leg. Technology has come so far. People make amazing recoveries with the help of therapy and the proper equipment. You could be back to more of your old activities with time and hard work instead of losing energy while your body tries to achieve the impossible here. We consult with a specialist at the hospital sometimes. Dr. Mackenzie Walton. She's the best in her field. She could be what you need."

"I don't think I've got it in me anymore. I'm tired."

"No, you're sick." She refused to quit trying. "Your leg is deadweight. Dragging you down. Listen to the experts. You've got all of us to support you. We'll be right there with you every step—"

"*Step.*" His disgruntled cackle broke her heart.

"It's true." Jambrea hoped her fellow nurse and the woman's husbands would hurry. Even as she watched, sweat ran down Lucas' face. He needed help, quickly. Or all his options would evaporate. They wouldn't operate if they didn't think his body was strong enough to endure the surgery. How much time had he spent persisting in a losing battle already?

He swayed and she steadied him, hoping she could lower his mass to the floor somewhat gently if he blacked out.

"I bet Ellie wouldn't leave your side for a second." Jambrea smiled when she thought of the other woman's protectiveness.

"She's crazy. She'd be better off worrying about herself." Unkind, his words would have stung the vulnerable girl.

Jambrea was glad her new friend hadn't seen him lash out because the underlying pain and fear causing his dismissal might not have been as obvious to someone with emotional problems of her own. "I don't want her around anymore."

Why couldn't things ever be simple?

"Jambi!" Matt's fist probably came within a hairsbreadth of knocking a hole in the door, solid hardwood or not. "Did you use your fucking phone?"

Oopsy. Before she could explain the necessity—that it really was life or death—he rattled the door handle.

"Get the hell out of there. Quit playing around and move. JRad picked up a signal from in here. If he did, I guarantee you he's not alone. We have to go before we have unwanted visitors."

"Son of a bitch." Lucas pushed to his feet with sheer determination and the thickly muscled arms that braced his weight on the bathroom counter. "And now I'll be responsible for getting you all killed too. Fuck me. Ellie's out there!"

"She'll go with you to the hospital. You, Ty and Mason can keep her safe on the way. Once you're away from me, you'll be fine." She couldn't help herself from bestowing one last hug. "It's going to be a long road, but you're not going to walk it. One day, you're going to run again."

"Jambrea Jones!" Clint joined in the ruckus. "Get your sweet ass out here this instant."

"Go." Lucas squeezed her back, for a second, before she turned. He'd barely hiked his pants up around his bonier than usual hips when she flipped the lock and faced her lovers' wrath. They didn't have their contented faces on like they had after they'd screwed each other senseless. That serenity had vanished.

"I'll explain on the way." She grabbed one of each of their hands and tugged them toward the door. "I'm so sorry, but it had to be done. Trust me."

"We do," Matt promised.

Without additional questions, they hauled her toward the exit.

Clint glanced over his shoulder at Lucas. "Mason said he'll be here in two minutes. Wait for him in the lobby, wherever the most people are gathered. Do you need help getting to the elevator?"

The trio paused before crossing the threshold.

"No, you go." Ellie stood tall, approaching her unlikely friend. "Together, he and I can make it."

"I think you're exactly right." Jambrea stared into Lucas's wide eyes, hoping he received her message.

Lucas nodded, then said, "Run."

Chapter Twelve

Matt and Clint hadn't been kidding. The moment they burst from their room, they linked hands with her and sprinted for the stairwell, guns drawn. Flying down flight after flight, they reached the ground floor in record time. Slamming through the fire exit, they hopped off the loading dock, then reached up to lower her to the parking lot. From there, it was a matter of seconds before they piled into Matt's truck and burned rubber.

Jambrea noticed a man in a black trench coat—far too heavy for the lovely weather—shouting to another guy who followed him as he tore along the sidewalk, running toward their vehicle. "Uh, Matt, you might want to floor it. I think someone's spotted us."

Clint swiveled his head, acting as his partner's eyes and ears while the other man concentrated on driving. "Confirmed. No delays now, Matt. Hop the curb if you have to get out of here fast. Jambrea, stay down. Pretty sure they're armed."

She grunted when Clint put his hand on the nape of her neck and shoved. Bent like a human pretzel, her head at his lap level, she giggled as she kept her inappropriate thoughts to herself. It was that or cry. Her life had gone from bored-to-death to out-of-control in a single twenty-four hour period.

Sexapaloozas. International men of mystery. Secret codes. Injured friends.

Dead ex-lovers.

She shivered. A keening whimper left her as she thought of poor John. He didn't deserve that kind of tragic end after all the people he'd served and protected in his lifetime. Certain she'd known his soul, even for a fleeting moment, she prayed for him. Something she rarely did.

These were special circumstances.

"Hang on, wild thing," Clint shouted. "We're going to have to swerve around the parking booth and pay the fine later. That or crash through it. Whatever you can do faster and with less chance of blowing a tire, Matt."

From the pitch of the cab, which knocked her first into Matt then Clint, Jambrea guessed they'd dodged the mechanical arm blocking their path.

"Great. You're losing them. I don't see any other pursuers on foot or any suspicious vehicles." An automated voice followed Clint's information, doling out curt directions. He'd programmed his GPS with the address Lucas had passed along. The electronic woman guided them down a main street that connected to the highway heading north out of the city.

A few minutes later, Jambrea asked, "Uh, guys, can I get up now or am I in training for mobile BJs down here?"

"Someday, when this is all sorted out, I might take you up on that." Matt's fingers pressed on the knots in her spine as he encouraged her to sit up.

"Not while you're behind the wheel." Clint shot him a glare. "If anyone's getting a BJ, it's me for having to ride along and put up with your crazy stunt driving."

"Came in handy today, didn't it?" The guys soothed her, even as they bickered. Familiar routines went a long way toward convincing a tiny part of her brain that everything was mostly normal, give or take a couple people who wanted to kill them.

Well, probably torture them for information, *then* murder them.

She shivered.

"It's going to be okay, wild thing." Clint wrapped an arm

around her shoulder, careful not to disturb the bandaged section of her arm. "Did you take your medicine before we left?"

"Don't think it's smart to be chomping down narcotics right now. It's okay. I doubled up on my ibuprofen and didn't skip the antibiotics." Though she obviously could take care of herself, it was nice to have him looking out for her too. Living on her own for so long had taught her how capable she was of independence, and also how ready she was to surrender a bit of it in exchange for this bond, deeper than friendship. "Although, now that you got me thinking about it...I'm pretty sure the prescriptions were on the bathroom sink. Shit."

"We'll figure it out. Why don't you close your eyes for a little bit?" Matt encouraged her to rest. When she snuggled into Clint's side and peeked at the gadget in his lap, she groaned. Three hours to go before they reached even the outskirts of John's property.

Maybe it would be for the best if she checked out for a bit.

"Sweet dreams." Clint kissed her forehead as she yawned.

"Naughty ones too," Matt added, caressing the inside of her knee before he put both hands back on the wheel.

"Are we stopping for gas?" Jambrea mumbled, checking her chin for drool as she sat up and squinted into the late afternoon sunshine.

"Nah. You slept right through that. There are a couple bottles of water and some snacks over there if you're hungry." Matt smiled at her as he stretched, lifting his arms as far above his head as he could in the confined space. "We're about a mile down the road from the address Lucas gave us. Pulled over to get ourselves together before approaching. Since we're not sure what to expect."

"Pretty certain it won't be an open-armed welcome." Clint

took her hand in his. "Are you ready for this?"

"I don't really have a choice, do I?" She blinked, trying to clear the fog from her mind. She'd had bizarre dreams. Of John calling to her from the top of a grass-covered knoll, leaning against a giant oak tree in a place she'd never seen before. Of Matt and Clint, changing their minds and breaking her heart. Or, worse yet, of the partners being hurt on the job. The funeral she'd attended for Lacey's brother Rob, one of the Men in Blue who'd been murdered in the line of duty, had blurred and melted into a horror reel about a similar service for her guys.

She shuddered.

As if reality wasn't bad enough. She peered at the woods around them. It was far too easy to envision their hunters hiding behind every tree.

"If you're not up to it, we'll take you away. Find somewhere safe to hide until the squad can come check this place out." Matt didn't hesitate, but they all knew if things were as they appeared, only Jambrea would be allowed inside John's family complex.

And maybe not even her.

They were gambling everything on the barest glimmer of a chance. For all they knew, John had hidden more relevant info in her apartment. "You know, we should have the guys go through everything they pick up from the hotel."

"I hope you don't mind." Matt cleared his throat. "We already told them to sift the boxes."

"Well, I hope Razor has fun detailing the contents of my underwear collection." Jambrea could already see those jokes coming. She liked silly prints, just like on her scrubs. Cherries, rainbows, stars, whatever cute things she could find to snazz up her practical cotton briefs.

"Oh hell. The kid and panties. You know he'll suddenly get really good at report writing." Clint snorted.

"He can say whatever he wants. Because that means you're here and your underwear are far, far away. Just the way I like it." Matt leaned in and kissed her.

The easy familiarity of the gesture caught Jambrea off guard. She appreciated his attempt at distraction. A successful one at that. Her lids fluttered closed as he used his thumb to encourage her jaw to open before gently sliding his tongue against hers, soothing her in a way rational discussion never could.

When he pulled back and smiled, Clint was quick to claim his turn. He tapped her shoulder so that she faced him. Not to be outdone, he finessed her mouth with seductive kisses that had her wondering how private the woods around them were.

"Okay. Let's not get carried away." Matt seemed a little grumpy that he couldn't take a second taste. She could relate. After a ten-year drought, she could probably soak in all the lust they rained on her and still take more. Hell, a downpour wouldn't be enough.

They'd have plenty of time to play later.

She hoped.

"Right." She ran her fingers through her short hair, using Matt's rearview mirror to do the best she could with her disheveled appearance. "This is as good as it's going to get. Let's see who's home and if they'll talk to us."

"We're with you," Matt vowed as he inched onto the tar and gravel road once more. Clint left his hand on her thigh, the heat of his palm reassuring even through her jeans.

"I know." And she really did have faith they would stick by her side, not only through this fiasco but also, maybe, far longer than that.

No more than two minutes passed before the GPS guided them to an unmarked turnoff. Matt looked to Clint, then shrugged as he slowed to a crawl. The dirt path had well-worn ruts that accommodated his truck. Grass grew between them and the trees closed in, forming a tunnel through the thick forest. On either side of the track, the two largest trunks had Private Property signs stapled to them. The next two said *No Trespassing.* And finally a third set about fifty feet in read, *Keep Out!*

Unlike the intelligent people they were, they kept right on going.

Daylight dwindled to mottled patches that littered the ground like golden snowflakes. Sunbeams—so bright she was transfixed by the dust and pollen floating through them—infiltrated the canopy to spear into the greenery below. A bunny hopped alongside the trail and when she watched it dive into the brush, several butterflies fluttered around a clump of flowers at the base of the scrub.

The idyllic scenery would have been captivatingly beautiful if it didn't give her the heebie-jeebies. There was no way out, only the two dirt tracks leading them deeper into this carefully crafted stronghold. They were essentially trapped, forced to go onward with no spot to turn around. If someone came in behind them they'd be stuck.

Fortunately, it didn't seem like John's compound got many visitors.

Inside the cab, Matt flipped off the radio, which droned on with repetitive blather about the murdered candidate from news reporters with no news to report. Worse were the endless sound bites from Bertrand Rice. Something about him made her skin crawl. The more she heard him express his false sympathy for the victim and the righteous revenge he promised to voters who hadn't supported him a few weeks ago, the worse he creeped her out.

Even still, the silence was unsettling. None of them spoke, all senses attuned to the strange world they'd transported to and any hint of a threat lurking on the other side of their windshield.

"Watch out!" Clint shouted, nearly giving her a heart attack as she scanned around them for psycho-commandos while Matt slammed on the brakes. An enormous buck bounded across the path, then into the foliage on the other side.

If she believed in fairytales, she might have thought it was John's spirit looking out for his home and his family—*if*, big if, his sister really did live here. Someone must, because for all the wilderness encroaching on the path, none of it had grown over.

They hadn't rolled forward again very far before an enormous stone wall topped with razor-wire came into view. A black, wrought iron gate with close-knit swirls and angled spikes at the top—too tight to permit someone to slip through—sat between two imposing pillars integrated into the wall.

More signs. These metal plaques inset into the stonework declared this a visitor-free zone and invited them to get lost.

They didn't let the lack of a warm welcome deter them.

Matt rolled down the truck window and waved at a surveillance camera mounted on top of the post. When no sign of life ruined the landscape, he withdrew his badge, flipped it open and held it toward the eye in the sky.

The drone of gears engaging sounded before a rock slid aside. Clint tensed next to Jambrea, leaning over to block as much of her as possible from the moving part. Instead of a weapon of some sort, the secret panel revealed a monitor and speakers built in to the masonry.

"Identify yourself." A woman's voice demanded their compliance though the screen stayed black.

"You mean you didn't run my plates as soon as we came down your driveway? Or maybe even on the mountain road back there?" Matt didn't let the chill in her request impact him. At least he made it seem like it didn't.

"What business does one of the COPD's Men in Blue have with me?" she asked.

"Actually, there are two of us here today." Matt gestured across the cab. "This is my partner."

"Clint Griggs." The woman affirmed she'd done her homework in the time it'd taken them to trek to her front door.

"Nice to meet you." Matt smiled, pouring on the charm that'd had Jambrea under his thumb in no time once he'd focused his attention on her. It rankled to see him apply that charisma to someone else. "We're actually just escorts today."

"Who's the woman you've brought?" The tone of her question changed, as if true curiosity was behind the inquiry rather than confirming truth or proving lies.

Matt looked to Jambrea. She nodded. "Her name is Jambrea Jones."

"Get out of the truck." The gatekeeper's command was as hard as the rock fence before them. Jambrea pictured a woman with slicked-back dark hair, bulging eyes, ultra-pale skin and an entire room of firearms behind her. At least she thought that might be what she saw if the screen had been illuminated. "Right now! I'm not fucking around."

"Wait for me to come over there." Clint exited first and rounded the hood to the driver's side.

"Stay behind us." Matt squeezed Jambrea's hand before sliding from the vehicle.

"Why do you guys always get to put yourself in danger?" she grumbled. This was her mess, after all.

Trying to calm the butterflies in her stomach, she took several deep breaths, then pictured John's face as he'd lain beside her in the moonlight. There'd been nothing aggressive in his touch. Circumstances aside, she had to believe the same would be true of his sister.

If that was who they were dealing with.

And if time and the world at large hadn't taught the woman she needed to be vicious to survive.

Or maybe John had found a wife who wouldn't take kindly to an ex popping out of the woodworks to make her life hell.

Well, shit.

As they shuffled together toward the gate, which was even more imposing from ground level, she murmured, "I feel like we're asking to see the great and powerful Oz."

"As long as there are no flying monkeys." Clint looked up to the puffy white clouds floating by. "I hate monkeys. They freak me out."

Silently, she thanked him for playing along, ratcheting down the intensity she couldn't erase any other way. His sense of humor would never cease to endear him to her.

"Below the screen is a fingerprint scanner. Have her put her thumb on it."

"I'm not sure..." Matt began.

"Too late to go home now," the woman snarled. "There are mines along every inch of the driveway. Try to leave and I won't allow it. If this is some sick game you're playing, you're about to be sorely disappointed. Enemies or competing spies are not tolerated at Camp David."

Seriously? Clint mouthed to Matt. *Camp David?*

A bad joke, maybe. But Jambrea could see how it fit. John had only wanted them left in peace.

"Five...four..." The woman had lost her patience. And maybe some of her sanity, up here in this lonely mountain retreat. Relentless vigilance had to take a toll.

Jambrea shoved through the tiny gap between her guys. She smooshed her thumb on the pad and waited. A few seconds later, green LED lights flashed, chasing each other in a rectangle around the perimeter of the scanner.

The gate creaked then opened inward.

"It really *is* you." A woman's face flickered to life on the screen. "Sorry about that. I had to be sure. I've heard so much about you, I sometimes wondered if you were real or a figment of John's imagination."

"Hi." Jambrea waved, unsure of what else to do.

"Listen carefully. Meet me at the main cabin. Get in your truck, drive north. There are a series of forks. From the left take the first, third, fourth, then second." She grimaced. "Don't screw up. The other ones are booby trapped."

Matt repeated the pattern several times before they were all satisfied.

"See you in about fifteen minutes." Again the screen went blank.

"Gee, Jambi. You have a knack for picking some fucked up boyfriends." Clint boosted her beside him once more. "That creeper must have lifted your print off a glass in your apartment."

"Or maybe he got it from her military files," Matt speculated.

For once they were all mute as they traveled deeper into the heart of Camp David. After what seemed like forever, and yet no time at all, they were there.

A meadow opened at the end of the tree tunnel that had persisted through the wooded maze. Flat and well-maintained, the grassy plane made sneaking up on the cabin centered in its green sea impossible. The stone and beam construction of the main house, complete with a thatched roof, had Jambrea thinking of bedtime stories all over again. In an alien landscape compared to the city only a handful of hours away, she felt as if they'd been transported to a place where the real world couldn't infiltrate far enough to touch them.

Maybe that was the point.

They rolled to a stop in the square gravel lot, edged with chunky rough-hewn rocks, then walked together—Jambrea in the middle—holding hands as they approached warily. When they got within ten feet of the wide porch stairs, the door opened. A woman, maybe five or ten years older than Jambrea, met them with her hand extended.

"Nice to meet you. I'm Shari David. John's sister."

"I guess you already know who we are, but hello." Jambrea smiled in an attempt to calm the jittery woman. Company probably wasn't a frequent occurrence at Camp David.

They climbed the stairs as one, but it was Jambrea the woman stared at. It was her hand Shari reached for to shake. The tremble in her fingers when they touched, and those very familiar wary, chestnut eyes—ones so like the pair she'd never forget in shape if not color—that scanned her tattoos as if for verification had her taking a risk.

Jambrea hauled John's sister—there wasn't any doubt left in her—into a warm embrace.

She may never have known the woman existed, but she could imagine how painful the past decade had been. Isolated. Forgotten. Alone.

As testament to Jambrea's guess, Shari burst into tears. She sagged against Jambrea. Something clattered to the hardwood decking.

"I'm going to pick that up before someone gets hurt, okay?" Clint spoke in his best nobody-panic tone.

The woman clinging to Jambrea nodded but didn't let go. "You're as kind and accepting as he claimed you were."

"Would you mind if we went inside?" Jambrea caught a glimpse of Clint retrieving a sawn-off shotgun from the ground and flicking on the safety.

"No, of course not. It's better that way. So no airbornes can spy on us. No satellite images either." Regaining some of her practicality, John's sister waved toward the truck. "Why don't one of you guys pull that in the barn over there?"

Matt nodded. "I'm on it."

Spread Your Wings

He jumped the rail and loped to his vehicle as if he couldn't bear to be separated from them for even a minute. Probably couldn't, given the odd circumstances of their visit. Clint glanced between his partner and Jambrea, unable to cover both simultaneously.

Fortunately, they'd hardly made it across the threshold when Matt rejoined them.

Inside, the cabin could have been anyone's home if it weren't for the complex surveillance system and the armory that stood in place of a coat closet. Other than a few red flags, the interior of the space was all log beams, cozy furniture and elaborate quilts hung on the wall. Family photos marched across the mantle like a line of soldiers.

Jambrea wandered closer to them. Her heart lurched when she saw a snapshot of a much younger John than even she'd known. He held a giant fish over his head while standing hip deep in a lake. Waders covered him from his belly down and an olive green short-sleeved T-shirt hugged his pecs.

In another, he sat on the floor at the base of a Christmas tree, ripping open gifts next to a pig-tailed girl that could only be Shari. There was one of the back of a teenager with unruly sandy hair she recognized as he accepted a burial flag from a uniformed soldier.

Is that who John had been fighting for?

Shari came up beside her. "Our mother died of cancer when John was seventeen. And before our father could be reached at his station in the Gulf, they came to tell us he wouldn't be coming home either. Probably for the best. He would have been devastated. They were madly in love."

Jambrea sat on the sofa closest to the fireplace and waited for Shari to sink down beside her. The woman had pretty brown hair and a light complexion that spoke of a great amount of time indoors. Or long winters. Maybe both.

"I think it's one of the reasons John refused to entangle you in his lifestyle. Even if he could have, he'd never have doomed a woman to suffer the way our mother did when our father was gone." Shari sighed as she relaxed into the cushions. "Worrying every night, crying herself to sleep, hoping for something that never happened. A homecoming that was never meant to be. And my brother was more than a simple soldier."

"He was special." Jambrea nodded. "I could tell that right away."

"So I suppose you came for the box he left you?" Shari used the hem of her knit shirt to daub the moisture at the edge of her eye.

"Excuse me?" Jambrea sat up straighter, and not only because Matt had come to stand by her side while Clint took a seat on the solid oak coffee table, perched so that he could cup her hand in his.

"I'm sorry. I hadn't gotten around to executing all the clauses of his will yet. It's only been a week since they let me bring him home. It still hurts so much." Sniffles didn't mar the woman's simple grace. Somehow she made weeping seem dainty. Jambrea would have been a red-eyed, snot-nosed wreck in her shoes.

Clint snapped his gaze to Jambrea and shook his head subtly, encouraging her not to correct their host's misconception. Something in her rebelled, though. This woman had no one to trust but her big brother. If she thought for one second things weren't as they seemed...

No, honesty was the best policy. Always.

John had appreciated her candor and she would honor his memory by giving the same respect to the person who'd been closest to him.

"Shari, it's okay. I actually hadn't learned of John's passing until today. And only then because I've been having some...trouble." She used her free hand to clasp Shari's. "I want you to know that if I'd had any clue of John's whereabouts all

Spread Your Wings

this time or had learned of his funeral, I'd have been there."

"Thank you." Shari squeezed her fingers. "I was afraid when I saw you today that maybe you didn't care as much as he did. If you could have seen his face when he talked about you..."

Matt growled a little. Clint flashed him a shut-the-hell-up look, but it rolled right off his partner.

"So it took two guys to replace my brother, huh?" For the first time, Shari showed her true colors and Jambrea had another gut feeling. They could easily become great friends. Sometimes you just knew. And she'd learned to trust her instincts.

"Sure did." She wiggled her eyebrows. "And honestly, it's a recent thing. I was hung up on John for...well, far too long."

Shari smiled. "I might be biased, but I think he was the greatest man in the world. So, tell me about this *trouble*. How can I help?"

"Well, I kind of got shot." She let go of Clint long enough to point at her arm. "That sucked. And then some assholes ransacked my apartment and rigged the stairs to collapse while we were coming down them."

Jambrea was almost sorry she'd shared when Shari went tense beside her. "These are the kinds of things he warned me about. Prepared me for. I have to say I started to get complacent. Until someone tried to break in here too. That didn't end well for them. Luckily, they gave up before I had to take measures more drastic than a little buckshot."

"Do you know who sent your intruder?" Matt leaned in closer, the cop in him bubbling to the surface. "What did he look like? Were there others?"

"Honestly, I can't say. He cursed in unaccented English when the pellets bit him in the ass, though." Shari grinned despite their predicament. "Look, my brother made a host of worldwide enemies in his career. But this didn't have the feel of some overseas terrorist. I think the people who caught up with him, and who are after us now...they're homegrown. They deceived him somehow. And that would not have been easy."

"I got that feeling too." Clint smiled at the blunt, self-sufficient woman. "You want a job on the squad, you just let me know, okay?"

Surprisingly easy to get along with, Shari built on their theory. "So maybe these dirtbags thought you already had whatever John left for you. I assumed the stuff in there was sentimental, but maybe it's more than that. Something important."

Clint winced a little at the word *stuff*, but Jambrea didn't let on that she'd noticed. If he was jealous of another guy, good. Maybe he could suffer a bit of the torture the partners had put her through lately.

"Frankly, Shari, to me affection is everything. Nothing could be more important than something that shows I wasn't a complete moron all these years. I lived in my shithole apartment for a decade because I wanted him to know where to find me if he ever came back." Jambrea hung her head.

"Oh, honey." Shari laughed. "He would have tracked you down anywhere if he could have. It's nice to know his obsession with you was warranted. I'm glad my brother had that to hold on to in dark places."

Before Jambrea could fall prey to the emotions wracking her, Shari stood. She crossed the hardwood floor silently in her quirky maple leaf and trolley dotted toe socks.

"You're doing great, wild thing." As Matt rubbed the tension from her shoulders, Clint leaned in and said, "Let's take this box and get out of here."

"You're leaving?" Shari paused across the room. "Where will you go? You're safe here. John would want you protected. No offense, guys, but if these bastards got my brother after all these years, they can get through you too. True, he was tired of the fight, talked more and more about trying to end the game. But still..."

"Maybe she has a point." Jambrea looked to Matt.

"How about we see what's in there first?" Clint mediated as usual.

Shari nodded and handed over a beautiful wooden container the size of a jewelry box or maybe a humidor. "He made it himself. All the carvings too. Out of maple from our own trees and bloodwood he brought back from his travels."

Studying the intricate piece, Jambrea fell in love all over again. Little birds fluttered around the lid's edges. They towed a banner behind them. *I never saw a wild thing sorry for itself.*

This time a tear did spill over. Not one borne of sadness, but one of sweet memory and the reassurance that she'd been right all those years ago to give her heart to a man who could create something like this. What she'd felt hadn't been one-sided. It hadn't been some crazy pheromone thing. It had been real.

With trembling fingers, she lifted the lid.

Inside, papers filled the velvet-lined space. Clippings about her graduation from nursing school and the hospital newsletter announcement of her awards. Beneath those was a letter. When she unfolded it, she was both thrilled and saddened to see it was short and sweet.

Wild Thing,

I may have been your first, but you were my last. My only true love.

No regrets,

John

Politeness only lasted so long before the curiosity of the three people ringing her took the upper hand.

"Jambi?" Clint towered over her, leaning in for a peek.

"It's personal." She snapped the top closed. Not that she

would hide the contents from him forever. Just for a moment she wanted to be selfish. Until she had closure.

"May I visit his grave, Shari?" She stared into those achingly familiar eyes and waited for John's sister to understand how much it had meant to her—that one wild night.

The pause extended until Jambrea wasn't sure the pretty mountain woman would grant her permission. Hell, she barely seemed to tolerate their presence on her land, let alone someplace so sacred.

Then she nodded. "He'd be so glad to have you near."

A single tear tracked along Shari's high cheekbones. She scrubbed it away with the long flannel sleeve of her shirt. "It'll be getting dark by the time you're done. Stay with me? For a little while. I'd like to get to know you a bit, if you don't mind. And honestly, you'll be safe here. John made sure of that. He talked sometimes of asking you to come home with him, but he knew it wasn't fair to take you from your life, your job, or your friends. I'm sure, though, he wouldn't mind you and your guys staying in his cabin. He'd approve of anything that made you happy, I'm pretty certain."

Jambrea didn't hesitate. She relied on her intuition and the well-honed bedside manner that had won her Nurse of the Year a couple times. She leaned in and hugged the other woman, who immediately broke down.

"You're not alone." Jambrea repeated the promise Clint had made to her this morning. Apparently it was as welcome to Shari as it had been to her. "No more will you have to defend yourself up here, be on constant alert. It had to have been hard to keep that going all these years. We have friends. Cops like Matt and Clint. They'll help us figure this out. Once it's settled, you should be free too."

"That's a nice dream," Shari murmured.

With that, she packed them a basket of fresh food to supplement the stores of nonperishable rations she'd maintained at John's cabin and drew a map with two X's. She gave them walkie-talkies that connected to her main house, a secure satellite phone with about a billion buttons Jambrea didn't understand how to use, directions on how to operate the surveillance system, and sent them on their way. "If you don't mind, it's still...hard...for me to go there."

"Of course." Jambrea hoped the other woman could sense her sincerity. "Thank you for everything. You're our only lead. I hope we can be more than necessity calls for, though."

"I think that's a pretty good bet." Shari hugged her one last time, then surprised Matt and Clint by doing the same to them. "I'm so glad to meet decent people again."

"Same goes, Shari." Matt patted her a little awkwardly on the back.

Clint covered by taking her off his hands. "You know, one of the things that gives me comfort about my job is knowing if anything ever happened to us, our friends would take care of Jambrea. I feel like you're part of our family too. John was. He had the same values. Hopefully you'll take advantage of that support system. We're here for you."

Unable to say more, Shari nodded and waved as tears streamed down her face.

This time they hopefully were more about relief than mourning.

They'd stayed at the main house talking with Shari long enough that even the gorgeous summer day finally faded toward twilight. The last full rays of sunshine streamed over them, lighting everything on fire as they climbed and climbed toward the site Shari had indicated.

They remained quiet until they parked at the base of the hill Jambrea had seen in her dream that afternoon. The guys would probably think she was loony if she told them that little factoid. Or hell, that she'd found such a crazy connection with a soldier passing in the night.

Except they didn't.

"He really meant something to you." Clint squinted slightly as he observed her struggle to swallow her despair. She lingered at the foot of the knoll, afraid to approach John's grave. No matter how hard she tried to bury the pain, she was sure they could see it. The two of them understood her like no one had before. Certainly not a man she'd only met twice.

"I thought I loved him." She cleared her throat and nodded.

"I'm pretty sure you actually did." Matt rubbed her back, his huge hand spanning most of her shoulders.

"I guess. But not in the way I imagined." She shook her head. "I never really got to know him. I just knew there was a connection there. Left unexplored. Forever, now."

Clint grumbled a little. "Much as I don't like to see you sad, I can't say I'm all that sorry it didn't work out. Otherwise we might never have gotten a chance to investigate what's between us."

"So you'll understand when I say I don't want to waste this." She waved her hand between them, then her and Matt, more vigorously than she intended. "How many times can a woman find this in her life and not take full advantage?"

She took a huge breath, filling her lungs with pristine air until they felt like they might burst, like her heart. Then she stared at Clint before shifting her gaze to Matt. "I know now that what I felt for John was real. And it could have become even deeper for both of us pretty easily, but...I know, because I love you too. Both of you dumbasses."

Jambrea spun on her heel, afraid they might not reciprocate. Even more, it terrified her that they might say they did to appease her or absolve any awkwardness between them. Kneejerk *me too*'s weren't what she was after.

Marching toward the only stone standing on the peak of the hill, she refused to slow lest she stall out completely. Death was a regular part of her life at the hospital, yet somehow this seemed different. So damn final. She imagined John's corporeal form lying six feet below her hand, now pressed to the churned earth beneath her knees.

To be this close again, and so very far away, stabbed her heart.

From her pocket, she withdrew a lined sheet of paper she'd ripped from her notebook earlier. The one she kept to herself most times. If anyone else saw the stream of consciousness she'd jotted inside, night after lonely night, it wouldn't be pretty.

The torn and ragged edges seemed fitting. They matched the wound on her heart that had scabbed over though never entirely healed. Even her connection to Matt and Clint wouldn't obscure the past. Not the beauty she and John had created or the damage that had been done. Hell, without these scars she never would have been bold enough to ask Lily to make her dreams come true. Fear was a decent motivator.

They might have been stuck in limbo forever.

She got comfortable on the ground before John's arched stone and petted the sparse grass beside her knees. Then she plucked a stone from the bare earth directly above his casket and placed it on top of the scrap that held her note to John. A quote from their favorite poet, actually.

Jambrea wondered if anyone would object to her adding the line beneath his name.

Permanently engraved, as he had been on her life.

Death is the only pure, beautiful conclusion of a great passion.—David Herbert Lawrence

"Thank you for your service to our country," Matt whispered from where he sank beside her, clasping her hand as he spoke. And she realized the quote could hold many meanings. He leaned in and touched the cold stone header simply marked *John*. The respect inherent in all men of service, military or otherwise, for their brothers radiated from the stoic lines of his grim-set mouth. It touched her, drawing fresh tears to her eyes.

"And for protecting our wild thing," Clint added as he threaded his fingers with her free ones, kneeling by her opposite side. "We know it had to have been hell to stay away. Thank you."

Seeing her pair of guys honor the only other important man in her life broke her.

Jambrea crumbled, weeping. Surrounded by nobility and strength, she let them carry her from the meadow. Into the light, out of the shade of the tree looming over John's grave.

Or maybe guarding it.

Goodbye, she mouthed over Clint's shoulder as John's final resting place faded from sight. *Sleep in peace.*

Chapter Thirteen

They'd piled into the truck none too soon. The cheery day and the heat radiating from the earth had fueled an angry sky. As cool evening air rushed over the mountains, it towed a storm, which rolled in behind it. Before they'd reached the turnoff Shari had indicated, rain splattered in fat drops that echoed on the roof of the truck.

Jambrea imagined even the clouds were crying.

It'd been one of the best and one of the worst days of her life. So much progress after endless stagnation made her head spin.

Physical and emotional exhaustion warred for top billing on her list of complaints. Clint didn't ask and she didn't protest when he carried her from the truck. Though he ran through the downpour, they were both soaked by the time he stood beneath the porch overhang and waited for Matt to open the door with the code Shari had instructed them to use on the keypad. She would know they'd gotten there without incident from the main house access center.

"I still think the numbers in the medal box were a combination," he muttered half to himself as he opened the door and flipped on the lights.

"But to what?" Jambrea had believed Shari when she swore she knew of no safes on the property.

"No idea. Gotta think about it more." He stopped talking as he took in their temporary shelter. Dripping on the welcome mat, Matt paused. "Wow, this is nothing like my old man's hunting cabin."

"No kidding, it's actually got plumbing and heat and shit." Clint nudged his partner aside so he could bring Jambrea in out of the elements.

With the rain firmly shut outside, the coziness of the place began to seep into her bones. She hung limp in Clint's arms. The interior of the log cabin was much more masculine than Shari's house, but its rustic charm called to Jambrea. She could see touches of her super spy in the functional yet artistic lines of the Shaker furniture.

Wondering if he'd made that too, she squirmed.

Clint put her down, then proceeded to strip off her shirt in one motion.

"What—" She glanced up at him, surprised to find he looked as tired as she felt.

"I'm not molesting you or anything." He shrugged. "I'm getting rid of these wet clothes. You can't sleep in them. Especially not with your arm."

"How is that, by the way?" Matt jumped in.

If she didn't squelch their concern quickly, they'd never leave her be. "It's good. Seriously. I've had worse."

"When?" Clint looked at her like she was crazy.

"Hell, it hurt more than this when I had my wisdom teeth out." She failed to mention how all four had been full bony horizontal impactions that required an oral surgeon to drill those fuckers out of her skull or how she'd had an infection in her jaw five weeks later, which had her sucking down pudding for nearly two months.

It had been a great weight loss plan, though.

"Can we *not* go back to the no-fondling bullshit?" Jambrea looked up to her guys. She finished shimmying out of her pants and underwear, then turned so Clint got a full rear view. "Get that bra clasp for me, would you?"

Contorting her arm behind her back would blow her cover.

It'd hurt like a bitch.

When Clint peeled off her polka-dotted cotton bra, he put her breasts on display for Matt, who whistled. "Are you asking him to reconsider? 'Cause I'm starting to think that might not be a half-bad idea."

"I just thought....with everything that happened tonight... Your memories. The John factor. The *stuff* we did this morning and yesterday, which you're not used to. That you wouldn't really be up for anything romantic with us." Matt blushed a little at Clint's description. She knew it was because nothing they did together anymore was about simply sex. Unless physical contact was a way to demonstrate their affection or the emotions running far deeper than their libidos.

They'd definitely moved from *stuff* to *romance* somewhere in the past two days.

That had to be harder to rationalize for Matt than when he'd allowed close contact with his best friend for the sake of jointly getting their jollies.

Still, it reassured her that neither of them had bolted for the mine-filled hills when she'd busted out the L-word earlier. Even if they hadn't said it back.

Hmm...

"I want to make this clear to you both. John's my past. You guys are my future." She bit her lip, cupping her hands over her breasts with her arms crossed as a sliver of uncertainty crept in. "I hope."

"There's no doubt in my mind." Clint didn't leave her hanging long. He caught her in his embrace, then descended. His breath warmed her smile a moment before he pressed his mouth to hers. He sipped from her lips, kissing her until even the heat his touch infused her with couldn't combat the persistent dampness of his shirt and jeans.

"Sorry." He chaffed her arm below the bandage before putting enough distance between them to shuck his clothes.

"I'm not." Matt ogled her hardened nipples.

While Clint had kissed her, he must have been busy because he stood naked to match her. It didn't take him long to close the gap between them. "I've never wanted something so badly in my life as I want you. Long term. I can imagine what it would be like. You, me, Clint—finding a place of our own. A house we could share and fill with laughter and the promises of a lifetime of tomorrows. I just didn't want to scare you away. I know it's only been two days..."

"Is that really as long as you've been thinking about this?" She squinted as she tipped her head, trying to read his expression. When would they stop hiding behind half-truths and trust each other enough to admit what they had?

"Shit, no." He easily grabbed her ass and tugged her to his body. The furnace of his chest encouraged her to snuggle up. "I actually have a whole folder I've been keeping of places that could work for the three of us. A couple out near Mason, Tyler and Lacey's house, sort of between the hospital and the station."

"You do?" Clint seemed equally as surprised as she was.

"Yeah." The shifting of Matt's gaze between her and Clint was accompanied by the skip of his heartbeat beneath her palm. "Does that freak you out?"

"Hell no." The waver in Clint's response cramped her gut. "I thought it'd be tough to convince you. You've seemed less open to this whole arrangement."

"I think because I want it so bad. I never guessed that's what my life would be like. I've never wanted to do things with another guy. Things I've thought of compulsively lately, of trying with you and her together. Hell, I practically lost my mind this morning. What was I thinking letting you mess with my ass like that?"

"That it felt good?" Jambrea stepped between the guys, wishing she could hug them both right then. "Why do we have

Spread Your Wings

to analyze so damn much when it comes to all this? Let's do what feels good and worry about the rest later. I'm guessing it'll all fall into place without so much drama. Nothing good happens when we try to work out all the possibilities in our minds. Life doesn't conform to our plans anyway. So it's better to adapt, no matter how uncomfortable it makes us to take a risk. We're too much alike on that front."

"Is all this emo crap putting you off?" Matt winced as he looked to Jambrea.

"Actually, it's making me want you more." She put a hand on each of their chests and shoved them toward the bed. Of course they didn't budge. At least not because of her insignificant push. They waited for her to pass by. "I want to remember that I'm not alone anymore. And not because I've settled or compromised my priorities, but because I found the men I was always meant to be with. Better yet, I'd like to be sure that if I put everything I am into this relationship, that it means something to both of you too."

"Jesus, wild thing." Matt took her with him as he charged the rest of the way to the bed. "How could you doubt that anymore?"

"I guess because we've been in limbo forever and spent only a day—a really fucked up day at that—as the new us." She couldn't believe the sinful smile that curled her lips. It just happened, she wasn't intending to be coy. They brought out all kinds of bad habits in her. She kind of liked playing dirty with them. "Maybe you should show me again what it's like now?"

"Not only for this minute either." Clint brushed stray hairs from her forehead. "This is how it will be from here on out. Or maybe better, even. You're not getting rid of us. Right, Matt?"

"Damn straight." He lifted her so Clint could strip the comforter to the foot of the bed. Soft flannel sheets caressed every inch of her back when he set her down as delicately as if she were an expensive vase.

Though Clint was quick to join her—lying partially over her as he resumed his tasting of her mouth, teasing her with nips and kisses that had her toes curling in the tangle of linens at her feet—Matt hesitated.

"Oh no, not again," she mumbled into Clint's roving lips before they meandered down her chin and onto the top of her neck.

"What's wrong now?" Clint paused his roundabout journey only long enough to shoot a don't-fuck-this-up glare at his partner. "Get your big ass over here."

Though he actually responded without an argument, surprising her, Matt settled in with less disturbance to the plush mattress than Clint's enthusiasm had warranted.

"I feel kind of guilty doing it in John's bed like this." He reminded her that the Men in Blue were men of honor, like her ex-lover had been. Yet another reason she'd so thoroughly lost her heart and soul to them.

People had often accused her of being too kind, too forgiving, too willing to turn the other cheek. But a positive attitude and consideration of others had always served her well. It was something she prided herself on, knowing she'd never allowed someone to drag her through the muck.

So she really considered Matt's objection. And how John might feel if he were still around.

"I'm pretty sure he'd be glad that I'm finally this happy." Her slow smile did a lot to lighten her heart and erase the bitterness that had begun to take hold after her string of relationship failures…or perceived catastrophes anyway.

"I don't know about that. He left you alone because it was the only way to keep you safe. Both from his enemies and from the devastation guaranteed by his ultimate fate in such a high-stakes game," Clint confessed. He studied the imaginary line the tip of his index finger drew in swirls around her belly button. "Not every cop comes home at the end of his shift,

Jambi. If I was as good a man as he was, I'd walk away and let you find a nice normal guy who works in an office. We both would."

"And that boring fellow could get hit by a bus on the way to work. Or catch some rare disease. I see these cases every day at the hospital. Don't tell me it doesn't happen." Jambrea rolled her eyes. "If you try to run..."

"What?" Matt dared her to make a threat she could live up to.

She leaned over, rummaged through the pile of discarded clothes he'd deposited there then held up some of his police accessories. "I swear to God, I'll cuff you to my bed and never let you go."

"That doesn't sound like a half-bad fate." Clint laughed. "Especially not if you're going to take good care of your captives."

"JRad and I are going to have a talk about what ideas his wife puts in your head." Matt glowered, though she knew he wasn't serious. "This is getting outrageous."

"Oh yeah?" She swung the cuffs around one finger. "You want to see *outrageous*?"

Before he could answer through his laughing, she took her chance. She snapped one of the cuffs on his right wrist then grabbed for Clint's left hand, since he now fondled her breast.

In record time, she'd linked them together. Hopefully they'd get the point.

"Hey." Matt shook his wrist, though he had to know it was pointless. Clint's arm jerked up and down on the other end of the chain.

"That's not funny." Clint sobered pretty damn quickly. He lunged for the key, but Matt's mass drew him up short. Jambrea palmed it.

"What's the problem?" She ducked beneath the chain and

got to her knees, propping one hand on her hip. "You don't trust me? Or is it being so inseparable with our guy that scares you?"

"Neither." Clint huffed hard enough to feather his short hair over his brow.

"Then come back over here and get down to business." Matt dared him with a soulful look. "We've practically been attached at the hip since the academy anyway."

Jambrea rewarded her boyfriend's honesty and frank sensuality by approaching him. She cuddled against Matt, and returned his lingering touches. He allowed her to explore however she liked. So she licked her way down his chest, thrilled to have free rein over his body. Her fingers trailed along his arms, enthralled with the build and dip of his thick muscles, before clasping his hips for balance.

By now she was bent over, teasing Clint with the full roundness of her ass. He groaned as he sidled up closer behind her, kneeling between her spread legs. His arm extended over her back to where he was connected by more than cold hard steel to the man in front of her.

They clasped hands—Matt's right enveloping Clint's left.

Her heart felt full to the brim with adoration as she peeked over her shoulder at their intersection. Their linked arms made a bridge that crossed the space between them, joining them.

Even better would be if she were the conduit spanning the gap in another unbreakable bond. So she arched her spine and pressed backward until the hard length of Clint's cock rode the crack of her ass.

They both groaned. Not as loud as Matt did, though, when she licked a wet path from the base of his cock to the tip, pausing to suck on the mushroomed cap. Her jaw protested his width a bit, but she managed.

"Are you sure you've got hardly any experience?" Clint squeezed her cheeks, separating them to give his cock more room to play. "You're dangerous, wild thing."

"Can you imagine once she's got some practice?" Matt's balls drew tighter to his body when she nuzzled them before taking one of his nuts into her mouth and lightly tonguing the sphere. "Christ, you'll kill me."

She might not have had a lot of hands-on experience when it came to pleasing men, but her knowledge of human anatomy was top notch. Employing all her book smarts, she lipped him then did the same on the other side, not minding at all the hefty weight of his shaft on her face as she subjected him to her experimentation.

Any shyness she'd had about bodies or their functions had evaporated long ago. Curiosity overflowed her instead. Having not one but two men to play with—to tease and test—had her ready to go all night long if they could keep up with her rapidly expanding personal knowledge.

While she began to nibble on the side of Matt's shaft, gauging how much of him she could take inside, Clint made some discoveries of his own. For example, he found out that if he nudged her back entrance with the head of his cock she shivered violently.

Maybe someday soon they'd both take her. At the same time. It'd be heaven to have Matt in her pussy—because she didn't know if she'd ever be able to take him in the ass—while Clint filled her rear.

She forgot what she was doing to Matt with her mouth for a moment when Clint slapped his cock against her ass, probably making her jiggle around him. That they treated her a bit more roughly pleased her. Moisture gathered between her legs as she took their lost kid gloves as a sign that they finally recognized how strong she could be, and that she was their match.

Or maybe it was simply instinct.

Fine with that too, she spread her legs wider. And next thing she knew, Clint was obliging her unspoken request.

Matt held her mouth off him while Clint made his initial approach. "No need to risk a bite, wild thing."

She laughed until the pressure of Clint's cockhead on her pussy turned amusement into wanton need. Backing up on him, she inserted some of his plump head into her opening. The gradual widening courtesy of his wedge-shaped tip had her gasping.

Taking full advantage, Matt inserted his erection into her mouth once more. The initial shock of penetration past, she devoted herself to guaranteeing he didn't feel left out because his partner got to fuck her this time around. Her tongue flicked across his frenulum. The inverted triangle of nerve-riddled flesh led straight to his head and another pleasure point. If his grunts and curses were any indication, he had no qualms with his post.

Strong hands banded around her waist. Three of them, since Matt and Clint were forced to cooperate. The angle of Matt's hunched body made it difficult for her to take all of his cock, though she was kind of grateful for the excuse. His girth made sucking him a workout.

A man's mouth would be a much more appropriate tool for this job, she thought.

"Are you laughing?" Matt growled. "I can feel that all the way up my dick. Clint, give her something to be serious about, would you?"

A spank caught her by surprise, turning her chuckle to a yelp. Apparently that felt good to Matt too, if the bulge of his shaft or the spurt of precome he released was a clear sign.

Following his slap, Clint rubbed the sting from her behind as he redoubled his efforts, advancing within her clinging sheath farther and farther until she wondered how much more of him there could be. Unable to sneak a peek at his invasion given Matt's cock pinning her, facing forward, she allowed herself to be awed by the new depths he reached on every grinding pass.

Her thighs quivered when he snaked a hand beneath her and palmed her belly, stroking the vulnerable flesh before sliding his fingers backward toward her pussy. Clint nudged her clit, causing her to hiss around Matt's cock, which now filled most of her mouth.

"That's better." The authority in Matt's commendation had her pussy hugging Clint's cock even tighter.

"She's soaking wet." He panted as he redoubled his efforts, retreating until he nearly fell from her strangling ring of muscles. When he plunged to the very limits of her body, he filled every bit of her.

Both men did in their own ways.

"Good, then you won't hurt her if you fuck her harder." The tensing of Matt's fingers in her hair turned her on even more. She mewled as she suckled his hard-on. "Come on, Clint. Give her what she needs. You know you want to. Ride her. Faster. Deeper."

"Who the hell are you and where did you put my partner?" Clint may have been as shocked as she was at this new side of Matt, but he certainly seemed to enjoy it. He picked up the pace, choosing to obey the call of their trinity of desires, which all three of their bodies seemed to have become attuned to in record time.

It felt so good to finally have what she needed and not be on some starvation diet, drooling over her guys from afar. She sucked harder on Matt, loving the guttural sound that fell from his chest as she treated him as well as she knew how.

"I'll always be your partner, Clint." For one instant they all paused, holding their breath.

Jambrea felt their hands shift on her back as if they linked fingers for a moment before returning their focus to her. A shockwave of joy ran through her at the idea of them meshing into one unit, closer by the minute. Clint's unfettered arm moved beneath her, supporting her even as he stole some of her strength with deft flicks of his fingers.

The tiny circles he rubbed over her clit guaranteed she wouldn't last long before shattering. Sex with them was a billion times better than even the most ingenious setting on her fancy, programmable rabbit vibrator. And that was saying something.

Sensing her impending orgasm, Clint ramped up his delivery of pleasure from both his pistoning cock and the swipes of his nimble fingers, which spread her own arousal over her swollen pussy.

"Careful, Matt," he warned his partner. "She's going to tip over the edge any second."

The big guy in front of her cupped her chin in his hand and retreated as far as the cuffs would allow. His cock slipped from her lips though he kept her close enough to lave him.

Unwilling to sacrifice the musky taste of him while she surrendered to the overwhelming rapture they gifted her with, she did as he soundlessly requested.

The edges of the metal that pressed into her back only made her explosion that much more powerful. With both guys supporting her, she allowed herself the freedom to feel. Clint's cock hammered into her spasming muscles. Unrelenting, he drove her to the pinnacle then let her soar. She let the currents of their ecstasy support her as she coasted to the ground, still hungry for them. For more.

Especially when he pulled out, leaving her to contract around empty space for the last lingering pulses of her climax. When she moaned in protest, he slapped her ass again. The fire only reignited her lust. "If I hadn't done that, I'd have come with you and ended the fun too soon."

"You were going to bust already?" Matt laughed.

"I'd like to see you last longer. She's hot and tight and so damn perfect." He groaned, then reintroduced his still solid erection with one continual thrust that buried him balls deep, as if he couldn't stay away a moment longer.

"A game for later," the big guy agreed.

When Jambrea could think again, she reapplied herself to pleasing Matt. She suckled the tip of his cock, then slid deeper, washing him with the flat of her tongue. The bulges made by his veins felt like a prize, rewarding her for pumping him up.

Clint jerked when he tried to adjust his hold and was drawn up short by the cuffs.

The reminder had her pussy squeezing him tight.

"Why don't you let us out of these things so we can do a better job of pleasing you?" Clint rattled his chain.

Jambrea pulled off Matt, who groaned at the loss of heat, moisture and suction.

"How could you already know what I enjoy most?" She wiggled her ass, thrilled when he smacked it with his free hand. Maybe Lily's clients had something there. She wouldn't say no to a full-on, over-the-lap spanking after tonight. "You feel so deep this way. I love it. Especially if it means I can taste Matt too."

"Well, who am I to deny a lady?" Clint thrust into her a little harder on his next entry.

"I-I do have one request." She had to try a few times to get the squeak out considering how well he fucked her. But taking advantage of his not so rhetorical question was an opportunity she didn't intend to pass up. "If you do a good job at fulfilling it, I'll let you guys turn the tables and restrain me the rest of the night."

No big sacrifice there. She'd love to see what all the fuss was about. Especially after her forays into Gunther's Playground. It'd sure seemed like some of those trussed women had enjoyed the hell out of the experience.

"Oh yeah, and what do you want, wild thing?" Clint asked, his voice strained and gravelly. Sexy as sin.

"Lean over me. It's a secret." She nearly choked on Matt's thick cock when she replaced it in her mouth for a few long, deep sucks. He was harder than hell. The motion of Clint's continually rocking hips made it easy to slide her tensed lips, which covered her teeth, up and down Matt's gargantuan shaft. The sweet taste of his precome nearly had her forgetting her devious plan.

Until Clint whispered in her ear, "What kind of mischief are you up to, wild thing?"

She let go of Matt and turned her face to kiss Clint deeply for a minute or two, getting lost in the bliss he granted her. Matt's fingers tensed in her hair and his cock brushed her cheek. The twin sensations brought her back to the present.

After a particularly bold stroke that had her crying out, she murmured in Clint's ear, "Look how close you are to his cock. Blow his mind. Suck him. Please, let me watch. Give him a blowjob while you make love to me."

"I can fucking hear you!" Matt roared. His cock jumped. "Don't kid around like that. Shit. I could shoot just thinking about it."

Both she and Clint chuckled, though their amusement was heavily tinged with desire.

"Go ahead." Jambrea put all her weight on her good arm and reached for Matt's cock. She pointed the dripping tip at Clint.

He licked his lips.

"Son of a bitch," Matt rasped. His free hand flew to his chest, pinching the hard disc of his nipple before gliding down his washboard abs. Desperate for stimulation, he provided it himself as Clint debated.

"Show him we're not joking. About any of it. This is serious, forever and ever stuff. If we can trust each other enough to take what we need. Come on, I'll feed you your first taste, okay?"

Clint balked, his shuttling hips stalling in their flawless rhythm, his cock slightly less firm than a moment ago. "What if I suck at it?"

"That's kind of the point." She kissed his cheek. "I've never done it before either, and he seemed to like it well enough. It's not rocket science, is it? Hell, you know what feels good to you. Do that."

He glanced out of the corner of his eye at her. "It's always the innocent ones you have to watch out for."

"Hell yeah." Jambrea encircled as much of Matt's shaft as she could. She lifted his erection and aimed it toward Clint. Holding it steady, both she and Matt waited for the man buried inside her to commit.

And he did.

He reached out his tongue first, barely skimming through the opalescent fluid decorating Matt's slit. The bigger guy groaned and flinched when every muscle in his torso contracted simultaneously.

"I barely touched you!" Clint shouted, his cheeks glowing red.

Sensing a possible meltdown, Jambrea distracted him by rocking back and reinforcing his hard-on with several short strokes of her pussy over his cock. Sheathing him fully, she swiveled her hips, loving the variety of sensations he could cause in her.

"Sorry. It just...it shocked me." Matt cleared his throat. "How good it felt. When I looked down and saw you, it was too much."

"Good, though, right?" Jambrea mediated their potentially disastrous exchange. "You mean it jolted you to see the man you'd dreamed of sucking you actually doing it."

"Yeah." He fisted Clint's hair, drawing the other man back where he belonged. "Do it again. I want you to."

It might be the closest to begging he'd ever come in his life. Clint knew it too. He didn't tiptoe around this time. He opened his mouth and slurped Matt's cock straight to the back of his throat. Though he coughed a little, he wasn't deterred.

As the taste of Matt must have settled on his tongue along with that fat cock, Clint reared within her. His cock twitched and stabbed deeper with every ram of his hips. Though less coordinated than he had been, the primal fucking affected her even more than his measured style had before.

All his swag evaporated and only honest urges remained.

"Oh. Shit." Matt couldn't manage more coherent responses than, "Yes!"

Clint must have blown Matt with as much enthusiasm as he fucked her. Because it wasn't more than a few minutes before the tree-trunk thighs in front of her began to bunch and quiver. Matt's balls were high and tight, nestled against his body, prepared to unleash their contents in a violent outburst.

Jambrea didn't dare speak or break the trance Clint was in, equally dedicated to devouring his partner and filling her with relentless strokes. Instead, she triggered Matt's demise by craning her neck enough to allow her to wriggle her tongue along the puckered skin of his scrotum.

He bellowed their names, begged to some god for endurance, but found no help, not when she and Clint worked methodically against his restraint. They collaborated to guarantee Matt's ecstasy.

Though he gave a mighty effort, he soon was warning them of his imminent climax.

Neither of them wavered from the course they were on.

And when Matt vented his desire, it was straight down Clint's throat.

Clint swallowed greedily, his powerful neck flexing even as his hips pounded her, driving her forward into Matt's abdomen until he braced one big hand on her shoulder, holding her in place for his partner to fuck even as he shuddered, grunted and called out for them to join him.

Now that was what she called multitasking.

As he drank every last drop of Matt's climax, Clint began to moan. Repeatedly. He escalated to shouts that matched the determined thrusting of his cock through her ever-tightening channel.

Jambrea let her head drop. It took too much effort to keep it high when all her energy was focused on holding out so she could come with the man who'd pleased her in so many ways tonight.

Witnessing their stalemate, Matt broke the cycle of torture they inflicted on each other. "You're both there. Come. Together."

He smiled down at them, one hand bracing each of his partners, steadying them while they lost control.

The first splash of Clint's release seared Jambrea's pussy. She couldn't resist the transfusion of such pure passion. Her eyes closed as she surrendered to the moment and the pleasure battering her senses.

"Yes. Beautiful." Matt's praise sounded so reverent it made her more aware of the splendor they shared. As if on autopilot, her entire body clenched in a powerful climax. Her enjoyment of the moment was enhanced by his appreciation.

Flooding her with his come and his affection, Clint draped over her back as he pumped every last bit of himself into her with strokes that ebbed to twitches and then grinds in time to the weakening clasp of her pussy.

Finally they both lay still as awe and gratitude mingled with the aftershocks of their orgasms. They collapsed into a pile of awkward limbs.

"The key, Jambi?" Matt nudged her shoulder.

She couldn't resist. "Oh, I thought you guys had it. I must have dropped it."

"What?" Clint lifted his head from the small of her back and stared at her with wide eyes. They scanned the rumpled sheets but found nothing. "We're stuck? Oh, shit. We're going to have to explain this to Shari."

Jambrea couldn't contain her laugher anymore. "Just kidding. I've got it right here."

She produced the key from her fist. The tiny piece of metal had impressed a red mark in her palm. Idly, she wondered if that might be her next tattoo. An eternal reminder that while she had the means to escape, she never wanted to flee these two men and what they had together.

"You're definitely getting a spanking for that later." Matt chuckled. "When I have energy to do it properly. Maybe in like ten years or so."

He smiled a little sadly at Clint, then unlocked their manacles. Free, they didn't move for a second or two. Until Jambrea shifted slightly to relieve the pressure on her arm, which throbbed a bit. Overexertion was worth it in this case.

Clint took the cuffs and key and replaced them in their leather case, which slid onto his belt when he was in uniform. Matt settled beside her, gathering her into his arms. The broad expanse of his chest felt marvelous beneath her cheek and her kneading hands.

Just when she thought she couldn't be happier or more content, Clint snuggled up to her backside. He toyed with the short hair at the nape of her neck, kissing her shoulder lightly as he breathed deep of the scent of their mingled perspiration and skin.

He nibbled her with exactly enough sting to get her attention. She tipped her face toward him.

Clint kissed her tenderly while Matt cradled her close to the shelter of his body. He didn't blink as he stared into her eyes, gliding his lips across hers. And when he paused, she struggled to catch her breath. That's when he whispered, "About what you said earlier... I love you too, Jambrea."

"Damn you, I wanted to say it first." Matt came closer to nuzzle her nose.

"Too late." His partner smirked.

"Well, I love you more," Matt insisted.

"The hell you do!" Clint reached across her body, which shook with laughter, to smack Matt's ass hard enough that the red print of his palm and splayed fingers would probably linger for quite a while.

The sight had Jambrea squirming, especially when mixed with the euphoria their declarations had instigated.

The two men stared at each other for a moment, during which she prayed they were on the cusp of admitting their attraction and something far deeper—a lifelong partnership—with each other.

But they didn't.

Stopping short, they reverted to their inner ten-year-olds. She wriggled aside, out of the danger zone, when they pounced on each other, wrestling for the top spot. Poor Clint had no chance at besting Matt when it came to a show of raw strength. It wasn't long before he was pinned beneath their hulking lover. For a moment, he looked like he might surrender willingly.

Why didn't he admit his feelings?

Saying it out loud would make it no less obvious than their loving exchange already had.

For whatever reason, neither of them seemed able to communicate so directly.

Clint jabbed his knuckles under Matt's ribs. He used his superior speed and agility to duck from the other man's hold. They broke apart, on their knees, laughing at each other until they both collapsed onto the bed, bracketing her once again with their strong bodies.

"Are you guys ever going to grow up?" She ruffled their hair.

"Probably not." Matt shook his head. "Is that a deal breaker?"

"Nah." She swallowed hard. "As long as you love me, we're good."

"I do." They both said at the same time.

"Jinx," Clint singsonged and they were off into another round of exchanged punches and tumbles that didn't fool her in the least.

Whether they admitted it or not, they loved each other too.

They had to. It was the only way their relationship could last.

Thunder rumbled outside, offset by brilliant flashes of lighting. Inside they burrowed, safe and warm, beneath the covers. For now.

Chapter Fourteen

The next morning dawned bright and clear. Overnight showers had washed away any stains on the earth. Birds sang. Matt might have been tempted to think everything was perfect if he didn't stretch, remembering too late he wasn't in his own bed and—better—that he wasn't sleeping alone regardless.

He clipped Clint on the nose with his fist, waking his partner rudely. "What the hell, douchenozzle?"

"Sorry, casualty of tight quarters." Neither of them had let go of Jambrea during the night. They were wadded into a mishmash of body parts. It took his sleep-addled mind a few seconds to figure out how to untangle himself from their human knot.

While he moved as carefully as he could, it wasn't always possible for him to be graceful because he was so damn big. Most people thought it'd be cool to be a giant. They were wrong. He'd felt self-conscious about his size most of his life. And now was definitely one of those times.

Jambrea whimpered as he shifted her. Still she didn't rouse.

Clint hummed from her other side. It sounded more like a thinking noise than a sleepy reflex or a happy sound.

"What?" Matt hoped he wasn't having second thoughts.

"Oh, nothing. Just keep wondering about the Rudolph Small case." His partner never stopped being a cop. Even when it wasn't their jurisdiction. "You figure Bertrand's behind it?"

"From the first second Small went missing, that was my guess." Matt scratched his chest. He enjoyed brainstorming with his partner as they had so many times before. "Must have done a good job of it, though, if they haven't brought him in for questioning yet, never mind arrested the sleaze ball."

"It's the perfect set-up, really." Clint kept his voice low to avoid waking Jambi. "Off the competition, then use his untimely death to rally the guy's supporters and drag them over to your camp. If he can frame someone, even better. He'll be a hero and Rudolph a martyr."

"It's a bitch when we have to play by the rules to prove what our instincts are screaming." Matt rolled toward his mates. "But that's the difference between us and them, isn't it? We believe in obeying the law."

"It's not justice when a killer walks free." A sigh came from the other man. "But yeah, you're right. They'll catch him eventually. I'm sure of it."

"It's just a matter of time before evidence turns up. They're digging, you know they are." Matt had faith in the system. It might not be perfect, but it worked the majority of the time.

"I hope the Feds catch a break soon." Clint went silent and his eyes drifted closed. He might have fallen back to sleep if Matt hadn't roused him again.

"It might be because we're all wrapped up like a ball of worms, but... Does Jambi feel hot to you, Clint?" Matt worried his lip between his front teeth, pressing the back of his hand to their girl's forehead.

That was when he noticed the sweat dampening her hair.

And still she didn't wake up.

"Oh, damn." Clint tested her pretty porcelain skin too. "Yeah. She's definitely got a fever. Let me radio over to Shari and see where she keeps the first aid kit. We're going to need some aspirin."

"It might be more than that." Matt paused Clint with a light touch on his arm. That dragon tattoo reared its head as if daring them to be brave enough to act like the lovers they were instead of the friends they'd been. But what if Clint felt differently today than he had in the heat of the moment yesterday? "She needs antibiotics. The ones she left behind at the hotel."

"Okay, I'll check with Shari. I'll bet they have a stash here somewhere. If we have to, we'll call one of the guys to get us supplies." Clint smiled a little shyly at Matt. It might have been weird if it didn't seem so damn natural. After all, they'd spent most of the past twelve years side-by-side.

Now they were a little closer, that was all.

"Okay, let me take a quick shower and touch base with the guys. If she's not up by then, we'll leave her a note before we go exploring." Matt couldn't help himself. He brushed her cheek with his thumb before climbing from bed. "Wouldn't want her to wake up alone and scared, thinking we ditched her or some shit."

"You know I don't plan to leave her. Ever. Right?" His partner grew very still, something that rarely happened. "I'm hoping what we're building between us is something I can count on for the rest of my life. Something like the friendship I thought you and I had."

"Why do you say it like that?" Wary, Matt watched as Clint curled protectively around their woman.

"Because lately I've felt like it was possible we'd break. Drift apart. Or worse, actively hate each other." He cleared his throat. "I don't ever want to go through that again. Not with you and definitely not with her. I'm a forever kind of man."

"So am I." Matt trusted that his promise meant something to his partner. The guy should know him well enough by now to keep from doubting his word. "Call Mason."

"I've got us covered." Some of Clint's usual personality returned. "Go clean up. You reek of sex like a hooker after a shift. Good job, big guy."

Matt flipped him the bird as he spun on his heel. His friend might not have been able to see his equally enormous smile or the hard-on that was difficult to blame on morning wood due to its delayed onset, but he could probably tell Matt's shoulders shook with laughter as he considered the promise of a new day. A new era.

When they'd swapped places, Clint taking advantage of the generous hot water heater, Matt had prepared Jambrea some breakfast—fresh fruit from the basket Shari had supplied along with a bowl of cereal. He laid the dishes on a tray he'd found in the kitchen and added a note, which he folded into a tent and placed beside the nourishment.

Shari tells us there's a storeroom in the boathouse. We're going to check it out. Need to round up some antibiotics. Take these aspirin and eat your breakfast. We'll be back before you know it.

Love you,

Matt

"Nice job." Clint nodded toward the tray as he whipped the towel from his hips and pulled his clothes on. Good thing the cabin had a washer and dryer running on the same generator as the rest of the house's conveniences. This place kind of rocked.

Maybe someday they'd have a home half as sweet.

The three of them.

Matt looked over in time to see Clint scrawling his name next to Matt's, unwilling to be left out. He didn't blame his partner.

"You finally set?" He decided to rib the other guy. "You take longer to get ready in the morning than a woman, I swear."

"Hey, it takes a lot to look this good." Clint tested out the spikes of his hair and the stubble left behind after his calculated almost-shave.

Together, they took one last look at Jambrea, who still slept peacefully, before heading outside then down the porch stairs. Without speaking, they broke into a trot.

Matt and Clint jogged, side by side, around the edge of the still, dark lake to the boathouse. This was familiar territory. They went for runs almost every morning they weren't on duty and even usually hit the gym together. On autopilot, Matt enjoyed the serenity around him and the company of his best friend.

He wished they could go for a few laps of the lake, through the woods and some of the other beautiful land surrounding them. Unfortunately, they made quick work of the distance between the buildings. With one last look over his shoulder, Matt said, "Maybe later we can see what kind of fish we can find in there. Add something to the dinner table."

"Sounds good. Only thing missing would be a case of beer and some of that processed cheese product stuff we used to pick up at the country store that sold bait." Clint laughed at their poor nutritional habits. On guy weekends, anything that could go in their stomachs did.

He couldn't wait for life to settle into a blend of the familiar old routines they loved and this new, uncultivated sharing that made everything a little more vibrant. The combination would be even more delicious than junk food.

Matt unlatched the door to the boathouse, sliding a weathered plank through the old-fashioned iron fixtures holding it, one square bracket bolted to each of the barn doors. Reaching in, Clint pulled one of the huge sliders to the side, admitting them deeper into John's realm.

He flipped the light switch near the entry, pleased to see rows of shop lights instead of dingy yellow bulbs dangling from exposed wires, like he'd first imagined.

"I guess this is where he made all that furniture. And practiced carving things, like that box he made Jambi. Probably had a lot of time to do that when he was out in the ass end of the world." Clint only sounded mildly jealous. Good for him. The thought of that dude giving their wild thing something so sentimental and precious had Matt in knots, because he wasn't sure that he could ever live up to those standards.

"Hey. Quit it with that death stare, would you?" Matt didn't sound super pleased either, though. The keen observation skills of the Men in Blue were pretty legendary. A requirement for their job. "He saved her life. If it wasn't for him, we'd never have met Jambi."

"It doesn't bother you to think of him stopping over for a one night fuck-a-thon then ditching her?" Clint's bugged eyes made it clear what he thought of that, even if his raspy question hadn't.

"Better than entangling her in his mess. And I'm sure as shit not going to complain about her being available now." He shrugged. "Things do happen for a reason sometimes."

"I'm going to be her reason." Clint nodded as he began to poke around. "*We* are."

"Yup." Content to work in silence, they methodically searched every inch of the shop including the cabinets and the mounds under every tarp. That was the only reason they noticed the difference in the floorboards beneath one of the freestanding tools, right where Shari had indicated the trapdoor to the cellar could be found.

"Got it." Matt rolled the heavy band saw a few feet to the left.

Clint opened the hatch and held it while Matt squeezed himself onto the ladder inside. Fortunately, the light had come on automatically when they lifted the trapdoor. This was no spider-webbed, dank hole. No, a smooth painted cement floor and walls reflected bright lights onto shelves of organized supplies.

It took less than two minutes to locate the antibiotics in the section containing medical essentials. Matt pocketed a bottle, thanking John again for his foresight.

As they turned to leave, Clint put his hand on Matt's arm. "Wait."

If his partner's urging hadn't done the trick, the electric current that shocked him at the guy's touch would have. He willed his boner not to make an awkward appearance right then.

Before Clint could notice his state, he scrambled up the ladder. He stopped when his knees were about floor level. He looked around a bit, then ducked into the cellar. Measuring the space with his fingers—held a bit apart—and one eye squeezed shut like he'd gotten something in it, he popped up again like a prairie dog on crack.

Finally satisfied, he descended.

"What was all that about?" Matt chuckled.

"The cellar walls line up with the beams supporting the center of the workshop and the outside walls. Except for that back part right there." He pointed. "I think the room is a little short on that side, smaller than it should be."

"Are you kidding me?" Matt stared at Clint. "How the hell did you catch that?"

"I don't know, something just felt funny." He pointed at the ceiling. "Why put a drop ceiling down here, unless to cover up that the joists aren't the right spacing somewhere."

"So we're going to move all this shit?" A wave toward John's inventory had him groaning at the thought.

"Have a better idea?" Clint asked.

"Nope." Rolling up his sleeves, he took boxes off the racks and stacked them neatly in the opposite corner. Fortunately, they'd only shuffled about a third of the heavy sacks of rice and canned goods before they found what they were looking for.

A door.

It sat in the wall behind the shelving, the seams nearly invisible.

"I've got this." Matt hauled one set of shelves into the center of the room, his muscles straining. It felt good to put his body to work. Useful for the moment, he cleared enough room for them to slither through the open-backed metal racks and open the white door to John's inner sanctum.

"Holy shit," Clint whispered. There was only one thing inside the three foot deep by twenty foot wide, false-fronted room.

A safe.

Adrenaline poured through them. Clint turned to Matt and slapped him on the back, except this time it was more of a hug. A manly embrace, but still. Definitely a hug. And Matt reciprocated.

This could keep Jambi out of harm's way and let them return to their friends. Their new-and-improved lives. He did a fist pump, then growled, "Hell yes!"

"Go ahead." Clint motioned toward it. "Do the honors. Use the combination from the medal box."

Matt stepped forward, spinning the dial first to the left, then to the right, then to the left once again. His fingers curled one by one around the lever to the door. He pulled.

Nothing.

"It was 4-14-50, right?" he asked Clint to confirm what he already knew.

"Yeah."

"Fuck." Matt tried once more. Still nothing. "You want to give it a go?"

"Shit, no. I watched. You did it right." Clint never fell into thinking he was a moron just because he was the size of an elephant. Sometimes brawn and brains did go together, although most people assumed they didn't.

Spread Your Wings

"Damn it." Matt smacked his palm on the cinderblock wall, kind of okay with the sting that reverberated up his forearm.

"Maybe we should try it backwards." Clint stepped up to the plate and spun out a few different variations on that theme.

"It's no use." Frustrated, Matt thought he did a decent job of hiding his annoyance. Clint put his hand on Matt's shoulder, though. "We'll figure it out. Let's go before Jambi gets worried. We can call JRad and see if he has any ideas."

"What if we try every combination?" Matt didn't mind putting in the time or hard work to figure this out if it was the key to moving on with their promising future.

"With ninety-nine options and three slots, although who knows if it's more than three digits in the combination, there's..." Clint did some mental math. "Probably close to a million possibilities. We'll rot away before we hit on it."

"Okay. I like your plan better anyway." At least part of Matt did. "Let's head back and let the rest of the team know what we found. We can amuse ourselves while they do some work on figuring this mess out."

"Nice thinking, Ludwig." Clint winked. "I could use some entertaining myself."

They didn't bother covering the hidden room or the safe since they planned to return later that afternoon. Whether or not the rest of the Men in Blue had a clue, they had to try something.

As they emerged from the barn, Clint replaced the beam. Matt stood staring out at the deceptively placid landscape that housed intrigue in spades. A glint off something in the trees caught his eyes, but when he blinked it was gone. A bird probably.

Didn't hurt to be safe, though.

"Yo, Clint. You see anything over there, by that big clump of fir trees?"

251

His friend studied the area, then shook his head. "Nothing but birds."

"Just checking." With that they took off in sync, jogging to the little cabin holding a big prize. They charged up the stairs. Matt flung the door open harder than he intended, eager to check on Jambrea.

He shouldn't have worried. They found her sitting cross-legged on the bed, toying with melon rinds and her empty bowl as she talked on the secure phone. Knowing there could only be a few people she spoke to, he yelled, "Honey, we're home."

Although a smile curled the corners of her mouth when she faced them, he could see she'd been crying and her amusement didn't entirely wipe the misery off her face. Frown lines marred her plump lips and creased the space between her arched brows.

"Oh, no. You don't feel well?" Clint rushed to her side.

"It's not me." She put on a brave face they both seemed to see right through. "It's Lucas."

Both he and Clint froze. Matt asked, "How is he?"

"They did have to take his leg." A tiny sob broke free from Jambi's chest. "He's in critical condition. The infection had started to spread. It was worse than I thought."

"I'm still stuck back on the first part." Clint rubbed his thigh. "*Took*? As in amputated?"

Jambrea nodded. "Right above the knee."

"Oh, fuck." Matt plopped onto the bed, clinking the dishes on Jambi's tray together unintentionally. "That's gonna kill him."

"No." She grew stern, which kind of turned him on. "Keeping it was going to kill him. Now he'll have a shot at full recovery. Or as close as he can get. Prosthetics are light years ahead of where they used to be. He'll be able to do nearly everything he could before. He's got friends. Ellie…"

"He won't let that girl near him." Clint put his face in his hand.

"Maybe not at first," Jambrea conceded. "But eventually. With lots of love and hard work. He'll get better."

"I hope you're right, wild thing." Matt held his hand out. "Can I talk to one of the guys, please?"

"Sorry, Lacey, I was filling them in. Is Mason around? Matt needs to talk to one of the Men in Blue." She paused for a few seconds. "I love you too. Everything's going to be okay, I know. You stay safe too. Later."

Jambrea handed the phone to Matt. She stared at him, eyes wide, as he relayed the progress they'd made this morning. "Yeah. A puzzle for JRad, I think. Uh huh. We're going to hunker down. Rest. Think of anything and we'll call you. If not, we'll check in again tomorrow morning. Please have something for us, Mason."

"We're doing our best. There's not a lot to go on. Your guy John was nothing if not thorough." Mason sighed, sounding as weary as Matt felt. "All right, we'd better get off the line. Take good care of each other."

"We will. I promise." He looked at Jambrea then Clint as he swore to protect them. "See you later."

The Men in Blue never said goodbye. They knew how final it could be.

"Later." Mason disconnected them from their friends and family.

"I have a present for you." The bottle of pills rattled as Matt pulled it from his pocket and tossed it to Jambrea.

"Aw, man." She stuck out her bottom lip. "That's not what I thought you meant."

"You're not operating at a hundred percent." Matt shook his head. "Why don't we pick a couple of books from that shelf over there and read?"

At least there was no TV in the cabin so they didn't have to stare at the talking heads debating the public ins and outs of the Rudolph Small case.

"Or better yet, why don't I grab a book and I'll read to you both?" Clint offered, already halfway to the sizable stash of classics. "Maybe in a while I'll make us some lunch. Then we can take a nap. After that, we'll see how it goes, okay?"

"Sounds good to me." Jambrea nodded vigorously.

"Who am I to say no?" Matt kicked off his sneakers and crashed to the bed, holding his arms out, open. It didn't take more than a moment for Jambrea to set the tray on the floor then cuddle up in his arms.

"*Pride and Prejudice* or *The Complete Works of Edgar Alan Poe*?" He held two books up for her to choose between.

"I hate scary things," she mumbled. "Mr. Darcy!"

"Oh boy." Matt prepared himself to be bored to tears. But lying there with Jambrea distracted him from a lot of things. And he found himself enjoying the twisted love story. The sound of Clint's voice wasn't bad either. They passed the book between them, each taking a turn reading a chapter before handing off the drama to the next person to continue.

It turned out to be a great way to spend a day.

The story also seemed to hornify their girl. By the time they'd finished dinner and Mr. Darcy was forking over Lydia's dowry so she could marry Wickham, Jambrea cracked. She was in full-on swoon mode.

"If someone doesn't kiss me right now, I'm going to throw that book across the room." Jambrea knelt between them. Two more doses of antibiotics and most of a day of bed rest seemed to have recharged her.

Clint seemed as full of restless energy as Matt was. His own foot shook beneath the covers even as Clint tapped on the book as he read. It wasn't like them to lounge around for so long, unless there was football on or a new videogame released. Even then they were likely to be shouting, hopping up and down from time to time or tossing popcorn at the TV.

Taking his silence as acceptance, Jambrea lunged up his body, sprawling across his chest as she laid her mouth against his. Like he could stop himself from making out with her then.

They exchanged liquid glides of their lips on each other's until Clint cut in. Matt used his free time to catch his breath and study how his partner and their lover meshed seamlessly.

When Jambi began to walk her shirt up her body, exposing first her midriff then her breasts—free from a bra—he closed his eyes and tried to think of why this might be a bad idea.

Her arm. Right.

"Are you sure you're up for this?" Matt double-checked.

"Yeah, it's a minor infection, which my body was fighting with a low-grade fever. It's not like I'm losing—" Her face went ashen.

"What?" Clint rushed to her side, as attuned to her as Matt himself was these days.

"I almost said, it's not like I'm losing a limb." Tears welled in her pretty eyes. She clapped her hand over her mouth and stiffened up.

"Lucas is going to be okay." Matt patted her on the back, feeling like a buffoon for not having something smarter to say. She would know better than him if the spin she'd put on his likelihood for a positive outcome was true. After examining his leg, her medical training would have given her a real clear picture. Maybe it wasn't as good a prognosis as they'd been told. "Isn't he?"

"Yes. S-Sorry." She sniffled. "I didn't mean to scare you. He's going to come through this. Although he almost waited too long. Bad things were starting to happen to his circulatory system. Damage that couldn't be undone by this procedure.

But, no, he still had time. It's just that... It's going to be a long and difficult journey. And I threw it out there like nothing."

"Jambi, you're the sweetest person I know." Clint came to the rescue when Matt fumbled for the right thing to say. "It was only a phrase. You didn't mean anything bad by it. Let's start over, okay?"

She nodded.

When Matt didn't speak, Clint poked him. Hard. "Ouch. Oh, right. Are you sure you're up for this?"

Jambrea laughed. The sound, as musical as wind chimes to him, was worth the small soreness in his ribs or even his feeling emotionally stunted for a bit.

If he didn't fuck this up royally, this could be his life.

Two partners.

People who'd be there to cover his mistakes and pick him up when he needed a hand. Two amazing human beings he could maybe offer something to in return.

And right then he knew what he wanted to do.

Confer.

With them both.

Jambrea first, because it was easier. At least for a little while, until he got used to this new layer in his relationship with Clint. Maybe today could be another step on that road. Finally, he was ready.

Staring into his partner's eyes, he smiled. "I want to give her all of us. Together."

"You mean..."

"Yeah." Matt nodded. "You'll have to take her ass, though. I would hurt her."

"Oh yeah, sob story material right there." Clint laughed. "*Problems My Giant Cock Causes* by Matt Ludwig."

Jambrea giggled, smacking Clint in the shoulder. "Stop that. You know not everyone loves the way they're made."

"No guy is disappointed that he's got a big dick." Clint's chuckle died when he saw Matt didn't join in.

"It's caused some issues." He shrugged. "It'd be nice to be normal."

"I know exactly how you feel." Jambrea hugged him.

"You'd better not be talking about yourself." Matt squinted down at her, inventorying her ideal form. What about her could she not adore? Pert breasts—not too big—a lush frame, the most smackable ass he'd ever had the privilege of touching and gorgeous eyes that he could stare at for days. She was amazing.

"Not when you look at me like that." She kissed him on the cheek. "You make me feel beautiful. Both of you do. But I haven't always."

"Crazy talk." Clint gaped at her. "But we can remind you later about how gorgeous you are. I plan to do it often, so deal. I want to hear more about this whole tag team proposal of yours, Matt."

"Well, I didn't think it was that difficult to grasp the concept." He found his amusement again. "You see, first I put my cock in Jambrea. We fuck a little and get her relaxed. Then I'll roll over and you can..."

"Stop talking. Start fucking." Their wild thing earned her nickname. She whipped her top off and flung it onto the chest at the foot of the bed. Then she shimmied out of her panties. Completely nude, she descended on them, divesting them first of their shirts, then mauling the zippers of their jeans one after the other.

Seeing her get aggressive, after nearly a year filled with passive and shy dealings, had him hard in an instant. He loved that she felt open enough to take what she wanted. He'd do anything to be one of the men to give her whatever she desired.

So far it seemed like she was onboard for his double penetration scheme. Would she prefer the variety he had in mind for the second stage of their loving tonight? He hoped so.

Even as nerves raced through his stomach, so did arousal. Fierce, driving attraction and longing had him sprinting right beside her toward the brilliance they could create together.

She shoved his shoulders until he fell backward on the bed. He loved the determined look on her face when she straddled him, rubbing her saturated pussy along his cock. She lubricated his thick shaft with her own arousal.

Without asking, Clint reached between them and spread the slickness up and down Matt's dick. The clasp of another man's hand, which could actually hold him more fully than a woman's, had Matt gasping.

Though nothing could match the searing heat of Jambrea's pussy when she lifted up enough so that Clint could position Matt's cock at the entrance of her body. She sank onto him, replacing the pressure of Clint's sure strokes with the undulation of her moist tissue, which sheathed him completely.

It still shocked him that she could take every bit of what he had to give.

Thank God she wasn't some dainty girl.

Before long, she was riding him like a cowgirl at the rodeo. He felt like the one who needed to hold on when the exquisite clasp of her pussy drew him too soon toward the temptation of an impressive climax.

"Clint," he called out to his friend, who watched with unblinking eyes. "Get in here. I'm not going to last at this rate."

And he had so much more he needed to do before he capitulated to the draw of ecstasy.

"Sorry about this, wild thing, but we don't carry real lube with us in our pockets or anything." He held up a jar of petroleum jelly they'd spotted in the bathroom earlier.

"Too bad my boxes are back in the city." She squirmed on Matt, grinding them together in a delectable figure eight that had him ready to wail for relief.

Clint pressed her forward and Matt caught her, drawing her fully onto his chest. Her breasts mashed against his pecs, delighting him with the hard nipples centered in mounds of softness.

He stopped kissing her only long enough to glance over her shoulder and monitor Clint's progress. His partner had a finger or two, he couldn't quite tell from there, working devilish magic on Jambrea's ass. From the moans she let fly, she had no complaints.

When Clint's fingers pressed against the thin barrier separating them, it was Matt's turn to groan. Too much more of that and his whole plan would be ruined.

"Hurry. Please, Clint." He didn't care if his begging seemed weak. If being overcome with rapture inspired by his two lovers meant he was feeble, he'd claim the insult any day.

"Are you sure, Jambi?" Clint leaned over her back, kissing her shoulder blades then down her spine until he got to her ass. He placed a peck on each cheek, then grabbed her bubble butt.

"Hell yes, just do it already. I'm with Matt." She bit his neck. Actually bit him! And he loved it. "I can't take this forever. I could come any second. But I want you inside me first. Both of you. Together."

"Then you'll have us." Clint aligned their bodies carefully. Even still, he struggled to fit himself within her. His cock slipped off the mark and rammed into Matt's balls. Matt moaned, and not entirely in discomfort, as their skin glided across each other.

The next time Clint attempted entry, he breached her tight rings of muscle.

Matt caressed her everywhere he could reach, trying to cover up any pinch of discomfort with the euphoria they brought each other. It seemed to be working if her incoherent cries—definitely of the *more-more-more* variety rather than the *oh-hell-no* kind—were any indication.

Her fingers curled against his pecs, digging those sharp claws into his chest. Her head tipped back, exposing her neck as she arched unnaturally. Matt sucked on the sensitive spot just below her jaw, not caring if he marked her. Let the world see who she belonged to now.

He'd let her do the same if she pleased. Hell, he might ask her for the badge of pride.

Clint began to thrust, in counterpoint to Matt's own upward spearing at first. Though he loved the rub of Clint's blunt head on his shaft through Jambrea, he wanted this to be about her. So, without words, they somehow merged their rhythms and began to impale her simultaneously then withdraw in time to one another.

It only took a handful of dual advances before she tensed, enhancing their rapture.

They were relentless, driving her past the point of no return.

Matt held her tight as she unraveled.

"It's a lot. Ohmigod. So much." Jambrea screamed as she came. She clenched around them so hard that Clint slipped from her ass. He held his cock at her entrance, but the spasms of her muscles made it impossible for him to penetrate as she danced on top of Matt. Though she scratched at his chest, he didn't complain, loving every bit of the stings that demonstrated her delight.

When she went limp, yet mewled for more, Clint attempted to advance again.

"Wait." Matt stopped him.

His partner locked gazes with him. "Are you kidding? I have to. That's the best thing I've felt in my life. Being with you both at the same time."

Matt knew he'd made the right decision. He smiled up at

Clint, then rolled over, still buried balls deep in Jambrea. He spread his legs, digging his knees in the mattress, both for better purchase as he drove into their wild thing, spiraling her higher again, and leaving himself wide open.

For Clint.

"Take me instead." He glanced over his shoulder, thrilled to see lust and not revulsion in Clint's lascivious stare.

"Because you're sparing her or because you want my cock?" The brat smacked his erect tool against Matt's ass.

"I think you know the answer to that." He didn't stop fucking Jambrea with tiny rocks that eased her from the fullest peak of her orgasm yet kept her riled and ready for more.

"Say it," Clint demanded.

"I want you to be my first." Matt closed his eyes. "My only. I want you in my ass because I need you. Like this and in my life. Always."

"You've got it." Greased fingers probed Matt's back passage before easing inside surprisingly smoothly. It wasn't long before Clint inserted a second and then a third, stretching him mildly with each addition. "How is that?"

"Damn!" Matt couldn't explain better. He hoped he wasn't crushing Jambi with his invigorated fucking. No way could he control himself with the increased stimulation.

"That's right, and it's going to feel even better when you're spread apart by my cock." The first press of Clint's blunt head against his extra-puckered hole had him jamming his hips forward, pounding Jambrea. Her moan guaranteed she didn't mind. "You've got me."

The promise inherent in his partner's speech had Matt relaxing a hair. Enough that Clint proceeded, dilating Matt's ass around the spear-shaped head. When he'd poked through Matt's initial resistance, he slipped in several inches at once.

"Holy fucking shit," Matt concentrated on breathing.

And this time it was Jambrea soothing him. "You're doing great. So sexy. Love to see you like this. You're going to make me come again soon. Would you like that? To feel me hugging you while he fucks you nice and deep?"

He could only moan in response. Though the jerk of his cock in her pussy should have been answer enough.

"He likes it, Clint. Don't worry. Fuck him. Like you fucked me. It felt great." She bridged the gap between them, eliminating any chance for the misunderstandings they'd all suffered from this past year. "Go ahead. Screw him. Shove him into me. I'm proud to take you both."

Matt couldn't ignore her generosity any longer. He kissed her long and deep, finding a way to fuck into her every time Clint plunged deeper into his ass. Soon his partner's hands were sure on his hips as he drove Matt, and Jambrea through him, hard and fast.

They may not have been graceful this first time around, but they'd get better. Smoother.

And he intended to practice a lot.

Jambrea opened her eyes and stared into his as they sucked on each other's tongues. She didn't have to speak for him to understand what was about to happen.

When she came, she set off a chain reaction. The milking of her pussy drew his come from his balls. There was no resisting it this time. His own orgasm did the same to Clint. It felt surreal when his best friend poured his hot release deep into Matt's ass.

Grateful for his big frame now, he held himself up to keep from crushing Jambrea while Clint blanketed his back. The weight of his partner made everything perfect.

Sandwiched between the loves of his life, he drifted.

Eventually Jambrea shifted, so he rolled over, depositing Clint on the bed then landing on his back.

To his surprise and delight, both Jambrea and Clint curled up to his sides. They laid their heads on his chest and met in a sensual kiss that had his cock twitching.

Catching him even more off guard, Clint looked up when he finished caressing Jambrea's mouth with his own. "Matt Ludwig, thank you for trusting me. For always being what I need in a partner. I love you."

Jambrea's breath hitched. When Matt glanced at her, tears dripped down her cheeks.

He decided to opt for simple words, when his actions and his heart screamed out so loud that Clint had to already know. "I love you too."

They took their turn, nibbling on each other's mouths before lashing each other with overenthusiastic tongues. Finally, they settled, thoroughly exhausted by their outpouring of physical and emotional energy.

"So it's the three of us forever, right?" Clint grasped one of Matt's hands and one of Jambrea's. "Promise me."

"I do." Jambrea smiled as she said it.

What the hell, Matt figured, why not? "I do too."

Minutes passed in utter silence and satisfaction. Until Jambrea sighed.

"What's wrong, wild thing?" Matt swallowed hard, as if she would be anything less than content after their heartfelt confessional.

"I don't want to get up, but I have to." She grimaced.

"Do you need your medicine?" Clint shoved onto one elbow. "I'll get it and a glass of water for you."

"Well, yeah, that too. But I really have to pee before I fall asleep," she admitted.

"Sorry, can't help you there. Golden showers really aren't my thing." Earning a slap from Clint, Matt grossed them all out.

He loved to do that as much as Razor treasured playing practical jokes on the guys at the precinct.

"Okay, I'm going. Don't miss me too much while I'm away." She swung out of bed. Or she would have except her arm had gone a little numb so when she pushed off it, she lost her balance. Flinging up her foot to right herself, she caught the edge of the nightstand.

Things went flying across the hardwood floor.

"Oops." She tried again, successfully this time, to escape from the cozy nest the three of them had made. Hoping she hadn't broken anything, she fell to her knees on the area rug and searched for displaced items.

After collecting a few knickknacks, she realized what the major clatter had been.

Her keepsake box from John. Oh no.

Jambrea ran her hands over the surface of the carved heirloom, searching for cracks. Thankfully it seemed all in one piece. She hugged it to her as she continued to trail her fingers over the relief that matched her tattoo. Except, something felt a little different to her than she remembered from studying it the past two days.

"Guys?" She scooted over so that she occupied the shaft of moonlight pouring through the window.

"Everything okay, wild thing?" Matt popped his head up so he could take a visual inspection of her safety, or possibly of her nudity in the silver glow.

She was good with either.

Except for once, sex wasn't the first thing on her mind while trapped in this cabin with them. "Maybe."

"That doesn't sound good." Clint rolled from bed a hell of a lot more gracefully than she had, coming to kneel by her. "What's up?"

She clutched the box to her chest so he couldn't cheat.

"What does the box John carved have on it?"

"It looked like this place kind of, lots of trees and animals. Some birds towing a sign that has your tattoo quote in the banner." He recited from memory generally what she recalled.

"No stars?" She asked.

Then Matt was suddenly at her side also. "There weren't any stars on the box. I'd have remembered that given your medal and the combination we found inside its case."

"Feel this." She bit her lip as she turned the masterpiece around.

Even his big fingers got caught in the divot she had noticed while groping in the dark. Then a second as well, a little farther down. "What the hell?"

Clint put his hand in the same spot when Matt withdrew. "Wow, I feel it too."

"I'm turning the light on, look away," Matt advised.

Once they'd all adjusted, they studied the box on the floor between them. Where they'd felt star shapes, there was only a depression between a tree and a bird on one side and the banner and a different tree to the right. Slight shadows there bore only a passing resemblance to what she'd detected nearly blind.

Ignoring what their eyes told them, they each took a turn feeling the carving again. The stars were evident to the touch, though only blobby shapes of varying degrees to the eyes.

"That can't be coincidence," Matt said.

"So why are there only two?" Clint wondered.

"How many should there be?" she asked.

"I'd guess three." He scratched his chin. "I'm not great at puzzles, but it seems to me like maybe we're supposed to take the three numbers from the medal container and use them with this. He left it for his sister to give to you. He had to know that would only ever happen if the shit hit the fan."

Jambrea stared at the box and the quote she knew so well. No secrets burst from the adornments to solve the riddle. Why couldn't life be like TV? "Maybe you guys should call the Men in Blue. We need help."

She headed off toward the restroom. By the time she returned, they'd relayed the critical information and disconnected. Though Shari swore the line was secure, they took as few chances as necessary.

"They're working on it. All we can do now is rest and be ready." Matt patted the gap between him and Clint on the bed.

"It's been a helluva long day." Her other lover yawned mid-sentence. "Come dream with us."

So she did.

Chapter Fifteen

Jambrea was pleased when a knock came on the door early the next morning. A delicious soreness pinged from different parts of her body as she rushed to put on her rewashed clothes. The guys filled Shari in on their discoveries from the day before while Jambrea cooked the fresh bacon, eggs and toast their host had brought over.

But all too soon, breakfast was done. Matt washed the dishes while Clint dried them. They tucked cobalt blue plates away in the solid wood cabinets, which Shari told them John had designed and constructed after building the home for himself.

The guys had only been inside most of the afternoon yesterday, but used to roaming their beat and living a very active life, they were going stir crazy already. They paced the perimeter of the cabin, staring longingly at the lake until even Shari caught on. "Why don't you two take a boat out? If you stay on this side of the lake you'll be able to see if we flag you down."

"Really?" Matt's eyes got as big as a kid's in a candy store. "You wouldn't mind?"

"I've got the phone manned, in case the guys call." Jambrea wiggled the bulky communications device in the air. It reminded her of a cell from the 1980s.

"It might be nice to have a chance for some girl talk." Shari rubbed her hands together. And that was all that needed to be said. The guys hightailed it out of there as if their asses were on fire. It was better than talking about any more emotional topics for a while.

From the porch swing, Jambrea and Shari had prime viewing of the guys as they ran together across the grassy area separating the outbuildings. Their coordinated strides and the flex of their muscled frames had both women practically drooling.

"You're one lucky bitch, Jambrea Jones." Shari surprised her by slapping Jambi's thigh.

Jambrea couldn't help but crack up. "I so am."

"I know I've just met you, but to hear my brother talk I'm sure you deserve every ounce of happiness you can find in this world." Shari smiled at her. "And with *two* guys. I'm pretty sure there's plenty to spare."

"Or extra headaches," she grumbled.

"I bet." Her friend chuckled. "But there have to be benefits too."

"It hasn't been easy getting here. Now that things are more settled, though, yeah, I think I could definitely get used to this." Jambrea glanced sideways. "You don't think it's weird? I wasn't sure if you could tell we were all together…"

"It's pretty obvious when you're sharing a bed." She leaned in. "I think it's hot, not odd. I mean, what about my life has been normal? If you've got two guys and they both care about you, I think that's double the awesomeness. And frankly, my brother would have said the same because two guys means an extra set of eyes watching your back, too."

"Uh, thanks." Jambrea nodded. It was hard to speak through the knot of emotions in her throat.

"While we're being all sappy, I thought I'd tell you I saw the note you left by John's grave." Shari's voice cracked, but she kept going. Tough ran in the David family, apparently. "I'm going to have it engraved on his headstone permanently. It's perfect. For you both."

Jambrea hugged Shari, thankful to have some closure. "I'm so glad we got to meet, though I wish it hadn't been under these circumstances."

"Me too. And I want to say, I'm happy for you, Jambi." Shari patted her hand. "It's nice to see good people get what they deserve for once. Usually it's the shit of the world piled on their heads because they're the only ones who will tolerate it."

Jambrea wondered where that left Shari. She didn't care to draw a dark cloud over their sunshine, though. So instead they sat quietly together, enjoying the day. It wasn't very long before they saw the partners carrying a rowboat inverted overhead.

They watched the guys launch the small craft through a row of cattails. A startled heron rose into the sky with agitated flaps of its huge blue-gray wings. Then the pair of men glided out onto the obsidian-mirrored surface, leaving only a faint silver V in their wake. When their oars dipped into the pristine lake water, they were in sync. They worked together, rowing as one, steadily progressing farther from shore.

Shari broke their mutual quiet time. "I wonder if they tried a few more combinations while they were out in the workshop gathering the rods and reels."

"Maybe." Jambrea figured it likely. The fact that they hadn't come rushing back, excitement burning in their eyes, had her shoulders slumping. She hoped to see that thrill of a mystery solved—a case closed, bad guys put away where they couldn't ruin innocent lives again—sometime soon.

It always gave her a rush when they charged into the hospital on a righteous high. Or when they celebrated with the whole team of Men in Blue. Not because they'd bested the criminals, but because they'd helped civilians and prevented anyone else from being harmed.

Their gallantry was their most attractive feature to her.

A half hour passed, or maybe a little longer. Jambrea had zoned out as she and Shari rocked in the swing. Her ankles were crossed where they rested on the railing. Something on the opposite bank caught her attention as it moved through her peripheral vision.

But when she tried to focus on the tiny motion, she didn't see anything.

"What's over there?" She pointed, the sound of her voice alien in the serenity they'd shared.

"I don't see anything." Shari yawned. She might have been half-asleep. "At least right now. There are a bunch of deer that come down that path to drink. Maybe you saw one of them? They could be staying barely out of sight because of your guys. They're not used to other people. Especially not ones like them."

She liked the way that sounded. *Her* guys.

"Yeah, that must be it," Jambrea agreed. "We've seen some really big bucks since we've been here."

"With no one to hunt them lately, they've been getting fat and happy." Shari smiled.

Just then, Clint hooted and hollered loud enough that his cheers and their echoes reached the women, who giggled. He reeled in—fast and furious—a fish big enough to bow his rod to the extreme. As the fish cleared the side of the boat, Clint stood. He gave them a preview of his catch. It seemed everything came super-sized at Camp David.

They laughed twice as hard when Matt barked at him to sit his ass down. As if on cue, Clint's arms windmilled, pitching their dinner back into the still waters of the lake. Concentric rings spread outward from the sizable splash their almost-catch made.

"The one that got away," Shari murmured. "Always brutal, eh?"

"I suppose it is. So what about you, Shari?" Jambrea angled her torso toward her new friend. "What are your plans? Is this your home or was it John's? I get the feeling that you're a fantastic caretaker, but is this what you really want for yourself?"

"I guess. I've invested so much of myself in guarding this place—*his* future—that I never really made a life of my own." Shari smiled. "That's not to say I don't love it here. I do. It's just...this is a lot of solitude for one woman. Having you all here the past few days has been terrific. Even if I wish your visit were for different reasons."

"Totally understand." Jambrea reached over and held Shari's hand. At least in all the time she'd spent alone she'd had the hospital and great friends like Lacey, not to mention Parker, to ease some of the stillness in her life. What if the quiet of her apartment had been her entire existence?

She probably would be insane by now.

"I've dreamt lots of times of running a resort instead of a fort. There's even more land here than we use today, since I can't monitor it all. If I could wipe away the need to look over my shoulder all the time. Well, maybe after we resolve this..."

"You'll be able to make some major changes." Jambrea could see it now. "Hell, I'd gladly be one of your first customers. Matt and Clint would go crazy for a getaway place like this."

"I'd love to have you. Anytime." Shari smiled.

Jambrea jumped when the phone rang beside her, shattering the tranquility of the mountain air. She bolted to her feet, with the secure satellite device clutched in her hand. "Hello?"

"Hey, Jambi. How're you feeling today?" Jeremy inquired.

"Pretty good." She smirked. "Kind of sore, but in a nice way."

He laughed. "Atta girl. Can I talk to the guys? Or have you totally exhausted them?"

She turned with one arm raised and waving, to signal them to return, but they were already halfway to the shore. "I did my best, but actually, they were distracted by the prospect of great fishing."

"Rough life on this job." He joked though they both knew the gut-wrenching tension that came from having a loved one in danger. It hadn't been so long ago that Lily was threatened.

"We're going to be okay." She told him.

"I think that's what I'm supposed to say." He grunted. "But I know you are."

"All right, incoming," Jambrea prepared him for the two men blazing a path like a tornado across the wide, natural lawn. "I'm putting you on speaker."

"Turn on the video screen too." Jeremy proved he knew more about her technology than she did. Eventually she found the button and mashed it.

Matt reached them first, with Clint a step behind. He held out his hand, pausing to kiss her quickly before getting down to business. She handed him the device though they all gathered around. So Matt went ahead, "Hey, JRad. How—"

"Clint's right," Jeremy said in a rush before Matt had even finished answering. "There's a third star."

"Did you hear that? You guys are my witnesses." Clint's chest puffed up. "I'm right about something."

"The code, dumbass. There have to be three stars." She caught Jeremy rolling his eyes as he kept going. "And sorry, but there's no one here to hear."

"Where is everyone?" Clint asked. The room Jeremy occupied at the station was curiously empty. Usually a half dozen or so cops would be bustling around on their various shifts.

His question got drowned out when Matt stuck to important business.

"What makes you say that?" Matt came close enough that his voice would carry on speaker phone.

Spread Your Wings

"Look at where they are." The Dom turned computer nerd turned reformed Dom counted out the letters with taps of his fingers on a printout of the image they'd emailed to him. "*I never saw a wild thing sorry for itself.* The first star is over the V and the second star is below the D in wild, right?

The stars still didn't show up well in the visual, although they'd circled the appropriate places for him in the image based on their manual manipulations.

"Yeah." Jambrea nodded.

"Those are the fourth and fourteenth letters in the quote." Jeremy cursed. "I'd almost think this was a standard alphanumeric code, a simple conversion once you have all the pieces of the puzzle. But, what the hell does fifty point to? *4-14-50.*"

"Are you supposed to wrap the text around and start again from the beginning?" Clint wondered.

"It's as good a guess as any." JRad blew out an extended breath as he paced the room, trying to sort through the clues that had stumped them. "If so, that would make the I in *thing* the last digit. Go try 23-4-9 in the safe."

Clint didn't hesitate. He hopped the porch railing and sprinted for the boathouse workshop without asking why. The Men in Blue trusted each other and knew the strengths of each team member. Jeremy understood data. Patterns. Analysis.

"You picked those numbers because..." Jambrea gave in to curiosity.

"V is the twenty-third letter of the alphabet, D is the fourth and I is the ninth," he explained. "It's one of the most basic codes out there, though some professionals would never think to look at it because of its simplicity."

"Nothing's been easy about putting all these bits of intel together." Matt groaned. "Motherfucker!"

"I take it that didn't work?" A bang sounded from the other

end of the line as JRad kicked a metal filing cabinet. It wasn't like him to lose his temper.

"Nope. Clint is flashing us a thumbs-down. He's on his way back." Jambrea took a moment to admire his long legs as he ate up the distance between them then settled into his place beside her, hardly winded.

"Damn it." Jeremy tried again. "You're sure there's no more..."

"Oh my God." Jambrea smacked her forehead.

"What?" Matt, Clint and Shari said in unison.

"There *is* more. It's just not here. Not written down or on the box. It didn't fit on my wrist either." She wracked her brain. "Shit. The quote is longer than this. I'm not sure I can remember it verbatim, though. The beginning was my favorite part. It gets the point across well enough."

Jeremy typed away in the background, probably looking it up on the web. "Yes! I've got it. The second line is, 'A small bird will drop frozen dead from a bough without ever having felt sorry for itself.'"

"That's it." Jambrea clapped.

"So that gives us a couple possibilities. It could be the fiftieth character of the second line converted into a number. Or the fiftieth character if you put both lines together... those would be 23-4-9 again, so that's out, or 23-4-15." Jeremy spit out possibilities like water splashing from a fountain as he mumbled to himself. "Do you have a piece of paper to write these down?"

"How about we all head over to the boathouse," Clint suggested instead. "I haven't been hitting the gym like I should lately."

"More like you're tired from your all-night romps." Shari wiggled her brows at the three of them.

"That too." He grinned. "Gotta keep my endurance high,

you know? Come on."

They all jogged for the building on the edge of the lake.

When they got there, they trekked down the ladder single-file and huddled around the safe the guys had uncovered the previous day. They tried the first suggestion Jeremy read off to them...no luck.

So they attempted a couple other possibilities using permutations of the second half of the quote. Everyone held their breath as Clint spun the dial. With the numbers input, his hand hovered over the latch.

"Do it." Matt urged.

So he did.

It didn't budge.

"Fuck, fuck, fuck!" Clint slapped the sold iron box stymieing them.

For a moment it looked like Matt might crush the phone in his grip. Jambrea hugged him. Even Shari tried to calm him with a pat on the shoulder.

Jeremy regrouped. "I have one other thought. Jambrea, what's the quote from your other tattoo, on the opposite wrist. It's by the same poet, right? Maybe if we concatenate them."

"What the hell does that mean?" Shari asked.

"Sorry." Jeremy laughed. "It means to smoosh them together."

"Okay, cool," Jambrea jumped in. "It says, 'I want to live my life so that my nights are not full of regrets.'"

Silence for a moment.

Clint rubbed his thumb across the script decorating her pounding pulse. He seemed as if he might kiss her.

"Holy shit!" Jeremy shouted. "Jambi, isn't that how John signed his note to you? The one inside the box? *No regrets.*"

"Yeah." She nodded. Shari laid her hand on Jambrea's forearm.

"That quote is exactly fifty characters long." He didn't wait for them to celebrate.

Jambrea's heart kicked up double-time. It had to be right.

"23-4-19." Jeremy repeated the numbers to be sure they heard.

Clint hesitated, as if afraid to dash their final hopes.

"If this doesn't work we can get a safecracker up there, but I'm guessing a guy like John has precautions in place against trying to force the door." Jeremy shook his head. "Maybe to destroy the contents, even. Then we'll never know what he protected so fiercely. He thought it important for someone to have whatever he put in there after his death or he never would have gone to Jambi—someone completely out of his circle—in the first place."

An icicle stabbed Jambrea in the heart. Had John only slept with her for access to her medal? A safe place to smuggle intel? She'd had about enough of her nice-girl side getting her trampled like a doormat.

"I disagree," Shari spoke up. "I think my brother went there for exactly what he got...a single night with the girl of his dreams. The only one he couldn't resist, though he knew he should. But he was spontaneous. He trusted his gut. And if instinct told him to entrust her with this secret, whatever it is, he would have done it then worked the rest out later."

Grateful for that perspective, Jambrea clung to Shari while Clint edged closer to the dial.

"Come on. Don't crap out now. This is it. It *has* to be right." Jeremy kept them on task. "Hurry. 23-4-19. Try it."

Jambrea didn't see the big rush. They'd been kicking up their heels for days. But still, she couldn't wait to see what would happen when Clint finished spinning the lock.

Matt, Jambrea and Shari held hands.

Clint tugged on the handle.

And the door opened.

"Holy shit." Clint hauled the heavy portal back until the contents were displayed to them all.

A single, thick, leather-bound notebook sat inside the container, perfectly centered on a pristine white cloth.

"Do you want the honors?" Jambrea asked Shari when no one reached to retrieve it.

"No, you should do it," Shari responded.

"Somebody open the thing. Quickly, please." Jeremy didn't seem as relieved as Jambrea thought he should given that they'd cracked John's code.

Matt squinted at the monitor on the phone, where the miniature version of Jeremy was gesturing furiously in the hand signals the guys sometimes used within their group. She didn't wait to see the two of them hash out whatever had Jeremy's panties in a bunch.

She put her trembling hand on the journal and took it from its resting place.

When she flipped open the front cover, she gasped.

"What is it?" Jeremy asked.

"It says, 'John David's Kill Log.' Beneath that he's written a lengthy paragraph about certifying the contents. Each entry contains DNA proof, according to this. He's also collected fingerprints from each of the bosses that hired him. No wonder he was able to lift mine so easily from my apartment. He'd been practicing." She wasn't sure she wanted to see this side of the man she'd idolized for years.

Shari sobbed quietly behind her.

"He only took jobs he believed in." Matt offered Shari what little solace he could. "It's a terrible burden to have to weigh right and wrong. I believe your brother made sound decisions in serving his agency."

"Thank you," she whispered, though she still winced when

277

their attention returned to the priceless evidence. Would the Men in Blue make it public record? Is that what John had intended all along?

Matt nudged her shoulder. "Wild thing, skip to the last page. Maybe if we can figure out who he was working for on this final job, we'll know more about who murdered him. It could easily have been a double cross. Especially if his employers found out about this. That'd be reason enough to take him out."

"Exactly." Jeremy almost hissed from the open phone line. "Hold the sat device so I can record this. Let's make it all official. Pick up the pace, kids."

Clint squinted at the tiny picture of Jeremy, then held his hand out. "Mind if I do this Jambi?"

A sigh fluttered from her lips as she let go of the book. Just touching it had given her the willies. Clint quickly flipped to the last written page. It was near the end of the journal. Shit, there had to be hundreds of completed entries. Jobs. Kills. Whatever you called taking a life.

"Oh shit," Clint whispered. Matt looked over his shoulder and threw in a few choice curses of his own.

"You knew this, didn't you?" Matt glared at the virtual form of their friend. "You figured it out somehow."

"If the man listed there is Rudolph Small, yes." Jeremy spoke in a grave tone she rarely heard him use. Maybe not since the night he'd announced to their group that he planned to infiltrate Morselli's sex slave ring and rescue Lily.

"But...isn't he a presidential hopeful?" Shari tilted her head.

"He was." Jeremy confirmed. "Until he disappeared while hiking in the Rockies last month. He's dead. Brutally murdered."

Jambrea recalled the disembodied heart they'd seen on the news. No. No way would John do that. He'd be more likely to be efficient and quick. As painless as possible. And certainly wouldn't brag or posture or use the death for his own means. Something wasn't right.

"John would never kill someone to advance his personal politics." Shari was outraged. "Sure, he didn't support that guy, but he wouldn't have offed him. Hell, he didn't like the opponent any better. This isn't right."

They didn't get a chance to debate her late brother's standards. Because just then alarms started ringing like they were at the center of a nuclear meltdown, or maybe an air raid.

Quickly, Matt placed the sat phone high on top of one of the shelves, in the corner, angled to best capture the entire room. Clint stepped in front of the women, who searched behind them for anything that could be used as a weapon.

It didn't matter, though.

They had nowhere to go and no way to escape when a team of men—in black cargo pants and matching midnight T-shirts covered by Kevlar vests—dropped into the basement and flooded their tiny hiding spot behind the storeroom's false wall.

Matt covered Jambrea with his body, acting like a human shield. But when no one immediately attacked, he loosed up a little. "Who are you?"

None of the modern ninjas answered.

Clint looked to Matt, but the man in front of her shook his head. There was no way they could beat these odds. Getting themselves killed for nothing wouldn't leave her or Shari in a better position. In fact, they'd be worse off.

Just in case he decided to do something stupid, Jambrea tucked her fingers in the waistband of his jeans and curled them tight. Then she did the same to Clint, beside her.

A moment later, their anticipation turned to realization. A well-dressed man took significantly longer joining them in their stronghold-turned-trap. Jambrea recognized him too. On the news he'd been blinking away stoic tears at the reports of his colleague's demise.

"Bert Rice." Matt laughed harshly. "Don't you know presidents don't do their own dirty work?"

"Well, I'm not the commander in chief yet. Besides, some things have to be seen to personally or they get all fucked up." The man was as smooth face-to-face as he was in the TV interviews she'd seen of him. Jambrea hadn't liked his slimy oil-slick vibe then. Like always, she should have trusted her gut.

"This country needs a leader who's willing to do whatever it takes to protect against modern threats. Including those that come from within. There's no way I'll lose now. Not with Rudolph on my side...in spirit." Good ol' Bert smirked.

Jambrea would have liked to have kicked him in his fake veneer smile.

Placing his hand behind his back, Matt squeezed her arm in warning.

"Right." Clint didn't give a shit about offending the corrupt bastard. "Or not. What we need is a leader who operates within the law and upholds the values of our forefathers. Fucknugget. Working outside our systems isn't going to get you anywhere but in a jail cell."

Bert chuckled. "Oh cops, you're all the same. Deluded with overly simple views of right and wrong. At least the honest ones. It's what made John so easy to trick. You would have thought after all this time, he'd have seen through the evidence I planted on my friend Rudolph that made him look like a terrorist infiltrating high echelons of our government. Now, the savvy ones..."

"The crooked ones, you mean?" Matt growled.

"Yeah, that I can work with. Wouldn't have had to destroy them. They could have been useful tools instead of a onetime use partnership that needed to be disposed of afterward. Along with their leftover trash." The guy glowered. "Enough chatting.

Spread Your Wings

Give me the book, and I'll leave you to enjoy your last minutes together. It's a generous offer, I believe."

Bert motioned for one of his henchmen to confiscate the notebook.

She hated to see it in his evil hands.

"Don't worry, I'll make sure we have a day of mourning for this tragedy in my constituency." He grinned. "It's horrible when four young people are taken so soon by God. If only they hadn't been so rebellious or chasing evil practices in their mountain complex, maybe that cave-in never would have happened."

"Do people really believe your bullshit?" Jambrea couldn't help herself. She laughed.

Bert didn't really appreciate that. When he rounded on her, snarling, the distraction was all the Men in Blue needed.

"Bertrand Rice, we have you surrounded. This is the COPD. Come out with your hands up." Mason's voice rang loud and clear across the valley.

Jambrea tensed, expecting their attacker to fight or maybe to take them as hostages.

But Bertrand wasn't even brave enough to shoot fish in a barrel.

"My lawyers will fix this. As long as I have the log, we can spin things any way we need to." He grinned. "People will fall for anything. I'll see you next year, when I'm president. We can revisit this then."

Matt swirled his finger around his ear. Yep, the dude was certifiable. But if he left them without a firefight, she sure as shit wasn't going to complain.

Jambrea kept her gaze affixed to the drone who'd tucked John's journal beneath his vest.

First Bertrand surrendered, then each soldier followed, one by one. She never let that guy, the one with her inheritance from John, out of her sight. When at last Matt climbed the ladder then hauled her the rest of the way up, she ignored the screaming of her arm and kept her focus on the goal.

So when the guy coiled, about to lash out, she screamed a warning to Clint, who was closest to the asshole. The thief wrenched away and sprinted toward the door to the boathouse and the lake beyond. If he got close enough to chuck the notebook into the icy waters, he could destroy all the evidence that was beyond reproach.

With a shadow of a doubt—about who'd killed Rudolph Small and why—Bertrand might have his way.

Clint's burst of speed impressed Jambrea. Though the thief had a few steps' advantage, he had no hope. Her boyfriend torpedoed at the suspect and tackled him neatly. Before they had finished rolling to a stop, Razor towered over them, gun drawn, daring the asshole to try anything again.

As Clint held the jerk, Mason approached and retrieved the notebook. "We'll be taking that, thanks."

Jambrea slumped, sinking to her knees in relief while the Men in Blue cleaned up the rest of the mess. After an afternoon of watching them work up close and personal, she had more respect for them than ever. Even if they had used her and the rest of their little gang as unwitting bait.

"I guess that explains where everyone else at the station was," she mumbled to herself, figuring Jeremy's sign language message had been something along the lines of *shit is about to hit the fan but we've got you covered.*

"As soon as I realized that, I knew we were in for an exciting afternoon." Matt hugged her tight. "With the recording from the sat phone in addition to the notebook, our guys have the unbreakable evidence they needed."

"It's over." Shari huddled in the corner, so Jambrea went to her, rocking her and murmuring reassurance. "It's finally over."

Epilogue

Jambrea had just finished her rounds when her phone buzzed in her pocket.

A picture of Matt and Clint smiling as they tickled Izzy and Razor's newborn son, Ezra, popped up on her screen. Her heart melted at the perfect combination of Iz and Razor, and the nurturing her big guys freely lavished on the baby. She picked up her pace, eager to see her men and their friends. Though her shift had technically ended twenty minutes ago, she never left before checking in one last time on all her charges, even if only to chat for a while.

As she passed by the wing housing trauma patients, she swung into it on the off chance that Lucas had changed his mind about his no-visitors policy. Maybe it'd be different if he went to them. Now that Izzy could have her own well-wishers, he could see the rest of their friends without them converging on his sick bed.

Jambrea knocked on Lucas's door before crossing the threshold. Bracing herself for his acerbic barbs, she called out, "I'm going to see baby Ezra—want to come take a look at the little guy?"

No answer. So she stepped inside.

The curtain to his bed was open for once, but he didn't occupy the rumpled bed and his wheelchair was missing. The bathroom was empty.

Could he have bailed on the hospital entirely? *Oh shit.*

Whipping out her cell once more, she speed dialed Matt.

"Hey, wild thing."

"I think we might have a runner." She winced at her hasty wording. "Lucas is missing."

"Actually, he's up here." Matt dropped his voice to a whisper. "I think he was sneaking a peek at the baby but got busted. Now he's kind of stuck talking because he hasn't let anyone see him lately. Since, you know..."

"Yeah. The surgery has been hard on him." She sighed. "Lacey and I both have tried to encourage him to spend some time with Razor while he's been hanging around the hospital, but he wouldn't."

"It's hard to see him like this," Matt confessed softly. "He's got a sheet draped over his lap. You can still tell, though. There's nothing there past his knee. Especially since he keeps rubbing his leg. It draws your attention. Then I feel guilty for looking."

"He's been having phantom pains for the past several weeks. It's not uncommon," she informed him.

"There are so many things I want to say, but I know he'll hate every one of them. They'd be for me, not him, you know?" Matt's heavy heart was obvious even over the phone.

"You don't have to address it. Just be his friend, like you've always been. That's enough." Jambrea jogged to the elevator. Her guys needed her. They didn't have her experience with the emotional wounds inflicted on recuperating patients. Especially not when paired with their own despair for a dear friend. "Remember it's the same him. Don't treat him any differently or he'll hate you. Right now he needs normal."

"So I should be a jackass? Is that what you're saying?" Matt had a little smile in his tone that time.

"Exactly." She clicked her phone closed as she hopped off the elevator and ran into Matt's open arms. "You're doing great. Get rid of the kid gloves and it'll be fine. The rest is up to him."

"I love you, Jambi." He kissed her lightly. "It's a gift, what you can do with people. For them. I hope you know that."

Spread Your Wings

"Hey there, no making out without me." Clint joined them in the hallway outside the maternity ward. "I missed you today."

Sometimes their schedules got crazy with their mix of unusual shifts, but they were starting to get things aligned so they all worked nights and had their days free to enjoy each other. And when they couldn't, well, it seemed absence really did make the heart grow fonder—or the cops grow hornier, however that saying went.

"Can you make it another half hour or so?" She spun from Matt's arms into Clint's, patting his ripped chest.

"Torture. But I'll try." He kissed her, making her debate the merits of a little time with their friends after all. She knew of enough maintenance closets in the hospital that they could probably take a quick break in before meeting up with the rest of the Men in Blue.

Except Jeremy and Lily exited the elevator right behind them.

"Look who we have here." Lily smacked Matt on the ass before hugging Jambi and Clint. "I hope you're not planning on slipping away."

"You guys are the newlyweds," Jambrea shot back.

"Mmm." Lily smiled, all traces of her hardass alter-ego gone in an instant. "That we are. Probably why we're kind of late to this party."

"I don't want to know." Matt clapped his hands over his ears. "Whatever monkey sex you and JRad were indulging in, I'm staying out of it. And so is our lovely Jambi. You've done enough to corrupt her already."

"I didn't hear you complaining after I taught her all about cock rings. Especially the vibrating kind." Lily raised a brow and her husband laughed as he slung an arm around her shoulder.

"Come on, kids." Matt shuffled forward, nudging them all

toward Izzy's room. "At this rate, Ezra will be eighteen by the time we see the fellow."

They filed into the bright, spacious room, which was blanketed in flowers. So different from the sterile environment Lucas had kept for himself. The man had donated any gifts brought to him, leaving standing orders with the nurse's station to get rid of them without even showing him the cards.

Jambrea had kept every single correspondence, refusing to trash the show of support from a variety of acquaintances she bet Lucas hadn't even realized gave a damn. Someday he would want to know who'd kept him in their thoughts.

It made her heart happy to see him surrounded by their friends. Not the center of attention, but just another one of the guys along to see the newest addition to their team. He rolled into the gap between the wall and Izzy's bed. She'd always been the most beautiful woman Jambrea had ever met. Now, with the glow of motherhood around her, she was radiant.

She dazzled Lucas with one of her perfect white smiles and asked, "Would you like to hold him?"

"Who, me?" Lucas looked around as if there were someone else sitting right beside him. "I-I've never held a baby before. I don't want to hurt him."

"You won't." Izzy extended the precious bundle to Lucas, supporting Ezra's neck.

"If Razor can manage not to fuck it up, so can you." Mason chuckled from across the room.

"Sure, okay," Lucas agreed, then kept very still as Izzy laid her son in the crook of his arm. The baby blinked up at the enormous-by-comparison man cradling him with the biggest, bluest eyes Jambrea had ever seen.

Ezra didn't cry. No, he cuddled into Lucas's hold and promptly fell asleep.

"Wow." The tough guy trailed a knuckle down the baby's

Spread Your Wings

cheek. "He's pretty amazing."

"Would you expect anything less of me?" Razor buffed his nails on his shirt.

"I think I had something to do with him too, you know." Izzy laid her head on Razor's shoulder.

"Thank you for being the best thing in my life and giving me more than I could have dreamed of." Serious for once, Razor hugged his fiancé tight. He smiled down at her. "So now that the baby is here, can we talk about setting a date for our wedding? Please?"

Izzy beamed up at the love of her life. "How about fall? When the leaves are turning and all the colors are rich."

"If that's what you want." He kissed her forehead. "I can't wait for it to happen. I want to call you mine. Officially."

"I'm already yours." She banded her arms around him. "That'll give me a couple months to get my figure back."

"I like your shape just fine." He ran his hands along her side to her hip. Tiny, she'd been one of those women who looked thin even pregnant. *The bitch*, Jambrea thought laughingly.

Lucas even chuckled from his seat near the bed. "You're so itty bitty you'll blow away if you lose a single pound."

The whole gang was teasing Izzy soon enough, making her cheeks blush with their indirect compliments. It was then that Ellie joined them.

"What's so funny?" she asked as she came inside, setting her purse on the only vacant chair. When she turned and saw Lucas, she froze.

"Let me out of here." He jerked as he tried to reach for the wheel of his chair with one hand. "Come on, Tyler, move so I can get through."

Startled awake by Lucas's barking, Ezra began to fuss.

"Shit, sorry. Sorry." He carefully handed the infant to Razor, who effortlessly quieted his son with a little rocking and some baby-talk.

Ellie rushed forward, "Lucas! How are you?"

"I gotta go." He glanced up toward Mason, who nodded. Closest to Ellie, the eldest of the Men in Blue reached out and hugged her to him. For once her attempt at wrenching away had more to do with running toward a man than running from one.

"Hi, Mason. Nice to see you too. I want to talk to—"

"He's not ready," Mason murmured into Ellie's hair.

Her eyes, already bloodshot, filled with tears. She whipped her head toward Lucas. "What have I done to you?"

"This isn't about you." Lucas zipped past them in his chair. "How self-centered are you? Jesus. Maybe it has something to do with the missing half of my goddamned leg?"

They all saw the impact his verbal assault had on Ellie. She flinched and turned into Mason's chest, which only seemed to incense Lucas more.

Irate, he snarled, "I knew I should have stayed in my room."

"You know, if I start to hate you it won't be because you're short a foot, asshole. It'll be because of your lack of heart." The only person brave enough to speak to him so directly, Ellie turned to glare at him.

Lucas stared at her for a moment, his jaw hanging open.

Izzy tried to diffuse the situation. "I hope you'll come back and keep me company tomorrow when everyone else is at work."

Lucas didn't respond to her invitation, though Jambrea would dance on top of the hospital naked if the wounded man returned.

"Don't let her follow me," Lucas ordered Mason. Then he disappeared down the hall in his wheelchair as if attempting to qualify for the Special Olympics.

"Lucas! Wait!" Ellie overcame her injured pride when Mason loosened his hold. She tried to veer in that direction.

Jambrea caught Ellie by the elbow and Mason let her take guardianship. "Hang on a second."

To keep from riling Ezra farther, they stepped into the hall. Matt and Clint were close behind.

"But he's getting in the elevator." Ellie's shoulders slumped when the doors smashed closed with her nowhere near joining Lucas for the ride. "I missed him."

"He really isn't ready yet. Mason's right about that." Jambrea softened her proclamation by hugging the girl. "It might take a while. We have to be patient with him."

"So he wasn't really sleeping all the times I called?" She sighed. "I guess I knew he'd still be allowed to have his laptop in recovery. I've emailed him...so much."

Somehow Jambrea didn't think Ellie referred only to the volume of the unread messages she'd seen cluttering Lucas's inbox when he left his email open on the screen. The content might be pretty weighty as well. "Sorry. Part of his recovery is social. Not exclusively physical."

"Maybe it's me he has a problem with, not his surgery. He was hanging out with all of you. So what's wrong with me?" Ellie scoured a tear from her cheek.

"Do you think it could be that he cares more about your opinion of him? Of how you perceive him as a man?" Jambrea wished she could make the young woman see what Jambrea did.

"No. He's struggling and I want to be there for him. Except maybe he's angry with me. I mean, it's *my* fault—"

"I never want to hear you say that again." Jeremy overheard them from his post at the door to Izzy's room. His Dom tone rang out, causing both her and her friend to stop short as he approached. "I was there. You were a prisoner. He's trained to fight for freedom. He would have sacrificed gladly for anyone being *violated* that day."

From what Jambrea knew of the Sex Offender lab raid, Jeremy had chosen that word carefully. Ellie had certainly been raped. Even if she'd begged for sex, it had been the drug talking, not her. How many times or how brutal the act had been were open questions. On those matters, she was as obtuse as Lucas. Certainly, she bore immense scars of her own, even if her wounds were invisible compared to a lost limb.

"Don't make me tell your brother..." Jeremy cut off when the man in question piped up from behind them, joining the party as the elevator burped out more visitors.

"Tell me what?" Ben and Ryan strolled into the gathering, which now spilled outside the room, with little Julie—Ben's niece—between them. Each man held one of her hands. Her mother had also been part of the Sex Offender fallout.

Only she hadn't been lucky enough to escape.

When Julie saw some of her favorite adults, she released a giddy squee, shook off her de facto fathers' hands and trotted into the room, getting hugs from every direction.

Tyler pulled a lollipop from his pocket, and she was in love. She crawled into his lap, swinging her feet while she smeared the treat all over her face.

Ryan ruffled his sister's hair. Though she was a young woman, he still treated her like a child most of the time. Maybe because it was easier to ignore all that had gone wrong that way. The things he'd done to rescue Ellie had been horrifying enough. None of them needed to relive those evil times when they had such cause for celebration. "What's the commotion, Ellie?"

"Your sister is looking at that nursery over there all googly-eyed." Jeremy shrugged. He would never betray Ellie's trust. Besides, telling Ryan the truth really would likely get Lucas's ass kicked.

"Ugh." Ryan groaned. "I'm not ready to be an uncle yet."

"You're pretty much Julie's uncle by default," Ben reminded him. The two men had become close and even lived together after their time in Morselli's dungeon. "And you're damn good at it."

"Yeah, well...doesn't matter. For that I'd have to have a guy first." Ellie pouted a bit as she stormed away, though by the time she'd gotten close enough to catch her first real peek of the tiniest boy in blue, she'd completely melted.

Jambrea laughed. No one could resist Ezra's charm. He'd inherited that, at least, from his dad.

After a quarter of an hour had passed, a soft knock came at the door. At first it went unheard in the riot of the overcrowded hospital room. Good thing Jambrea and Lacey could shoo away the glaring nurses from this ward, who would prefer their patients rest. Otherwise they'd all have been kicked out ages ago.

The next time she heard the light tapping, Jambrea wiggled through her friends in time to spot Shari David's rich brown hair pulled into a messy ponytail that still managed to look utterly lovely with her off the shoulder floral blouse and skinny jeans. Her boots may have been functional at Camp David, but they were just plain sexy with her outfit.

"Shari!" She ran to the woman and wrapped her in a hug, almost tipping them off balance in her enthusiasm.

"Careful," Mason rumbled as he braced them. Tyler laughed from his spot right next to his partner and husband.

Lacey reached out from her place on their laps, which had been abandoned by the fickle little girl when her candy had all been eaten, to squeeze Shari's shoulder. "So good to meet you. I've heard a lot about you and your brother."

"Thanks." She smiled and swallowed hard. It couldn't be easy to be surrounded by the chaos of so many people after years of solitude. But with these men and their wives, she'd find a family that understood the sacrifices some people made for the freedom of others who didn't know or care about the cost of maintaining their rights. "I hope I'm not interrupting. I had to come to the city to finish some paperwork and I thought I'd stop by the hospital to see Jambrea."

"Don't be silly." Izzy smiled serenely, looking effortlessly glamorous as always, despite her frumpy hospital gown and the plastic bracelet she wore instead of the jewels of her socialite days. "Friends are always welcome. Friends of friends, even."

Ryan got up quickly and offered Shari his seat, though he stammered over his greeting and offer. Ben was quick to make introductions, starting with himself.

Jambrea smiled as she imagined the possibilities. No one quite knew what Ben and Ryan's relationship was these days, but Lily swore they were more straight than bi, or at least they had been before their lives had been changed forever by the unwanted captivity the Mistress had discovered them in.

It seemed kind of fitting that their group might end up with three groups of three.

Jambrea looked to Lacey. Her friend smiled and nodded as Ryan and Ben fell all over themselves to ensure Shari's welcome and comfort.

Matt and Clint each put a hand on her shoulders. She leaned back into them, knowing they'd always be there to support her. After baby Ezra had been fed, he made his rounds of the room.

Just like his dad, he had all the women wanting to pinch his cheeks.

Until Matt coughed. "Holy crap. What is that smell?"

"I think it's literally crap." Clint's eyes watered.

"Well, I guess we know he's really your son, Razor," Tyler teased their ex-rookie. As youngest and mouthiest of the bunch, he still took the brunt of the ribbing. "I've come across that odor before in the station bathroom after you've had too much cheap coffee to wash down a box of six-day-old donuts."

"Gross!" Lily whacked her brother-in-law on the arm. "You know you shouldn't eat junk like that. My sister needs you healthy to grow old with her and take care of your spawn."

"Don't worry, Aunt Lily. You and JRad are his godparents. Ezra will be your problem if I croak." He beamed at them, true affection wiping away any faux insult in his snark.

"I think it's time Razor learned how to change a diaper." Lacey snagged him by the elbow.

He lifted Ezra, holding the baby as far away from his nose as possible and followed her to the nursery. "Yeah, yeah. I see how it is. The rookie always gets the shit jobs."

They all burst out laughing, including baby Ezra, who gave a tiny gurgle.

He was already a Man in Blue in training.

About the Author

Jayne Rylon is a *New York Times* and *USA TODAY* bestselling author. She received the 2011 Romantic Times Reviewers' Choice Award for Best Indie Erotic Romance. Her stories used to begin as daydreams in seemingly endless business meetings, but now she is a full time author, who employs the skills she learned in her straight-laced corporate existence in the business of writing. She lives in Ohio with two cats and her husband, who both inspires her fantasies and supports her career. When she can escape her purple office, she loves to travel the world, avoid speeding tickets in her beloved Sky, and, of course, read.

Jayne loves to hear from fans. You can reach her by email at contact@jaynerylon.com or chat with her while she's procrastinating on Facebook (www.facebook.com/jayne.rylon) or Twitter (@jaynerylon).

For the latest news about what Jayne's writing, where you can find her at events or to win one of her prize packs given to random subscribers in each addition of her newsletter, sign up for the Naughty News: http://bit.ly/Y523Db

What will grow from the seeds of desire?

Hope Springs
© *2013 Jayne Rylon & Mari Carr*
Compass Girls, Book 2

Hope Compton never considered her parents' unconventional relationship a dangerous thing. Until, after a few too many drinks in a crowded bar, she admits her desire for a ménage to her college boyfriend—and uninvited guests try to turn her fantasy into a nightmare.

When Wyatt catches some thugs harassing the pretty daughter of his bosses, he doesn't hesitate to call on his partner Clayton to kick some asses. But then he realizes what a temptation the sweet, sheltered Hope presents. Especially her naughty wish to unleash her inner vixen—with both of them.

Hope has no doubt her playmates want to fulfill her every desire, but something's holding them back. She has an idea what those *somethings* are. With luck, and a little help from her Compass cousins to hold her fathers off, she'll find what she needs in the shadows of the past—and convince them she's found two men of her own who are worthy of her love.

Warning: Compass books bring love in every direction and every season. But not all of life's moments are filled with joy. Take the good with the bad, and the steamy.

Available now in ebook and print from Samhain Publishing.

Romance

HORROR

www.samhainpublishing.com

CPSIA information can be obtained at www.ICGtesting.com
Printed in the USA
LVOW07s2054211014

409819LV00005B/713/P